SPOTLIGHT

FAMOUS BOOK 2

EDEN FINLEY

SPOTLIGHT

CHAPTER 1
RYDER

COFFEE. Need coffee.

Caffeine is the magic elixir that will allow me to function like the responsible single father I supposedly am.

Supposedly, because photos of me during a sweet moment with Kaylee leaked, and now the tabloids think I'm this patient, down-to-earth, hands-on type father.

You know, the type of single dad that makes ovaries sigh all around the world.

The honest, goddamn truth is this parenting thing is the hardest job I've ever had. It's more grueling than nine-month-long music tours where I got no sleep and traveled around the world without a break. Jet lag and exhaustion were not in my vocabulary because I couldn't afford them to be.

Exhaustion is now my life.

I swear, nighttime potty training means I get less sleep than when Kaylee was teething. There're only so many times a night I can get up and change sheets before I give in and try to put Pull-Ups on the kid. Of course, then she reminds me that she's almost five and doesn't need diapers.

She picked up toilet training so easily, but we struggle with nights. If she didn't sleep like the dead, maybe she'd wake up to go to the bathroom.

As if sensing my increasing level of tiredness from sleep deprivation, the girl behind the kitchen counter at the kids' play center finally comes over with my order. Large coffee for me and a giant cookie for my daughter. I swear it's the size of her head.

I'm going to regret the amount of sugar later.

Future me can deal with the crash. Present me wants peace.

I tug my cap lower on my head and keep my gaze down as I say, "Thank you," to the server. It's rude and not how my momma raised me, but even two years after Eleven broke up and I disappeared out of the spotlight, I'm still recognized and mobbed on the street. Even when I'm with Kaylee, and especially by the waitress's demographic.

Being part of the biggest boy band in the world for seven years means it's hard to slink away into oblivion no matter how hard I try.

Unless another big act comes along, this will be my life for the foreseeable future.

Come on, teenage boys, join a boy band! For my sanity, please.

More importantly, for my daughter's safety.

Kaylee stares up at me with the big green eyes she got from her mother while a deep brown ringlet falls in her face because the stubborn hair won't stay where I put it. Daddy and pigtails don't mix.

Her mouth is full of cookie, and as she chews, she gives me the biggest smile. It's so big that crumbs spray out between her teeth.

"I can't take you anywhere." I reach over and wipe the table.

"Why not?" More cookie falls from her mouth.

"Because you're messy."

"But I'm cute."

I laugh. "That you are."

"Momma always says that."

My heart twinges. "Yeah. She does."

"When she coming home?"

No matter how many times I explain, she never understands. She's too young. "Umm …"

"Can I have a pony for my birthday?"

And this is why I love the attention span of four-year-olds. "No. Not until you're old enough to ride."

Technically, there's a riding camp that would take her at four years old, but no way in hell I'm telling her that.

I've never had an ever-growing need to protect someone with my life until Kaylee came along. Fatherhood changed everything.

Everything I used to take for granted, I don't anymore. Like five minutes of complete silence.

At the table behind us, a young boy starts singing an Eleven song.

Because I like you. Ooh, ooh, ooh. I like you.

I change my mind. I wish I had five minutes where I wasn't reminded of *that* song. It was our biggest hit, the most annoying to get in your head, and it got so much radio time that I think even the die-hard fans got sick of it.

"Nuh-uh," a deep voice says. "What have I told you about singing Eleven songs?"

"I like them!" the boy protests.

"Their lyrics are lazy and cliché. They suck."

I can't help it, I snort. Loudly.

Oops.

I clear my throat and then cough, trying to cover that I'm eavesdropping on a private conversation.

Subtly, I glance over my shoulder.

The boy looks a little bit older than Kaylee, and the guy he's with is younger than I'm expecting. Midtwenties at most. I guess he started having kids young. Not that I can judge anyone.

I was twenty-two when Kaylee happened, and she was definitely not part of my life plan.

My gaze finds my daughter's, and the familiar heaviness of guilt fills my chest. She might not have been planned, but in no way was she a mistake. I wouldn't trade her for anything.

In fact, I gave up my whole life for her, and I'd do it again in a heartbeat.

And again, and again, and again.

The kid behind us starts humming the song now, and I have to get up and leave before I burst into laughter when the guy with him groans.

"Come on, Kaylee. You can go play, and I'll watch."

My fearless daughter races up the padded stairs to the jungle gym of tunnels running throughout the place while I sip on my coffee and try not to lose her. The tunnels have windows, and I track her by following the Elsa dress she *had* to wear because wearing anything else was not acceptable.

Not that I can't afford to replace the dress she's determined to destroy, but that's not the point. I don't want her growing up thinking everything is replaceable and money is never an issue.

I don't want her to become like those spoiled kids at her school. I didn't want her to go to pre-K at all, but socializing with kids her own age is supposedly "psychologically beneficial" or whatever. Apparently, if I don't want her to grow up to be a sociopath, I have to let her get bitten by other children.

When I asked her teacher about the bite marks that first week, she lowered her voice and said, "We have a biter," like it's normal to let kids bite other kids and there was nothing they could do about it.

This, coming from the most expensive school in the LA area where all the stars send their children.

The worst part is they won't even tell me which child it was who bit her. I bet it was one of the Kardashians' kids.

The guy who thinks Eleven sucks moves in my periphery and stands a few feet away from me as his boy runs up into the tunnels.

It's tempting—so tempting—to make eye contact with the guy just to get a reaction out of him, but if I'm recognized by anyone else, it'll take a few autographs and selfies to get me and Kaylee out of here.

I am at a better angle to check him out properly, though.

Eleven definitely has haters out there. It's not hard to when, as this guy puts it, the lyrics are lazy and cliché. We never claimed they weren't. But the other thing those songs are? Multiplatinum-selling hits.

They might be shallow, but they're damn catchy, and the biggest demographic out there is people wanting to dance and scream the words at the top of their lungs.

It doesn't make Eleven or any of us who were in the band any less of an artist than this guy.

And there's no doubt he's an artist. Music, I'm guessing by his pretentious attitude.

He's wearing ripped, black skinny jeans, a white T-shirt, an open black vest, and he has leather bands around his wrist.

His long golden surfer-boy hair is in a man bun at the nape of his neck.

And he's hot. He's all smooth skin with just a touch of stubble on his chin and jawline.

I want to keep staring at him, but eventually he'll look my way, and then I'll be fucked. And not in the way I'm close to fantasizing about right now.

I miss sex. There's something to be said about only getting laid once in five years.

An ear-piercing screech fills the space, and I know without a doubt it's my daughter.

Another kid wails, "Stop!"

I don't know if I put my coffee down or I drop it, but all I know is when I run up those stairs and into the tunnels, I'm only thinking about Kaylee.

Someone climbs up behind me, and I may or may not accidentally kick them in the face.

Oops.

I turn to make sure it's not a child and I haven't hurt them, but all I see are the hazel eyes of the pretentious douche glaring at me, so I keep on climbing.

I'll apologize when he tells me I don't actually suck. My award for maturity should be coming any day now.

I'm not sure what I'm expecting to find—my thoughts go to worst-case scenarios like my daughter bleeding or with a broken bone—but when I reach a flat area through the first set of tunnels, what I find is startling, confusing, and a little laugh-worthy.

I can't laugh though. If I do, my daughter will think this sort of behavior is acceptable.

She stands with her foot on top of the boy who was humming the Eleven song but is now lying on the floor.

I pull myself through the tunnel exit and stand, though the roof is about six inches too short. I hit my head but ignore the pain, craning my neck to fit properly. "Kaylee Margaret Kennedy. Let that boy go."

My voice is the firmest it's ever been with her, so she does it immediately.

"But—"

"No buts. Say you're sorry."

Behind me, the boy's dad gets to his feet.

He's my height, so he headbutts the roof like I did as he stands. "Ah, mother flipping f—ire truck." He glances at the kids. "Chase, what happened?"

"She kicked me!" the boy yells.

Kaylee faces me with big, round, green eyes that are welling up because she knows she's in trouble. "He pushed in front of me. And you said if someone hurt me, I have to 'fend myself."

I drop to my knees so we're eye to eye. "Honey, I meant if someone bit you at school. Or hit you. It's never okay to kick someone. You *know* that."

"Chase, are you okay?" the boy's dad asks.

I turn to face him. "Hey, man, I'm so sorry. She's just learning how to be social with other kids. She might not have the hang of it yet."

And after almost five years of parenting, I'm beginning to think I have no fucking clue what I'm doing either.

The guy doesn't reply to me, but his eyes do widen. His hypnotic, softer than I'm expecting, hazel eyes.

The look he's pulling now is one I've seen a million times on a million different faces. Recognition is hitting him.

"Uh, umm … yeah. Okay. I mean, no problem. I mean, it is a problem, but kids test boundaries all the time. Umm, you, uh, handled that well."

I have to admit I really like him fumbling for words and getting flustered.

"Thanks. Not bad for someone who's lazy and cliché, am I right?" I smirk.

"I-I'm sorry. I … I mean, it's you. And aww, shi … vers. I'm sorry."

While the blubbering is cute and I want to see more of it, I need to leave before he tells the whole place who I am. "It's all good. Come on, Kaylee. Let's go home."

"Lyric, who is that?"

Ah, the boy is young enough to know my songs but not old enough to know what I look like.

Also, did he just say *Lyric*? Really?

I reach my hand out for the boy. "Hi, I'm Ryder from Eleven."

Chase's face lights up. "You are? Really?"

"Really. I always love meeting a fan."

He shakes my hand so hard I think it might fall off. He's adorable. His blond hair flops into his eyes.

"I'm sorry my daughter kicked you."

"And hey," *Lyric* says, "I'm sorry too. For, uh, you know, what I said."

I half want to lecture the guy on sticking to his opinions. Eleven's music isn't for everyone. He doesn't have to kiss my ass because he realizes I'm an actual human being and not just a celebrity figure who doesn't exist in real life.

People think being famous means you're fair game when it comes to criticism. They don't realize we're just like everyone else.

I stand tall again, ducking my head under the short roof. "No need to be polite now. But we really should be going before anyone else recognizes me."

"We won't tell anyone," Chase says.

"I don't want to go!" Kaylee yells.

"I know, bub, but—"

"We won't," Lyric says.

I meet his gaze and hate that mistrust is my first instinct. It's always my first instinct because it has to be. For all I know, he'll say that now, then as we go to leave, I'll face a wall of paparazzi.

As if sensing my distrust, he offers a small smile. "I'll even buy you a coffee to replace the one you practically threw at my head."

Oh. Now it might be my turn to apologize. "Sorry. And for, uh, kicking you. I heard her screaming and—"

He holds up his hand. "I get it. Parent's instinct. I'm the same way with Chase, and he's not even mine."

I cock my head.

"Oh, wow, that totally sounded like I kidnapped him, huh? He's my brother's kid. I babysit him. I promise. Chase, tell him I'm your uncle."

Chase grins up at me. "He's my uncle. He likes boys not girls, but Mom and Dad say that's okay because boys are allowed to love boys and girls can love girls."

Lyric covers his face. "*Too* much information, Chase."

And an interesting turn of events.

"I think kissing is gross," Chase adds. "Boy or girl."

I try not to laugh but fail.

"Wanna play?" Kaylee asks Chase.

My laugh dies. "Kaylee—" I call after her, but they're both already climbing to the next level of tunnels.

"Oh, to be a kid again," Lyric says. "Quick to forgive and make friends."

"You know what's a good way to make friends? Not saying people suck is a good start."

His mouth drops open, then closes again. I guess he can't tell if I'm being serious or joking.

I want to torture him more, but if I do, there'll probably be an article about how I'm rude and treat people poorly. Anything for a story.

"I'm messing with you, man," I say. "Well, sort of. I'm not actually offended, but I still make a good point. Spread love, not hate."

"I have an excuse, I swear."

"Can you maybe tell me after you buy me that coffee? I don't know how long I can stand here like this." I rub my neck.

"Deal. You want to go first, or shall I?"

I step aside and gesture for him to go. "By all means."

He walks by, and naturally, my eyes focus on his ass in his tight jeans.

Damn.

We climb down together, but when we get back to the main floor, I see a staff member cleaning up the coffee I threw.

I pull my cap down, trying to shield my eyes and face as much as I can. "I should—"

Lyric grips my bicep to stop me, and the move feels natural and completely different than when fans do it to try to get my attention.

We lock eyes.

"She'll recognize you as soon as she sees your face. Let me." He approaches the waitress. "Sorry about that. We heard the kids screaming and thought they might be in trouble. Here, let me clean that up."

She waves him off and says it's fine as she smiles up at him. "I'll bring you a replacement."

"Thank you." Lyric's face when he smiles is … there are no words for it.

Shake it off, Ryder. Stop staring at the pretty guy.

The waitress is as enamored with his smile as I am because she blushes as he walks away.

Lyric joins me at my table. "So, I'm sorry. Again. For saying you suck."

I laugh. "Hey, it's not a lie."

His eyes widen a little, and then I realize what I said. It's true either way, but that's not exactly public knowledge.

"We didn't get a lot of artistic control with Eleven," I elaborate. "I probably hate those songs as much as you do."

"Didn't you and Harley write a lot of the songs?"

I lean back in my seat. "Not a fan, huh? Most people don't know who writes what."

"I, uh, well, I graduated from Montebello. Music studies. That's how I knew you wrote the songs."

"Ah. Well, even though we wrote those songs, we wrote what we were told to. Mindless shit is what the label wanted, so we gave it to them because we didn't get much choice. You'll learn that as soon as you're signed with someone."

"How do you know I'm trying to get signed?"

"You went to Almost Famous. That gives away *a lot* about you."

Montebello is a private college that has one of the most competitive performing arts programs in the country. It's nicknamed Almost Famous because getting in is almost a guarantee you'll make it in LA. A lot of stars went there, and I could tell this guy was an artist just by looking at him. Makes total sense.

"How so?" he asks.

"Well, Lyric for one. Has to be a stage name."

He grimaces. "Honest to God, it's my birth name."

"Really?"

"No shit. My brother is named Chord, and I have a sister called Melody."

I bite my lip to keep from laughing.

"Don't hold back now. None of my childhood friends ever did. But, hey, it does work in my favor. It's totally fit for a musician."

"True. Very marketable. I'm guessing your whole family is musical, then?"

Lyric glances away. "Not so much. Mom hates it. Chord went into entertainment law, so similar vein but not performing."

"How can your mom hate music? Is she a zombie? She's a zombie, isn't she?"

Lyric laughs. "Sometimes I wonder, but no. Mom wanted a more practical career path for me, which is why I did a double degree at Montebello. Music and early education. And that's also how I ended up being my nephew's nanny for no pay while I go to audition after audition and get turned down by, oh, *everyone*."

"Ah. Hence the boy band hate. Because we had it so easy."

"I never said that. I said—"

"It's okay. Trust me, we're all used to the hate by 'real musicians.'"

"I didn't mean that. It's just disheartening being rejected so many times—"

"That's the business."

"I know. And you have to have thick skin, which I think I do. It's not like I cry over bad auditions or anything, but my latest rejection was this morning, so I was cranky. While I still don't think Eleven had super inventive and touching lyrics, that doesn't give me the right to whine about it to my seven-year-old nephew, and I'm sorry for that."

"Apology accepted." I eye him as a look of relief crosses his features.

The waitress comes over with my coffee, and Lyric slides it over to me.

"Try not to throw this one."

I huff a small laugh. "Okay, I'll try."

I take a sip, but it's scalding hot, and I spray it all over the table. "Ouch," I hiss. "Hot."

Lyric laughs. "Not off to a good start." He grabs a napkin from the dispenser on the table and wipes down his shirt.

"Sorry."

"Does this make us even yet? I insult you, you throw coffee at my head and then spit on me."

I can't help laughing with him. "I'm so sorry. I wasn't expecting it to be that hot."

"That's what all the boys say about me."

My laughter doesn't die even though it probably should.

A comment like that would normally have me searching the room to make sure no one overheard. Whether it's because we're seated away from others or there's something about the pretentious nice guy that calms me, I want to keep talking to him instead of doing what I should be doing which is going home.

The longer I'm here, the more chance of being spotted.

I glance up at the tunnels and remind myself that Kaylee doesn't get to do this type of thing often. She should get to play for as long as she wants without her famous father ruining everything for her.

I turn back to Lyric. "So, you're a nanny?"

One of Lyric's eyebrows rises, and it amazes me how people can do that. Kaylee can do it too, but it's like I have an invisible mono-brow or something—like my eyebrows are attached to each other—because I can't separate their movements.

"Umm, you don't look like a typical nanny," I say. "Kaylee used to have nannies when I was on tour."

"I'm technically Chase's nanny, but I've really gotta find a gig that'll pay me. Though they do let me crash in their pool house for free."

"Have you thought about teaching or something?"

Something like sadness fills Lyric's eyes. "Teaching is a backup. Music is my first priority."

Wariness replaces the warm, happy feeling I'd had while sitting here with Lyric. If this ends with him asking for help connecting with a label, I'm going to be disappointed.

It's not every day I meet someone where the conversation flows and they make me laugh. Like honest to God laugh.

I direct the conversation away from music. "I'm sure you'd make a great teacher. Better than the one Kaylee has right now. Then again, a turtle would be better than the teacher she has now."

"She's having trouble at school? Already?"

"First year. She's in pre-K, and it's not going well. I've been getting back into working on music, and I need someone to look after her, but she's coming home with bite marks and an attitude, and it's supposed to be the best school in LA. What are the shitty ones like?" Why did all that just fall from my mouth? I don't know this guy, and he could go and tell anyone.

"What school is it?"

I hesitate.

He holds up his hands like he's a busted perp. "I won't tell anyone where your kid goes if that's what you're worried about."

It's not, but I also don't want to get into how paranoid I am. How paranoid I always am.

"I worked at some of the best schools as a teacher's aide during college. I'm wondering where she's going."

"It's, uh, Vista Point."

"Whoa, dude, no." Lyric shakes his head. "Most expensive doesn't mean best. I can give you some names of actual good schools."

"Really?"

"Really. But hey, if you don't want her in pre-K at all, I'm available." Lyric's so confident in his delivery, it makes it hard to shut down the idea immediately.

"That was really subtle."

"Like a sledgehammer. I really need a paying job so I can stop mooching off my brother."

It's tempting, but again, I don't even know this guy. "I was told she needs to socialize with other kids."

"I practically act like a kid, does that count?"

I laugh. "I don't think so."

"In all seriousness, kids do need socialization, but there are playgroups and other ways to achieve that than sending them to a terrible school where they're all brats." He catches himself. "Not saying Kaylee's a brat. She's adorable, and, umm, oh God, forget I said anything. No way you'll hire a guy who calls you lazy and cliché and then says your daughter is a brat. I'm on fire today."

"You really are. Are you this disastrous during auditions? Because I'm starting to see where you may have a problem."

Lyric leans back in his chair. "I don't know. I sometimes think I'm overconfident. They tell you to go in there and own the auditions, but when I do that, I come across as—"

"A pretentious musician who thinks boy bands are lazy and cliché?"

He groans. "I thought we were even. You're not playing fair."

I pretend to think about it. I may not be playing fair, but it's definitely fun *playing* with him. "I might drop it if you give me the names of those schools."

"I can do one better. Give me your number and I can text them to you. Then you can call me if you have any questions."

Ah. There it is.

The industry connection he's after.

But even though he's using me, one look at his breathtaking smile and I know I'm going to cave.

What can I say? I'm a sucker for a pretty man.

CHAPTER 2
LYRIC

RYDER KENNEDY.

The cap he wears is old and ratty denim. His jaw is unshaven.

He's not the stunning, put together man he is in the media. Although, he's definitely, without a doubt, stunning. Just rougher around the edges than I'm expecting.

It's weird. Sitting here with him. It's like an out-of-body experience.

And did I really ask for his number?

What is wrong with me?

I've seen my fair share of celebrities. I live in LA. It's impossible to live here and not run into someone famous occasionally. Having an entertainment lawyer for a brother makes it easier too. But I've never had a legit conversation with one.

Ryder Kennedy seems so ... *normal.*

I take out my phone and hand it to him before I lose my nerve.

He eyes it.

"I'm not going to sell your phone number for money. I'm not that broke." In all honesty, I am *that* broke, but I have a roof over my head and my brother feeds me. The little money I do earn from weekend gigs goes into buying equipment and shit.

Ryder still hesitates.

"Would an email address be better? Since you're clearly worried about me calling you at three in the morning and breathing heavily to creep you out." I'm only half-joking.

"Email addresses are easier to change than phone numbers." Ryder types in the address and hands it back. "Sorry."

"I get it. Guys like me only wish we could reach the level of fame where our privacy is under constant threat."

"You say that like it's a good thing."

"No, I understand it's a nightmare, but it's also an indication of success. If that makes sense."

He takes a sip of his now cooled coffee. "It does. Doesn't make me feel any better about it, though."

"I don't suppose it would." I type the school names into a new email, and I'm about to hit Send when I pause.

I glance up at Ryder, then back down at my phone, doing something either bold or stupid. Perhaps both. I punch in my phone number and hit Send before I can stop myself.

"I left you my number in case you change your mind about the nanny thing."

"Right." Ryder tries to cover a yawn. "Nanny thing."

There's something in his tone I can't pinpoint. Disbelief, sarcasm, or maybe it's just exhaustion.

"Not sleeping?" I ask.

"Not enough." His bright blue eyes, the brightest blue I've ever seen, pierce through me all of a sudden. "Okay, *Mr. Nanny*. Here's a question for you. Your kid is wetting the bed. Every. Night. You spend most of your time redoing their bedding, and neither of you are sleeping. What do you do?"

"Easy. You layer the bedding. Mattress protector, top sheet, mattress protector, top sheet. So when the accidents happen, you rip the top layer off and put her back into bed. She'll grow out of it eventually."

Ryder's mouth drops open. I guess he wasn't expecting me to have an actual answer. I don't look like a typical nanny, and it's not like this is my first choice in career, but I do know a few things.

I'm currently doing gigs on the weekends at different clubs, auditioning, and trying to get my name out there.

Either my degree from Montebello isn't worth the paper it's printed on or mine's defective or something.

Then again, no piece of paper can count for auditioning well, and I suck at that. I get too in my head and come across as fake and arrogant. When I try to be humble, I sound like I'm not confident. I need to learn to sell myself as myself. Hold the side of douche.

"Layer the bedding," Ryder mumbles. "It's so simple and logical. Why didn't I think of it?"

"Sleep deprivation is a real form of torture."

"My child has tortured me for over four years. She's sadistic."

I can't help laughing.

His head swivels fast, looking around the space. "I didn't mean that."

"I know." I have the urge to reach for his hand to comfort him. Which is crazy.

People don't meet like this. This isn't how you make friends in this day and age. But it's easy with Ryder.

In the short time we've been sitting here, it already doesn't feel like I'm talking to *the* Ryder Kennedy from Eleven.

I'm sitting with an exhausted parent.

He still looks guilty over what he said.

"You've gotta cut yourself some slack. Parenting is hard. I'm only Chase's uncle and it's hard some days I have him."

He relents. "You're right."

"For future reference, I'm always right. So, I get the job, then?"

Ryder scoffs. "There is no job, but if there was, you'd be the first one I call."

"That doesn't really help me out with my current situation."

Ryder flattens his lips and looks confused. "If you want a connection at a label, you can just ask for it. You don't need to pretend to be interested in being my kid's nanny."

Wow. Okay. Guess this isn't going the way I thought it was. "You think this is a ruse to get industry connections?" I can't say I blame him, but it kinda hurts. Though it's not like he knows me. Clearly.

"It wouldn't be the first time someone's tried to strike up a conversation only to show their true colors." Ryder shrugs. "I'm trying to cut out the middle part and get to the point."

I've never tasted fame. Have never been anywhere near close to it. But the dejection in Ryder's eyes is utterly heartbreaking.

What would it be like to live like that? Not knowing who's in your life for you and who's in it because they want something.

"You can keep your connections. I want to make it in this business on my own. I want my music career to be earned on merit, not who I know."

"That's admirable—really, it is—but it's also a little naïve. The industry doesn't work like that."

"If I keep pushing and pay my dues, I'll make it one day."

I can tell Ryder wants to say more, but he doesn't.

Instead, he glances out to the maze of tunnels and slides this place has. "Do you think they're okay up there?"

He says his daughter drives him nuts, but it doesn't take long for those fatherly instincts to kick in.

"Chase is a good kid. He'll look out for her. Besides, I think Kaylee has proven she'll scream if something's wrong."

Ryder smiles proudly. "Yeah, she will."

Movement outside on the street catches my eye, and fuck …

"It wasn't me. You've been with me the whole time, and the only time I touched my phone was to email you."

Poor guy thinks I'm using him for a label contact, and now paparazzi are outside waiting for him.

Ryder looks confused until he turns. His skin turns ashen when he sees the cameras and two nosey paparazzi trying to see in here.

"One of the staff or someone else must've recognized you and tweeted about it or something."

I feel guilty even though I didn't do this. I did promise him no one else would find out, though. Not that I can control other people.

He's out of his seat immediately. "Where's Kaylee?"

"Let's go find her."

We both rush toward the steps to go back up into the tunnels when a loud laugh I know to be Chase's comes from the slides. He pops out at the bottom, landing in a giant ball pit, and then a few seconds later, Kaylee shoots out the bottom of the second one.

"Over here," I tell Ryder.

"Kaylee, sweetie, we have to go." Ryder tries to hide his panicked tone but doesn't completely pull it off.

I've craved fame ever since I could sing. I would kill to have those cameras out there looking for me. Maybe it's because I have no plans to have kids of my own, but I've never thought about having to deal with paparazzi while trying to protect a child.

"I'm having fun!" she yells.

"I know, bub, but there are cameras here."

She huffs. "Again?" She sounds exasperated and beyond her age. "Tell them to go away."

"You know that's not how it works."

Uh-oh. I know that face. Her bottom lip droops, and water fills her eyes. I don't know if Kaylee's the type to throw tantrums or just have a cry, but if the paparazzi get that on camera, TMZ will report on Ryder's parenting skills within the hour.

She's still in the ball pit, so I go to the edge and kneel down to her level. "Kaylee, you and your daddy have to go, but I gave him my phone number, and if you ever want to play with Chase again, get your daddy to call me, okay?"

"Can I play with Chase?" she asks Ryder.

Ryder stares down at me with a frown marring his breathtakingly beautiful face. His lips look like they've had fillers, and his jawline is a work of art. All the Eleven guys are hot—there's no doubt about that—but there's something about Ryder that's alluring.

He's probably thinking I'm trying to use him again, but I'm trying to help him here.

"We can set up a playdate for another day," Ryder says warily. "Right now, we need to go before any more cameras turn up."

"Okaaaay." The poor little thing sounds so dejected.

Ryder helps her get out of the ball pit. "Now, how to get out of here without them getting a usable picture." He lifts her into his arms.

"Well, it's you they want, so leave Kaylee with me while you bring your car around."

There he goes, staring at me with mistrust again.

Although, I get it. Leaving your daughter with someone you don't know is stupid even for a few minutes.

"Or if you don't trust me with Kaylee, then Chase and I can go get your car for you. Risk a stolen car instead of a child."

"It's not that I—"

"I get it. I do. I'm just hoping it's stranger danger more than me being gay."

He looks confused at what I'm saying, but he can't stand there and deny there's a stigma about guys in general in the childcare industry. Gay guys are ridiculed and kept under a microscope even worse. It's all bullshit, but you never know when you're going to meet someone who thinks that way.

The things my brother's colleagues and friends have said to him about having me look after Chase is enough to make me avoid socializing with them. Chord stands up for me, but there's no teaching stupid, and I'd rather not deal with them.

"It's definitely the 'I don't trust anyone around Kaylee' thing. I don't … there's not … I'm cool with the gay thing. Trust me." He hands me his key fob. "It's the Tesla in the middle row." He rattles off the license plate, and Chase and I head for the parking lot.

The paparazzi are forced to stay outside by law, but they're growing in number. And when we walk past them, they don't even blink.

Oh, the joys of being invisible.

Kind of ironic when all I want to do is stand out in a crowd.

It's all I've ever wanted.

Not that I don't love my life. I just want more.

I put Chase in the back seat and pull Ryder's car around as close to the entrance as I can get.

Ryder makes a break for it as soon as I pull to a stop. He's got Kaylee in his arms, and she's got her head buried in his shoulder so they can't get photos of her face.

Ryder's expert-fast at buckling her into her seat, and then he jumps into the passenger side while asking paparazzi to back up.

I take off before his seat belt is even on.

For a few blocks everyone in the car is silent.

I'm stunned speechless, Ryder looks pissed off, Chase is generally good at picking up tension in a room, and I can't tell if Kaylee is still upset she had to leave or if the big, bad men shoving cameras in her face scared her.

"Shit," Ryder hisses.

Kaylee gasps. "Daddy said a bad word."

Damn, that's adorable.

"Your car," Ryder says to me.

"We caught the bus. I can pull up to a stop on line fourteen to get back home."

"Where do you live?"

"Beverly Hills."

When he looks at me surprised, I remind him, "Crashing in my brother's pool house, remember?"

"Oh. Right. We can take you. It's the least I can do to thank you for helping back there."

"It's not out of the way?"

"Don't worry about it. I insist. Drive to your place, and then I'll take Kaylee home."

"Thank you."

We fall back into silence.

The easy conversation we had back at the play center is gone.

"Does that happen a lot?" I ask stupidly. Of course it happens a lot. "I thought it was illegal for them to take photos of Kaylee? Didn't Reese Witherspoon's diva fit make new laws?"

"The law actually states they can't *harass* the children of celebrities. They're free to post any photos they get."

"And that back there isn't considered harassment?"

"The law is vague. I can bring charges against them and try to sue them in a civil suit, but the one time I inquired how to do that, the lawyer advised me it would be more detrimental to Kaylee's mental health having to go through something like that—talking to psychologists and giving testimony that she felt threatened and harmed—than if I just let it be."

"That's the stupidest thing I've ever heard."

"Uncle Lyric, don't say stupid. It's mean."

"Not if something really is stupid," I mumble under my breath.

Ryder's easy smile is back. "Don't say bad words, Uncle Lyric."

Damn, why do I like his teasing voice so much?

"But, Daddy, you said *shit!*"

I bite my lip to stop from laughing at Ryder's defeated slump.

"I'm not going to hear the end of that," Ryder says.

"Kids swearing is so adorable."

"Adorable is one word for it."

I almost hate that there's little traffic for once and we make it home in relatively good time. Good time for LA, anyway.

Ryder Kennedy is nothing like I expected him to be. Not that I'd thought much about him at all before this.

In the media, he's portrayed as the humble one everyone wants to be friends with. I can totally see it.

When we inevitably pull into the circular driveway of my brother's ranch-style home that screams old Hollywood, I reluctantly turn off the car.

"What does your brother do again?" Ryder asks, dipping his head to stare up at the house through the windshield.

"Entertainment lawyer. He has some pretty big names on his client list."

"Ah. That explains some more things. I'm learning a lot today."

"What things?"

He side-eyes me. "This isn't me being conceited or anything, but you don't treat me like I'm a celebrity."

"Sorry, should I be kissing your a—"—I glance at the back seat where the kids are listening intently—"feet?"

"Not at all. And after overhearing what you really think of me, I'd be disappointed if you suddenly did. But, I don't know … most people—even the ones who hate Eleven's music—gush and fawn over us. It's unnerving."

"I'm fanboying on the inside."

Ryder laughs. "Good to know."

"The way I see it, the difference between a celebrity and a struggling artist is a record deal."

"That's so true it's scary."

"Thanks for dropping us off. Saved us a long bus ride."

"Thanks for your help with the paparazzi."

"No problem. I have Chase Thursday and Friday afternoons after school and alternating Saturdays if you want to set up a playdate with the kids."

"Yeah!" little Kaylee says behind us. "I want a playdate!"

Ryder nods. "I'll contact you."

"And don't forget, the nanny offer is always open."

"Do you ever give up?"

"Never. Don't know the meaning of the word." Apparently, I'm as stubborn as my father. But unlike him, I won't let the industry suck me in and then spit me out.

We get out of the car and meet around the front while Chase runs inside the house.

"So, I'll, uh … call you, then." Ryder looks down at his feet.

I like his awkwardness. It's cute. "Hey, who says you can't make friends like kids do? Insulting one minute, fighting the next, now look at us."

"I believe that was you."

"Oh. Right. Well, yeah, I think we, like, totally just became best friends."

Ryder shakes his head with a smile. "If you say so."

I watch as he climbs back in the car and pulls out of my brother's driveway.

I hope he uses the number I gave him, but I doubt he will.

Especially not for what I want him to use it for.

CHAPTER 3
RYDER

THE DEEP RASP of Cash Kingsley's voice fills my home studio. As front man of the latest rock sensation, Cash Me Outside, he's got an amazing range and soulful tone that I'm a little jealous of.

I'd be lying if I said I wasn't wishing I was inside the booth instead of in front of a soundboard, but I'm just thankful to be doing something with music again.

When Kaylee started school, I wanted something to fill my time. My studio is small and not suited for bands, but it has great acoustics for vocals, and that's what Cash wants for his next album.

We work well together, but it's trying. He tries my patience and my self-control.

I broke once, and since then he's been pushing for a repeat.

Today, he's decked out in tight pants and a button-down that's basically undone all the way, and the sexy smolder he sends my way while he sings is so not subtle.

Cash is the only person I've been with since Kaylee was born. He's the one selfish act I allowed myself, and I felt guilty immediately afterward.

He was fun, but I can't be that guy.

I don't think he's used to rejection because it was his idea to make it a onetime deal, and when I agreed, suddenly he was interested in making this some sort of fling while we work together.

No, thanks.

He finishes his song and hangs up his headphones.

I end the recording and lean back in my seat, watching as he stalks through the door and toward me. "Dunno if that was the take," I say. "Felt like you were rushing it."

"We'll redo it later." He doesn't stop moving toward me.

Mischievous brown eyes lock on mine, but for some reason, all I can see are hazel ones.

I see blond hair in a man bun instead of Cash's long brown locks.

I shake away the image of the cute guy I met a few days ago. It was weird how that whole day transpired.

What's even weirder is that I can't stop thinking about him. I keep replaying his offer to be Kaylee's nanny and how he could take her to playgroups and give her the attention she needs.

I have this strong gut instinct to hire him, but I'm not completely sure it's coming from my gut. I think it could be coming from lower than that.

As if answering me, my dick twitches, and it has nothing to do with the rock star in front of me basically offering himself as a sex toy.

"Ry?" Cash asks, and I blink out of the inner argument I've been having with myself for days.

"Sorry, spaced for a second."

"Should I be offended?"

"I'm a bit distracted. Kid stuff." I wave him off.

"You know what's good for getting your mind off kid stuff?"

I roll my eyes. "Let me guess. Having sex with you again?"

"See." He waves his finger between us. "Same page. It's like, fate."

"Keep telling yourself that. It shouldn't have happened the first time. It's not going to happen again."

Cash presses his lips together. "This is … weird."

I laugh hard. "You really don't know how to handle rejection, do you?"

"I really don't!" He laughs.

"Look, I like you, and we're friends, but I don't date. It's that simple."

"This is sex, not dating. I don't date either." He shudders.

"I don't need sex that bad."

"Okay, *now* I'm offended."

I laugh. "No, you're not."

"Okay, no, I'm not. It's just, you can't get the opportunity for release too often with the kid being home and the world thinking you're straight. I'm offering no strings attached, and you're looking at me like I'm offering a plate of your least favorite dessert. You'll eat it once but pass on it the next time."

I don't know how to explain to Cash that my priorities the last few years have all revolved around one little girl, and that everything—including sex—isn't important in the broader scheme of things.

If it were to get out that I was having sex with Cash Kingsley, out and proud artist, Kaylee's life would be turned upside down.

"When you're a parent, you'll understand."

"Eww. No kids for me. Ever." He still looks disgusted at the suggestion. "But hypothetically, if in some alternate universe where I did have a kid, I don't understand why that means you can't have fun when she's not here."

I lean forward in my seat. "Okay, maybe I'll put it another way. What's your earliest memory? How old were you?"

He thinks about it. "Maybe four or five? I guess. I remember the old house we used to live in before my dad took off and it became just me and Mom."

Wow, okay, I didn't expect him to share that much, but it does prove my point. "Know how old my daughter is? She's almost five. I don't want her first memory to be strange men in her face asking if the rumors about her dad's sexuality are true. I don't want them telling her she's adopted or a test tube baby or any of those other stupid rumors out there. She already calls them *the bad men with cameras*. You remember your dad leaving. Imagine the kind of mental toll it would've taken if paparazzi were there taking photos of that moment and asking you about it. I need to keep her out of that life as much as possible. Even if it means I don't get a social life."

Cash frowns. "Okay, but you've hidden your sexuality from the public forever without it getting out. I don't know why a kid changes anything."

"Because before, the only person coming out could hurt was me. It's not worth the risk."

"Are you saying you don't trust me to keep it between us?"

"It's not that *exactly*. It's ..." I don't know how to explain it. "Okay, I can't believe I'm going to say this, but I actually learned something from all those 'God is great' schools I went to as a child. You know how they're all about 'the only form of safe sex is abstinence'? Same motto. I don't have to worry about anything getting out if there's nothing there."

Cash opens his mouth to say something when my phone starts vibrating on the table next to me.

"Shit, it's Kaylee's school."

I give him an apologetic stare as I answer the phone, but I'd be lying if I said I wasn't thankful for the opportunity to get out of this conversation. "Hello?"

"Hi, Mr. Kennedy. It's Tiffany from Vista Point." Her voice is the annoying, cringy type of bubbly. No one is that naturally happy. It's impossible.

"Is Kaylee okay?"

"Oh, well, we had a little incident." She's still bubbly. *Like, so sorry, sir, your daughter is in the hospital, but look on the bright side, she's not dead yet. Yay.*

"What type of accident?" I growl into the phone.

Fuck this school.

"Another ... biting incident. Though, this time she's asking for you."

"I'm on my way to pick her up." I hit End before she can tell me in her bubbly way that she'll see me soon.

She should be apologizing for not providing adequate care to my child.

"Rain check?" Cash asks.

"Sorry." I stand and shove my phone into my pocket.

"All good. When can we rework the song?" he asks.

"I was lying. You nailed it. We can move on to another song during your next session."

Instead of getting pissed for giving him shit, he laughs as he grabs his jacket and we walk out together.

Cash climbs onto his Vulcan motorcycle parked in my driveway and reaches for his helmet.

I eye the sexy bike but can't help asking, "Does the label know you ride around on that thing?"

"What they don't know won't hurt them."

"If you die because a semi flattens you, they'll hurt lots."

"Nah, they'll love it. Imagine my album sales if I die."

I cock my head. "I guess that's a positive way of looking at death?"

"It's not like I have anyone who'll miss me."

His sad confession hangs in the air, and I feel like I should say something.

As if sensing my concern, Cash dismisses it. "I mean, I have no responsibility like you do with your kid. I realize that might've come out more emo and depressing than I intended it."

I'm not entirely convinced, but whatever I sensed is gone as he sends me a cocky smile.

"Until our next session. I'll get my people to call your people."

I snort. "I don't have people anymore. Just a connection at the label who's throwing some producing work my way."

He puts on his helmet and fastens it, giving me a wave when he starts his bike and takes off.

As I get into my car and start the drive to Kaylee's school, my anger starts to simmer.

The school is doing nothing to help Kaylee.

My mind goes back to the guy offering to fix this situation for me.

There's something about the guy. He looks like an artist but has the soft touch of someone who works in childcare, and I can't help thinking he would be good for Kaylee.

At least, that's what I tell myself until my dick perks up and makes me think I'm contemplating hiring him for my own selfish reasons.

Though, it's not like he's unqualified. He's already saved me hours of sleep this week with his bedding trick.

Then I think about what it would be like to actually hire some random guy off the street to be my child's nanny. It's an insane idea and one my usually overprotective self wouldn't even contemplate. It would be safer to go through a nanny agency.

I can't remember the last time I had fun just talking with someone like that. Most of my conversations over the last few years have all been with a tiny human who asks things like, "Why can't we live on the moon?" or with musicians who are all professional. Well, except maybe Cash.

The way I got along with Lyric is part of why I don't want to hire him. I'm worried my intentions aren't entirely selfless, and like I told Cash, Kaylee is my priority, not my love life.

Yet, as I pull into Kaylee's school and then see my little girl in tears, sitting in a chair in the office, I know there's no way I can keep bringing her here.

"Mr. Kennedy." Tiffany approaches.

"Save it," I bark. I'm not the type of person to get angry—at anyone—but I'm mad now. "How do I unenroll her from this place?"

Kaylee's little ears prick up at my voice, and she runs right into my arms.

She has a bandage over her forearm.

Tiffany looks confused. "Unenroll?"

"Yes. Unenroll. As in Kaylee will no longer be going to this school."

"I don't … I mean, I can assure you this won't happen again."

"Hmm, you said that last time. I should've pulled her out then. Do whatever you have to do. Kaylee won't be coming back."

I pick up my daughter, and I'm vibrating with rage.

I never should've left her. Nope, she's not ready for school. Nope, nope, nope.

As I put her in her car seat and buckle her up, she looks up at me with her glassy green eyes. "Am I in trouble?"

"Oh, honey, no. Not at all. The school is. And the boy who bit you."

"My teacher says he has 'motional problems."

I'd hope so if he has a fascination with biting people.

"You don't have to go back there, okay?"

"But you said I have to make friends."

Oh, how my own words come back to bite me in the ass. It's on the tip of my tongue to say *I'll buy you new friends,* but I want genuine relationships for Kaylee.

"We'll work something out, honey," I say instead.

When we get home, I send Kaylee to her room to play with her toys while I jump online and look at the other schools Lyric recommended.

They all look great online, but my trust is a little shot.

I don't know if another school is the right move for Kaylee. She'll have to go next year, but right now, it's not compulsory. Why send a kid to school longer than she has to be there? I hated school growing up, mainly because it was all God this and God that, Texas is great and so is God!

I pick up my phone, hitting a number I rarely get to nowadays even though we were inseparable at one point in our lives.

Harley Valentine, ex-Eleven member, answers right away. "Please tell me you've considered my offer to get Eleven back together and you're jumping at the chance to go on tour with me again."

Of course that's the first thing he says. When he called a few months ago to tell me about his harebrained idea of getting Eleven back together, I told him he was drunk and hung up on him. Apparently, no, he wants it to be a thing.

"I told you, man. When we're forty."

"Can you really wait thirteen years to see my beautiful face again?"

"Who are you talking to?" comes a growly voice in the background.

"Ooh, someone's boyfriend is jealous of how beautiful *I* am," I taunt. "We both know I'm hotter than you."

"Calm down, Rambo," Harley says to his bodyguard boyfriend. "It's only Ryder."

"Nice to know you think so highly of me, but anyway, I'm calling because I need a favor."

"Yes. Yes, I will get Eleven back together for you. It's a sacrifice I'm willing to make."

"Not that."

"One day." Harley sighs.

"I can *hear* you pouting."

"Just wait. After I finish this tour, I'm coming after you … in a nonthreatening way."

I huff a laugh.

I'll never understand why he wants Eleven to get back together. Since splitting, Harley has gone on to win two Grammys on his own. He has the most success out of any of us, so this whole *get the boy band back together* thing doesn't make sense to me.

I'd jump at the chance if not for my current situation. The reason I left Eleven—to protect Kaylee—still hasn't changed. I don't know if it will until she's a grown-up, and right now, I can't even imagine her as a teenager, let alone an adult.

Oh God, a teenage girl. Nope, nope, nope, she will stay my baby forever.

"I need a favor from your badass boyfriend," I say.

"Need a bodyguard? Because mine is taken."

I laugh. "No, but I assume he and his badass friends you've told me about can do a background check on a nanny I'm thinking of hiring?"

"Background check? Wouldn't a nanny agency do that sort of thing?"

"Well, uh, he's not with an agency."

Silence.

"Harley?"

"You know you can't fuck your daughter's nanny, right? That'd be like …"

"Like a famous person fucking their bodyguard?"

"Touché."

"And I don't want to fuck him. I want to hire him to look after Kaylee."

"Male nanny … interesting."

"He's just a nanny. Why do you have to put his gender in front of it?"

"Sorry."

"Anyway, can he?"

Harley's voice goes quieter as he dips the phone away from his mouth. "Hey, Brix, can you do a background check for Ryder on the guy he says he doesn't want to fuck but really he does?"

"Harley," I growl.

But I no longer care about him giving me shit when his boyfriend says it's easily done. I give them Lyric's name and the phone number he gave me, and Brix promises to get back to me as soon as possible.

If it all comes back clear, I'll have no reason not to hire him. He needs the job, and I need a nanny.

I can put my attraction to Lyric aside for Kaylee. I've practically been a monk for years. Minus that one slip with Cash.

Easy.

Totally easy.

CHAPTER 4
LYRIC

LITTLE SECRET about those so-called talent shows: majority of people who get through the large cattle-call casting audition are handpicked and selected after private auditions first.

Which is how I've ended up here. At yet another audition where I'm failing miserably.

Rumor has it, Denver from Eleven is one of the judges on this new show. It's supposed to reinvent all the *Idol*, *The Voice*, and *X Factor* shows there have been throughout the years.

I was hoping Denver would be here so I could break the ice with, "Hey, I met Ryder the other day," but no, I'm standing across from two producers who are wearing passive expressions after I finish my rendition of "It's Time" by Imagine Dragons.

I blink at them.

They blink back.

I know how this ends. "Thank you for your time."

Crouching down, I start putting my guitar away when they whisper to each other. I can't hear the words, but I don't need to.

I'm already running the audition over in my head and trying to pinpoint where I went wrong. My pitch was great, my guitar-playing flawless. The only thing I can think of is that they don't see that thing inside me. The spark. The *it* factor.

Story of my life.

"Mr. Jones, can you hold a second?"

Hope blooms in my gut, but I don't have faith it'll last. I'm waiting for the inevitable "Thanks but no thanks" speech.

That's not what they give me.

"You have an identity problem." This coming from a guy with a bland face, even blander suit, and the personality of a walnut, but sure, I have the identity problem.

"How so? If you don't mind me asking."

"You dress like you want to be a rock star and sing like Kurt Cobain, but your face screams pop. We're willing to give you the on-air audition if you dress trendier and sing a Harley Valentine song."

Oh dear God. I've died and gone to hell, haven't I?

"Like I said earlier, thank you for your time."

I turn to leave, catching their stunned expressions as I do. They're probably not used to being turned down, but my dad spent his entire life changing his image because of advice "the professionals" gave him. He sold his soul to become famous. I want fame but not at the cost of being myself. If the public doesn't want me as me, then I'm happy to teach kids to become better humans than those who judge us solely on our looks or what we're into.

Maybe Ryder was right when he said that's naïve of me, but I won't give up my life the way my father did.

Regret might haunt me for the ride home, and I might scold myself for being stupidly stubborn, but by the time I pull into Chase's school to pick him up, I'm over it.

I'm going to stand my ground. And hey, if this industry kills me before I'm famous, at least I can say I went down with dignity.

While waiting for Chase in the long-ass pickup line at school, my phone starts vibrating, and I hate that I hope it's the producers from the show saying I can audition as myself.

It's a blocked number.

It could be them.

I hold my breath and barely get out a "Lyric Jones" as I answer.

"Hey, uh, Lyric." The warm voice sends a jolt of want to my dick. It's definitely not the producers. "It's, umm, Ryder. Uh, Kennedy."

Holy shit.

Holy fucking shit.

"Hello, Ryder, uh, Kennedy."

"This is awkward." He lets out a chuckle. "So, I've been thinking."

"Is it always awkward when you think?"

"Yeah." Ryder's voice is quiet. "Pretty much."

"You calling to set up a playdate for the kids?"

"Actually, no. Well, yes. I mean, if you're going to be Kaylee's nanny, I assume Kaylee and Chase will be spending a lot of time together."

I pause, not entirely sure I heard him correctly. "Nanny … You want me … to nanny."

I have to contain the urge to fist-bump the roof of my sister-in-law's car.

"I took Kaylee out of that school, and as much as I trust your judgment on the others, I'm thinking maybe she's not ready. We can try again next year somewhere better."

"Hmm. I don't know how I feel about this. I mean, working for my best friend might be crossing lines."

"Ha, ha. Still going with best friends, are we?"

"No one can dispute our best-friend meet-cute. What are we talking in terms of the job? Full-time for at least six months?" That would be perfect for what I need. Money and temporary.

"If she likes you and the arrangement works, yes."

"I'm in. Do you need to see my credentials or run a background check? I can get all the info—"

"Already done. I have connections."

"Impressive. And a little creepy."

"Oh, I know things about you that you probably don't even know."

I have to be reading into his flirty tone. Have to be. "Like what?"

"Stuff …"

"What kind of connections do you have? If I say I need two producers whacked, can you do that?"

Ryder's laugh is warm. "Scarily, I think I could. Not that I would. Another bad audition?"

"Yup. You'll get a kick out of this. They wanted me to sing a Harley Valentine song."

Instead of laughing his head off like I thought he would, Ryder makes a noise like he's about to say something but cuts himself off.

I can practically imagine his mouth opening and closing.

"Are you sure you want to use me for a nanny job instead of a meeting with a label head?" he eventually asks.

My stubbornness rears its ugly head again. "I'm sure. When do you need me?"

"When can you start?"

"I have a free day tomorrow."

"Then tomorrow. I'll email you the details and a standard contract I used to have with the nannies on tour."

"I'm not being cocky when I say you won't regret this. I'll be the best nanny your kid has ever had."

"Hmm, we'll see. I expect you to do all those things you said you would. Like taking her to playgroups and having her interact with other children."

"Whatever you want, boss."

I'm met with silence again.

"Umm, hello?"

"Call me Ryder. Not boss." His friendly tone holds something I can't decipher, but I shrug it off.

"See you tomorrow. *Ryder.*"

His name feels weird rolling off my tongue without including his last name.

I'm gonna have to get used to that real fast.

Ryder's house is off Mulholland Highway in Calabasas, hidden behind a large gate.

Brenna, my sister-in-law, reaches out the driver's window and hits the buzzer.

The gate slowly opens, and she crawls up the long drive. When the house comes into view, she lets out a loud whistle.

The U-shaped resort-style home is overwhelming. I stare up at the two-story beige house with a three-car garage and windows everywhere that must belong to countless rooms. It has been easy to forget how famous Ryder actually is until now. He didn't come across as the "mansion in the Santa Monica hills" type of guy the other day.

It makes sense because, duh, *Eleven*, but the house doesn't seem to fit the Ryder I met. Because talking to him for a couple of hours means I know him so well and everything.

"Let me know when you're finished, and I'll come pick you up," Brenna says.

"It's okay. I'll get the bus, but thank you."

"It's no trouble—"

I give her a smile. "I mooch off you guys enough. You don't need to be my personal taxi too."

"Lyric, it's not like that, and you know it."

"The bus is good. It's only one change and two and a half hours. Easy."

"I'm picking you up." She's cute when she thinks she can beat me at the stubborn game.

"You can't do that if you don't know when to pick me up," I sing.

"Then I'm staying right here. All day."

"You have to go pick up Chase at some point. Also, I don't know how good an impression it would be to have my own babysitter while I'm babysitting."

She grunts. "Fine. You win. Have a good day." It doesn't sound like she means that.

The front door to the house opens, and Kaylee comes running out with Ryder not far behind her. He yells for her to get back inside, but she ignores him.

Brenna laughs. "Oh, this could be super fun for you."

"Nah, he's straight." At least, that's what most of the media says.

Brenna laughs harder. "I meant because she seems like a handful, but good to know where your head is at. Or, not your head."

Oh. Right.

I clear my throat. "My head is nowhere near Ryder Kennedy. Only in the game."

"Right. Hey, can I buy one of the flying pigs you're trying to sell?"

"You're lucky my brother loves you. For some reason."

Before she can say anything else, I grab my bag and jump out of the car, giving her a wave as she pulls away.

"Lyric!" Kaylee bounds up to me. "Where's Chase?"

I kneel to her level. "Chase is at school."

"Daddy says I don't have to go to school anymore."

"You don't. You get to spend time with me instead. Does that sound fun?"

"It be funner if Chase was here too."

"Kaylee," Ryder groans.

I laugh. "It's okay. I'd rather hang out with Chase than myself too."

"Is tact something you can teach her?" Ryder asks.

"I can try. Doesn't work with Chase though."

Ryder gestures to the house. "Let's go inside so we can go over your contract."

I stand to full height. "Right. About that …"

"Already a problem?"

"No. Well, not really. I told you my brother's an entertainment lawyer. Contracts are his life. Well, he read over what you sent and has some changes."

"Then let's discuss them."

He leads Kaylee and me inside, and I try not to trip over my feet when I see the grand staircase in the foyer or the formal seating area around a fireplace to the left. Everything is pristine and clean, and every little thing has its place, like the potted cacti in the long windowsills and plain white knickknacks on the mantel above the fireplace.

Maybe my eyes give something away because Ryder turns to me.

"We don't use this half of the house. This is, like, the display part where if anyone comes over, it looks like I have my shit together."

Oh, to have so much money you can divide your house into *everyday use* and *special occasion*.

We walk down the hall behind the staircase, past a large marble kitchen on the left, a formal dining room after that, and then we take a right where there's a large living room with a sectional couch, big-screen TV, and glass coffee table.

All I think is thank fuck cleaning is not in my job description.

Ryder pauses outside two large sliding doors and turns to me. "I apologize in advance for the chaos you're about to witness. This used to be the nanny's quarters when we had a live-in when Kaylee was younger, but since we haven't had anyone working for us for two years, it's kind of turned into a play area."

I don't have the heart to tell him the carefully decorated and meticulously placed *everything* on this side of the house probably scares me more than anything that's behind those doors.

But as he slides them open, nope, I'm wrong.

So wrong.

"Did a toy store explode in here?" I step into the room which is another large living area.

Every toy known to man covers the floors, the shelving … everything.

There's another, smaller, single-counter kitchen in here, and a bedroom at the back.

"I did ask Kaylee to tidy for your arrival, and then I found her forcing her GI Joes to kiss right before you buzzed. I probably should have supervised the cleaning part."

"Guess so. Though, are you sure she was *forcing* them to kiss each other? Growing up, my GI Joes were all for kissing other boys." I wink at Kaylee.

Kaylee tugs on Ryder's hand. "Told you, Daddy."

Ryder smiles down at his daughter. "And I told you to clean up this mess. How about you do that while I talk with Lyric?"

"How about you clean and *I* talk to Lyric?"

"This isn't a negotiation." He boops her on her nose and then gestures for me to follow him.

He leads me through a side door and down a narrow hallway to an office. This part looks newer than the rest, though. Like it's an addition to the original building.

"Dude, you have your own recording studio?"

Glass separates us from a soundproof booth with microphones, and a glass-paneled door to my right leads to a control room.

"Built it back when Eleven was still together. Before …" He glances at the door.

Before Kaylee.

"Ah. Got it."

Ryder pushes a seat out so I can sit and then takes one for himself.

"So, what's wrong with the contract?" He reaches for the desk drawer and pulls out a copy of the one he sent to me yesterday.

"Nothing wrong, per se, but the contract is for a live-in nanny situation, which this isn't, and it also has clauses pertaining to tour schedules and bonuses which don't apply to me because you don't tour anymore. So, factoring in the live-in wage being lower than average, and touring bonuses I don't qualify for, the base pay … in my brother's words is, umm … shitty."

"Shitty?"

"Like, isn't even minimum wage kind of shitty."

Ryder looks horrified and starts flicking through pages. "Really? Fuck."

"Daddy said a bad word!" Kaylee yells from down the hall.

"Doesn't sound like a whole lot of cleaning is going on in there!" he calls back.

I try not to laugh.

"I'm so sorry," he says to me. "I had no idea."

"It's okay. It's obvious you weren't doing it to be cheap. Your previous nannies were paid really well, but the situations were different."

"I, hmm … I used the contract my old nanny agency sent me. I guess I can't call them and ask for a blank one so I know what to put in it."

I reach into my bag and pull out the contract my brother drew up. "I have this. Chord did it for me. It's basically the same as your old one, but it adjusts the wage to my situation, factoring in an hourly rate based on what nanny agencies typically charge, and then overtime clauses as well if you need me to stay late for whatever reason. Like, if you have public appearances at night or something."

Ryder scoffs. "Won't be any chance of that happening. I stepped away from everything when I left Eleven."

"A date, then."

He levels me with a look I can't figure out. "There's more chance of me making a public appearance. I don't date."

My eyes widen. "*Ever?*"

"Ever."

That might be the saddest thing to happen to humanity.

The urge to ask about Kaylee's mom is on the tip of my tongue, but I hold it back. There's not much to find about her on the internet. Either his PR people did an amazing cover-up job or she didn't want fame. I don't know. All I've found out is she's his childhood friend.

The tabloids claimed she was a fame whore who wanted attention, but if that were the case, surely everyone would know more about her. Others say she was paid to disappear. Then there are the rumors that the whole daughter thing is a hoax and a publicity stunt to cover the fact Ryder's gay.

As much as I wish he were gay, I'm pretty sure he wouldn't have full custody of some random publicity stunt child or give up his career for her to cover that up.

"Single by choice?" I blurt out and then realize it's an inappropriate question to ask my new boss. "I only ask because I'm the same way. Only, not on purpose."

He eyes me, but it's more scrutinizing than anything else. "Please, like it'd be impossible for you to get a date."

"You'd be surprised."

Ryder's brow scrunches as he gives me another once-over.

I clear my throat.

He snaps out of it. "What were we saying? Oh, right. Nights. I might need you to stay late sometimes if recording goes over schedule like sessions tend to do. I know Kaylee will be asleep, but I'd feel safer knowing you'd be here if she was to wake up or something. Artists tend to get diva-y on me if I leave them waiting. Crazy, right?"

"I can work weeknights, but I gig on weekends."

"That should be fine. I was only booking sessions for when Kaylee was in school, but I figure by hiring you I can extend my available hours. I'll make sure to block out weekends."

We talk more about schedules, and I'm happily relieved Ryder's more than okay with me keeping my afternoons with Chase.

Cars are an issue—mainly, I don't have one—but Ryder's even flexible on that too.

"I have my sister-in-law's car on the days I have to pick up Chase from school, and on the other days, I figure if Kaylee and I want to go out, we can catch the bus."

"No bus. The public shouldn't recognize Kaylee without me, but she is known by paparazzi and superfans. I'm not comfortable—"

"That's okay. Umm, I could maybe work it out with Brenna to get her car more or—"

"No need. On days you don't have a car, you can take mine, and I'll use one of my … toys if I need to go out."

"Toys?"

"You know how some people collect coins or stamps or, I don't know, old video games? I might collect cars. Just a little bit."

"How many do you have?"

"Eight. Nine including the Tesla, but that doesn't count."

"Right. Because a Tesla is an everyday kind of car. Got it."

Ryder smiles in a way that really makes me want to see what other cars he has in his garage.

"Is that everything?" Ryder asks. "Any more questions?"

"I think I'm good for now."

Ryder stands. "I figured you guys could hang out here today while I work in case you had any problems or whatever."

I pick up my bag, and we make our way back down the hall toward Kaylee's playroom. The hallway is narrow, and our shoulders bump as we walk side by side. "I'm sure we'll be fine, but if you're more comfortable with us staying in for the day, that's okay."

"Am I that transparent?"

"Yep, but it's all good. We all have to grow to trust each other, and that takes time. It's not like I was sent here by an agency or have references or anything. And now I'm probably talking you out of hiring me. Good one, Lyric."

Ryder laughs. "No, I stand by my decision. I can't explain why my gut is telling me this is the right move. I guess I'm a sucker for guys who insult me."

I swear I hear a flirty tone in there, but then I remind myself it's probably my dick hearing it, not my ears.

I pause outside the door. "It'll be fine. It won't take long to get into a routine. I promise."

CHAPTER 5
RYDER

IF THE BIGGER MESS Kaylee made while we went over the contract didn't scare Lyric off, I was sure my involuntary innuendo and compliments might've done it.

Like it'd be impossible for you to get a date.

I cringe just thinking about it and keep trying to delete it from my mind, but it replays over and over again.

All day while I half-heartedly work on Cash's new single, I keep an ear out for them. I have my headphones on with one ear still exposed so I can hear.

Every time Kaylee's little laugh filters down the hallway, I want to run in there and see what she thinks is funny, but I don't. I don't want to be that overbearing father who uses any excuse to go check on them. It's true what they say about parental instinct. I worry all the fucking time, and it's exhausting.

I should be here, focusing on the sexy rasp of Cash's voice, but instead, I want to go down that hallway and see what they're doing.

When I finally cave and take a break around lunchtime, I find Kaylee sitting and waiting patiently at the little table next to the kitchen while Lyric makes her a sandwich.

The sight is wrong on so many levels. Not only because one, my daughter is quiet, and two, the bomb site this place was this morning is gone and replaced with a neat and tidy area where every toy is in its place, but the most important thing is the way Lyric smiles as he makes my daughter food.

I was never attracted to any of Kaylee's other nannies before. They were pretty women, and they'd flirt with me, which was more annoying than charming, but while I reside on the gayer end of the Kinsey scale, I don't think that's why it's different with Lyric.

I'm starting to regret using his number to hire him instead of asking him out. Not that I would actually go out with him anyway.

This was a mistake.

Lyric's gaze finds mine. "I asked her if she had any allergies, and she said no. I figured the half-empty peanut butter jar meant she was right."

"Yeah, no allergies here. At all."

"Good to know. Landing in the hospital on our first day wasn't on my list of goals."

"That's a good goal to have. If you could stick to that one, I'd be grateful."

Lyric's lips curve up at the sides. "Can I make you anything for lunch? I have mad sandwich-making skills."

"I usually have a frozen meal for lunch and do the home-cooked meal thing for dinner." I go to the freezer. "There're heaps in here if you wanted something other than peanut butter."

"You live on Lean Cuisines?"

"They're easy and healthy and tasty."

"If you enjoy the taste of cardboard," he mutters. "I'm good with PB and J, thanks. I told you I'm basically like a child. My eating habits also reflect that."

"Why am I not surprised?" I throw my meal in the microwave and lean against the counter as I watch him finish the sandwiches.

Damn it, why does blowing off work to spend the afternoon in here with them sound more appealing than doing the very thing I begged the label to let me do.

I wanted to go back to work because, after two years, not only did I want a break from parenting but I missed music. I missed being in a studio and creating art. Even if Lyric thinks what I do isn't considered art.

Music is an outlet that's good for the soul and should be about emotion, and while we didn't get a lot of that in Eleven, that doesn't mean I don't have notebooks full of "real" music I want to record or produce one day.

One day when Kaylee's old and married.

When the microwave beeps, I move toward them and sit at the table.

Lyric shoves bread in his mouth. "Enjoy your cardboard."

Kaylee looks confused. "Daddy isn't eating cardboard."

"Mmm, vegetables," I say and take a bite.

"Eww, gross," Kaylee says.

"High five." Lyric holds up his hand, and Kaylee doesn't hesitate.

"Part of your job is to get her to eat her vegetables, you know," I tell him.

"That's okay. I have a trick."

"What's the trick?" I ask.

"I can't give away all my secrets."

"PB and J!" Kaylee yells. "No vegetables."

"Don't worry. I won't torture you with veggies," Lyric promises, but he winks at me.

My stomach flips.

At a fucking wink.

I definitely made a mistake in hiring him, but do I regret it? Not one bit.

I force myself to go back to work after lunch because I get the feeling Lyric thinks I'm checking up on him. Which, okay, technically I was, but that's not the point. I wanted to be out there for more reasons than just my daughter's safety, and that's not okay.

I knew hiring him was a risk because of how drawn to him I was the day we met, but I thought it would be easy to compartmentalize. Clearly, I'm a dumbass.

When I finally manage to put it out of my mind, I get lost in what I need to do and then lose track of time.

It's not until Lyric knocks on my office door and I blink out of my stupor that I realize it's dark outside the single window in this part of the house.

"Shit, what time is it?"

"Seven thirty. Kaylee just went down."

"Sorry I kept you. You should've come to find me at five."

He shrugs. "Overtime, right? And I didn't want to disrupt whatever you were doing in here."

"Thank you, and yes, you'll be paid for your time. I'll set an alarm or something so I don't go over tomorrow. I've been working on this album for Cash Me Outside, and—"

Lyric's mouth drops open. "Cash Me Outside? As in Cash Kingsley was here? In this room?" He glances around as if saying his name could summon Cash.

His excitement is cute. "Fan?"

"A little … Okay, a lot."

"You want to hear it?"

"Fu—dge yes." He throws himself in the seat next to mine.

"Kaylee's asleep. You're allowed to say fuck."

"I'm trying to break the habit. Not just for Kaylee but for Chase."

"I should probably try that. The other day, Kaylee threw her shirt across the room and said, 'It fucking itches.' I mean, it was kind of adorable, and part of me was proud she got the right context, but you know, it's not so great for school."

"We could start a swear jar."

"I would go broke," I mutter.

"You could probably pay my wage right into the jar." Lyric smiles, and that's dangerous. Because he's so goddamn gorgeous it's not even funny. Or fair.

And now I'm staring.

Shit. *Stop staring.*

"Okay, the song." I unplug my headphones so it will play through the speakers.

"Am I allowed?"

"Are you going to record it on your phone and leak it before it's out?"

"Fuck no."

"Dollar in the jar."

"Fuck."

I laugh. "We'll start tomorrow. Tell me what you think of this." I hit Play.

The song I've listened to countless times fills the room, and instead of analyzing the sound and the quality and listening to it as a product, I watch as Lyric gets into the song the way a fan would.

I see the moment he falls in love. His lips curve upward, and his eyes are full of awe. His gaze flicks over to mine, and even though I've been caught staring, I don't avert my gaze.

I can't.

The music speaks to him in a way it's not resonating with me, and I need to search his face to figure out if it's just me being overbearing and controlling over my work or if he's placating me to be nice.

He clears his throat. "It's ... good."

"Good? That's it?" I run my hand through my hair. "Cash is so gonna fire me."

"No, no, it's amazing. It's his best song. Like, shit, I'm jealous over here. I couldn't think of a word that would do it justice."

"So you settled for *good*? Maybe when we save up enough money in the swear jar, we can buy you a thesaurus."

Lyric's phone pings the telltale sound of a Grindr notification, and he stiffens. Not that I've ever used Grindr. Okay, I did for a while, but I could never go through with anything other than some messaging back and forth.

"Hot date?" I ask.

"Uh, I, umm, it's probably Brenna, my sister-in-law. I texted her to see if she could come pick me up since I stayed late."

That could be the truth. Maybe he set all his alerts to sound like the default Grindr tone, but I get the feeling he's lying.

I don't know what I hate more: the lying or that he's active on a hookup app. Not that he's not allowed to be, but ... no. Just ... no.

"You really should have come and disrupted me. I promise I don't mind."

"I will tomorrow, then. Are you sure it's okay for me to bring Chase back here after he finishes school?"

I wave him off. "It'll give Kaylee someone to play with."

"Speaking of which, I have a list of playgroups I can take her to if you want to have a look." Lyric hands his phone over which is open to a website.

While I'm scrolling through and clicking on each one, I realize I have no idea what to look for. "I trust your judgment."

"Maybe I can check out a few of them and see which one fits best."

"Sounds good." I go to pass his phone back when a notification pops up on his screen.

There's definitely no mistaking it this time. Especially considering part of the Grindr message shows, and it's a request for dick pics.

"Well, I really hope that's not your sister-in-law asking to see your dick."

He turns red as he takes his phone back. "Shit, shit, fucking shit."

"That's four bucks in the swear jar."

He doesn't appear amused. "I want you to know that Kaylee won't see any of those messages or anything on my phone. The full display only comes up if the phone is unlocked, and I keep it in my pocket when I'm working. I don't—"

I touch his arm because he's borderline freaking out. "Lyric, I believe you. It's okay."

He lets out a relieved breath, and I have to remind myself to let his arm go. His surprisingly toned arm. *Damn it, Ryder. Stop.*

"Thank God. I thought I'd gone and fu—dged this whole thing up."

"Not at all." But I swallow the lump in my throat. "Though, words of advice? Dick pics aren't cool."

Lyric bursts out laughing. "No, they're not. And yet, I still get requests daily."

"I thought you said you have trouble getting dates?"

He looks at me like I'm a moron. "I have no trouble finding hookups. Actual dates that could lead to a boyfriend? Nope."

"I don't think Grindr is the place to do that. It's a cesspool."

He pauses, and I realize I tripped up.

We stare at each other, and his curious eyes almost have me blurting my sexuality all over him like a unicorn vomiting rainbows.

"I'm guessing it's like Tinder." I hold my breath.

"It really is," Lyric says.

It's not that I'm purposefully keeping it from him—okay, maybe I am—but the thing is, if I tell him now, it would seem sleazy as fuck.

First day on the job and I'm all "Oh, by the way, I'm not as straight as everyone thinks I am."

It would look like I'd only hired him for one reason, and I didn't.

I didn't.

He's good for Kaylee, or he will be.

Minus a few industry people and those closest to me, no one knows the truth about me. I've pretended to be straight for this long; I can keep it up in Lyric's presence.

"You really don't date?" Lyric asks.

"I couldn't imagine dating again. I haven't since … basically when Kaylee was born."

Lyric's eyes widen.

I laugh. "That look on your face says it all. I don't have time to date and no one to look after Kaylee if I did."

"You have me now."

That idea excites me until I realize he's talking about looking after Kaylee while I go out on a date. With someone who isn't him.

"I really can't see myself sitting across from someone at a restaurant and doing the whole 'getting to know you' thing. Not to mention the press would have a field day. I'm trying to disappear from the spotlight here."

"Can I ask about …" Lyric hesitates.

I know what he's going to say because it's what everyone wants to know. "Kaylee's mom?"

"It's okay if you don't want to get into it. It's just no one really knows much about her."

"Her request." I know he wants more, but I don't know if I can give it.

The truth of what Maggie and I had is a little sad and somewhat bitter, but we got Kaylee out of it.

"We were childhood friends."

"How did you end up with sole custody?" His phone chimes again, and this time it's a regular message tone. "Oh. Brenna's outside the gate."

"Story for another time, then." Or never. I'm good with never too.

Lyric stands. "I'll see you in the morning." He's halfway out the door when he turns at the last second. "Oh, and there's leftover spaghetti with a million different vegetables hidden in the sauce if you're hungry. Kaylee ate it without complaint."

Lyric leaves with a cocky smile and a huge chunk of my respect.

CHAPTER 6
LYRIC

I THINK I'm impressing Ryder with my awesome ability to hide vegetables in Kaylee's food. All week, she's eaten whatever I've made her without even a hint of hesitation.

If she were ever to figure it out, all trust between us would be shot, so I have to hope she's like Chase and remains oblivious.

Because I like working for Ryder and Kaylee.

It's only been a week, but we've eased into a routine without too many hiccups.

The only big issue was a superfan who recognized Kaylee at one of the playgroups. We left early and haven't been back.

The group I ended up choosing is a mixture of low-key nannies with only one or two high-maintenance moms.

So far, it's been great.

I use my key to let myself into Ryder's place, and I find both of them in Kaylee's playroom. Her bright green eyes look up at me, and she puts a finger to her lips. "Shh. Daddy's sleeping."

As if on cue, Ryder lets out a little snore.

"Did you wake him up really early?" I whisper.

"No! It was almost light out!"

It's my turn to put my fingers to my lips and shush her, but it's too late.

Ryder startles awake, sees me, and groans. "Five more minutes."

I laugh. "Want me to make you coffee?"

"An IV drip would work better, but that's not part of your job description."

"What are best friends for?"

Ryder shakes his head at me with a smile.

"Kaylee, come help me make coffee."

"I can't make coffee." She giggles. "I'm only four."

"You're almost five. Five-year-olds can make coffee."

She screws up her cute little face. "I don't think they can."

"I'll let you pour the milk into the frothing jug."

That gets her moving. I'll have her making lattes before she knows it. Ryder can thank me later … or lecture me about child labor laws. One or the other.

Ryder's face is the definition of grateful as he sits up and I hand over his mug.

"She ended up in my bed last night. Which, of course, doesn't have your mattress protector trick going on. Murphy's Law."

"Aww, I'm sorry you had a rough night. Have you got much planned for today?"

"I was actually hoping to come see Kaylee's playgroup."

I must make a face or something because he pauses.

"Not a good idea?"

"I think it would be good for you to see Kaylee interacting with the other kids, but I don't know the mothers and other nannies well yet. I'm wondering how they'll react to Ryder Kennedy crashing the class."

"My guess is they'll be fine with it. Probably too fine with it."

"That's what I mean. It might be a pain in the ass for you. And then they'll know for sure who Kaylee belongs to."

"If you think it'll make things weird—"

"It won't be weird for me. I'm worried for you after the play center thing."

Kaylee looks at her father with the biggest puppy dog eyes I've ever seen on a human … or a dog for that matter. Holy shit, it would be impossible to say no to that face. "Please come, Daddy. I want you to meet my friends. I have *friends*!"

"I'd like to meet them," Ryder says and then looks up at me. "If that's okay."

"I guess we're about to find out just how cool everyone at play-group is. Or isn't."

Hopefully they won't react like that other playgroup mom did.

We get ready for the day, and Ryder watches as I prepare a plate of celery and carrot sticks to take.

"Healthy snacks only," I tell him.

"Are you *sure* this is the right playgroup?"

"Hey, at least I only have to bring this. I think they took pity on me since I'm the only male in the group and gave me the easiest job. Also, the less sugar I feed your kid, the easier she is for you to deal with after I go home."

"Oh. True."

"Ready to go?" I ask.

Ryder turns to Kaylee. "Ready to go, bub?" When she runs toward the front door, a line forms in Ryder's forehead. "She was never that excited to go to school."

"She's doing great."

Ryder loses some tension in his stiff shoulders. "I still wonder if I made the right decision. I never know if I have when it comes to her."

"Welcome to parenting. I remember my brother freaking out when Chase came along. Thought he wasn't doing anything right." I give him a reassuring smile. "All you have to do is see how excited she is to know you did the right thing. And I'm not just saying that because I have an actual paying job now and I want to keep it."

"Good to know."

Ryder lets me drive since I know where we're going.

The whole way there, Kaylee is her normal chatty self.

"Will Wicker be there?"

"No reason he wouldn't be," I say and try to cover my laugh as Ryder gives me the side-eye.

He mouths, "Wicker?"

"How do cows fart?" Kaylee asks.

"The same way dogs fart," I say simply.

Ryder looks horrified in the passenger seat.

"How do dogs fart?" Kaylee asks.

I don't miss a beat. "The same way cats fart."

"How do—"

Ryder turns around in his seat. "The same way every animal on the planet farts."

It's cute he thinks that means she'll stop.

"How do aliens fart?"

There it is.

Ryder groans.

I answer like any sane person would. "We don't even know if aliens have butts. If they don't have butts, they can't fart."

"Can we stop talking about farting?" Ryder asks.

"I'm trying to educate your child," I argue.

"On alien farts?"

"It's important she learns about the entire universe. Be thankful we haven't gotten onto Uranus yet."

Ryder levels me with a look. "It's pronounced Ura-ness."

"I like the other way better. More fun."

Out of the corner of my eye, I see Ryder shift in his seat.

"Why are elbows called elbows?" Kaylee asks.

Ryder throws his head back and mutters, "Holy mother of Jesus, are we almost there?"

"Almost," I sing.

I pull into the parking lot of the playground we're meeting at today and find a parking space near the entry.

Kaylee clicks herself out of her booster seat and moves like lightning to get out of the car and run across the field to where a group of women crowd around picnic tables.

"And she's gone," Ryder says as we climb out to follow her.

"Yeah. I've been trying to get her not to do that, but she gets too excited and doesn't think. She definitely keeps me on my toes."

"You and me both."

We watch as Kaylee runs off with two other children to climb the jungle gym.

"So, who's this Wicker kid, and how judgy are we over that name?"

"Hey, just because you refuse to conform to celebrity norms and name your child something weird doesn't mean you get to judge others."

Ryder narrows his gaze at me.

I laugh. "I'm fucking with you. We judge very much. But he's a good kid. The mom is your typical gluten-free, sugar-free, all organic type of mom."

"Ah."

We move toward the table where the moms and other nannies are sitting and watching the kids play.

Ryder adjusts his cap, and I can tell he's holding his breath as we reach them.

I put the plate of celery and carrot sticks in the middle of other snacks. "Hey, everyone, this is Kaylee's dad—"

It starts with a gasp. And then another.

And now all eyes are on him.

I'm sure he's used to this, but I wonder if it ever gets any easier.

"Hey, I'm Ryder."

They stare blankly at him.

"If you're pausing for me to say my last name, I won't."

I get what he means. Thinking of Ryder as just Ryder has been an adjustment. It's hard not to add Kennedy to the end.

"He's only Ryder. Nothin' special." I shrug.

Ryder tilts his head in my direction. "Really? That's what you're going with?"

I turn to the group. "If you tell him his music is bad, he'll give you a job."

Kathy widens her eyes at me. "Lyric Jones, please tell me you didn't do that?"

"I soooo did, but it worked out for me."

"What can I say? There's something about Lyric's bluntness I like."

Kathy nods. "He does have a certain way of charming us all, which is why he gets away with bringing the easiest share platter."

I grin. "I'm unapologetically me."

The mom I told Ryder about approaches him. "I'm Ria, Wicker's mom."

Ryder glances at me over her head with a knowing smirk. "Nice to meet you."

"Welcome to playgroup."

"I was under the impression playgroup was more like a classroom thing."

"Oh, we have classroom days too," I say.

"We're what we like to call a pop-up playgroup," Ria says, "so each day we do something different. You came on a fun day where the kids get to play and us *single* parents get a break."

I don't miss the way she emphasizes the word single, and my automatic response is to frown.

Ryder's all charm as he asks about what other activities the kids do. The women flock to him, and ugh, ugh, ugh.

I knew they might be a bit crazy because he's Ryder Kennedy. I didn't even think about them all trying to get into his pants.

Doesn't take a genius to work out I'm jealous.

My wee little crush on my boss might have an ugly side.

"I was so devastated when Eleven broke up," Ria says.

Ryder shifts uncomfortably. "I'm, uh, sorry about that."

"Was it really a big fight like they say?" Kathy says.

The forced smile on my boss's face says it all. "No, it really wasn't. The others were ready to move on, and I was ready to focus on Kaylee."

"Because her mom's not in the picture? What's her deal?" Ria asks.

"Whoa," I cut in. "I told him you were all cool. Don't make me take that back."

"Sorry," Ria whispers.

"I'm gonna go check on Kaylee," Ryder says, maybe a bit too loudly.

As he walks away, I turn to them. "I like coming to this playgroup. Please don't make it so awkward I have to find a new one for Kaylee."

"Sorry," everyone murmurs.

"It's …" Kathy watches Ryder's retreating form and lowers her voice. "It's Ryder Kennedy. My inner teenager is squealing."

"You're married," I point out.

"I have a hall pass." Kathy winks.

"I'm not married," Ria says.

I wave my finger, pointing at all of them. "Don't make me go get some cold water. Ryder told me he hasn't dated since Kaylee's mom, so put your hormones away."

Ria gasps. "He doesn't date? *Ever*? That's such an injustice to all womankind."

And I'm out. "I'm gonna go check on Kaylee too."

"We'll behave," Kathy says. "We promise."

I wave them off and move toward Ryder anyway.

He's pushing Kaylee on the swing when I get to him.

"Daddy! I can do it myself!" she yells. "Lyric taught me how."

Ryder eyes me. "Did he now? This I've got to see."

We step aside and watch as Kaylee swings her legs to make herself go higher and higher.

"You were right about coming here," he mutters while making impressed faces at his daughter.

"I'm sorry about them."

"Eh, I'm used to it. Not so used to the bluntness about Maggie, though."

"Maggie?"

"Kaylee's mom."

"Sorry. I wasn't sure how they'd react to you, but I didn't think they'd actually cross personal boundaries."

"You'll find out for yourself one day when you're famous."

I scoff. "Yeah. Okay. At this rate, I don't think that'll ever happen. Had another rejection over the weekend. A manager came to see me play. He didn't even stay for my whole set."

"Sorry. That sucks."

I shrug. "I'll just keep plugging away."

Ryder touches my arm. "Until you become famous, you can continue to be my protector."

"From horny moms?"

Ryder laughs. "I was going to say from all the personal questions, but I guess yours works too. Thank you for butting in over there. Not everyone would have. People come to expect celebrities to deal with stuff like that. We don't get personal boundaries."

"Maybe I don't want fame after all." I'm only half-joking.

"Nah, fame is awesome. It's just ten times harder when you're trying to protect someone else." He looks at his daughter as if she hung the moon.

But behind his proud blue eyes lies a whole lot of guilt.

"Into the unknoooooown!" I sing at the top of my lungs along with Kaylee, who's wearing an Elsa dress that's almost two sizes too small for her. She has more in her wardrobe, but this is her favorite one.

Apparently.

Kaylee and I are still getting to know each other better, which happened to include learning the backlog of every *Frozen* song ever made. Even the outtakes that never made it into the movies.

The only reprieve I've had is when we've picked up Chase and they've entertained each other for a few hours before it was time to go home.

I try to work out where Ryder's genes play into her looks, but there isn't much of a resemblance. She has hair a few shades darker than Ryder's brown locks. Her eyes are pale green unlike his piercing blue. Their noses are different too. Hers is narrow and petite. He's not carrying around a giant Barbara Streisand nose or anything, but it's fuller than Kaylee's.

"Again," she says.

"Again? Can it be another song?"

"No! 'Into the Unknown.'"

"Hon, why don't you *let it go*?" *Frozen* puns. My new life.

"No, I don't like that song anymore. 'Into the Unknown'!" She jumps up and down on the couch that she should not be standing on, but every time I try to get her to sit down, she screams. Luckily, Ryder's not here to see me handling this so well.

Brenna might be right when she says Kaylee's a handful, but honestly, she's mostly well behaved. She's at that boundary-pushing stage and gets in moods of stubbornness, but that's normal.

It's what kids do.

"One more time," I say.

"Two more times."

"One more song and then reading. If you finish the book without help from me on any words, you get another song."

I was surprised to find out Kaylee's already able to read some words. She's above where she should be at her age, and I figure if we can hone her reading skills, it'll make kindergarten next year easier on her.

Kaylee contemplates it, but I'm expecting her to say no. She's only learning to read and hasn't gotten through a book yet without any help.

"If I finish the book without help, I get *three* more songs."

"Deal." And that's how you negotiate with terrorists … I mean children.

Only, I learn extremely quickly that either she's smarter than she lets on, is desperate for more songs, or I'm a really excellent teacher. Let's go with the last one.

She reads an entire early reader without any help, and I'm wondering if she knew how to do that the whole time.

"Kaylee," I say, my tone laced with suspicion, "do you already know how to read?"

She giggles. "No. This is my favorite book. I 'member all the words."

The little cheater. I can't even be mad because she's too smart for her own good.

"Now, sing," she demands.

With a sigh, I mutter, "Hey, Google, play 'Into the Unknown' from *Frozen*."

Her little face lights up as she sings the intro.

She has an amazing voice even at four-years-old. I guess she got that from Ryder.

I join in, though I push to sound more like Brendon Urie and less like Idina Menzel.

Kaylee spins in her Elsa dress, and I laugh through the lyrics at how adorable she is.

We dance around the play area, jumping over her scattered toys.

When we get to the bridge in the song, I get down on my knees as I belt out the words.

Of course, that's when the sound of a throat clearing fills the room.

As if my hot boss seeing my Grindr notifications wasn't embarrassing enough, he just happens to walk in the moment I'm singing and dancing to the *Frozen* soundtrack.

Hey, Satan, if you could open up a hole in the ground right about now, that'd be great. Thanks.

Play it cool.

I nod to Ryder, who's leaning against the doorjamb.

"Brendon Urie, eat your heart out" is all he says.

Still playing it cool.

"I could totally kick Brendon Urie's a—uh, butt in a singing competition. How was your meeting with the label?"

"Daddy!" Kaylee yells and runs to hug her father.

He picks her up and cuddles her to him but doesn't take his eyes off me. "Meeting went well. They're going to throw me some more producing work."

My chest warms at the sight of him with his daughter. I have no idea why I find his protectiveness and softness toward her so appealing. Probably something about daddy issues, but anyway.

He has this weird look on his face I can't decipher. It's part mocking, but it's as if I can see the gears turning in his head. "How has your day been?" He glances around at the mess we've made.

Playing it cool. Cool, cool, cool, cool, cool.

"It's been fun. We've done some reading, some singing …"

Ryder still looks … something. I don't know if I've done something wrong. It doesn't feel that way, but he doesn't stop staring at me.

He puts Kaylee down. "Okay, little miss, how about you clean up in here. I need to talk to Lyric."

Uh-oh.

I must have done something wrong.

"It feels like all I do is clean around here." Kaylee pouts.

Ryder grabs his chest. "Oh, the pain of having to clean up after oneself. It *hurts!*"

"Not funny, Daddy."

I want to laugh at them, but all I can do is think about whatever it is I could've done that Ryder wants to talk to me about. I mean, I guess bribing the kid into learning how to read isn't how the books say you should get children to do stuff, but fuck that, bribery works. And how long was he standing there?

Maybe Ryder hates the music industry so much he's taking a *Footloose* approach to his daughter and doesn't want her singing and dancing. Though, if he hated it that much, he probably wouldn't be producing music for Cash Me Outside.

I still can't believe Cash Kingsley has been in this house.

"We won't be long, bub." He bops her on the nose the way he always does, and I follow him down the hall with my head held low.

"Is something wrong?" I ask as he gestures for me to take a seat.

"Yeah. A big something."

I blink at him.

"You can *sing*."

"I'm sor—" I blurt. "Wait, what?"

"When you told me you kept bombing auditions, I thought it might've been because you sucked, and then I didn't want to ask to hear you sing because I didn't want to be the one to have to point out you have no talent. No one likes being that person."

"Uh, I've met with many label heads who would disagree with you on that, but thanks? I think. I mean, wow. Umm, yeah, I feel super great now that I know you thought I had to be bad at singing and that's why I haven't been picked up by a label."

Ryder purses his lips. "That's the thing. I don't understand why you haven't been picked up yet. What auditions are you going on?"

"Cattle calls, mostly."

"No manager or booking agent?"

I shake my head.

Ryder leans back in his seat. "Just how bad are you at auditioning?"

I huff a humorless laugh. "I don't know. The most feedback I've gotten was from my last one where they said I'd get a callback if I changed my image and only sang the songs they want me to."

"What did you sing?"

"Imagine Dragons, 'It's Time.'"

Ryder screws up his face.

"Come on. What's wrong with that?"

"Nothing. I mean … apart from it being a big 'Fuck you' by saying you won't change who you are? Not only that, but when you sang that *Frozen* song, it at least showed off your range. If you really want your voice to shine, you need to sing something marketable that will showcase your amazing pipes. What did you wear?"

"What I usually wear." I gesture to my tight jeans and white T-shirt under a black vest.

"Hmm. It's too much. Lose the vest and you're good. Plain clothes are best for auditions because they can then mold your image to suit your voice."

Same shit, new person. "I've heard all that before, but I want to audition as *me*. I want to sing the types of songs I want to record, and I want to wear what I'm comfortable in."

Ryder's eyes lock on mine. "I want to help. Let me make some calls—"

"No. I don't want it that way."

"What way?"

"I appreciate you wanting to help, I really do. And I'm humbled that you see talent in me. The thing is, I need to do this on my own terms in my own time and as *me*. I'm after the right record contract, not just any deal that will make me famous. I won't sell out."

Ryder huffs. "Right. Like me. Because I'm just a guy from a boy band with lazy lyrics and cliché songs."

I don't want to get into this with him. "That's not what I mean."

"Mm, isn't it?"

"Not this time." I stand. "Look, I've said it before, but apparently I have to say it again. I didn't take this job for your connections. I don't need them."

"Don't you?" His lips twitch.

How this guy can be patronizing while trying to be nice is beyond me.

"No. I don't. I'll do this on my own time."

"Fair enough." Ryder stands too and takes small steps until he's right in front of me. I'm only the tiniest bit shorter than him—not even an inch—so we come face-to-face.

He hasn't shaved for a few days, so there's scruff on his face that frames his perfectly plump lips even more.

Not what you should be focused on, Lyric.

"You might not like how I got my career," Ryder starts. "You might think signing to a label and doing as they say is selling out, but if you fight every single little thing and refuse to compromise on trivial things like your clothes or your hair or your image, you won't go far in this industry."

I swallow hard. "I know you didn't mean that to sound like a threat, but either way, I'm okay with that. I'd rather die a struggling musician and stand on my principles than become a shell of the person I used to be and die not knowing who I truly am anymore. I'm not going to kill myself changing and conforming to their demands only to land on my ass anyway."

Ryder assesses me, taking in my words. He goes to say something, but I cut him off.

"Can we drop this? Please? I'm going to see if Kaylee needs help cleaning because *that's* my job here."

Ryder looks confused as I leave the room.

I never asked for him to step in and help, and I never asked for his opinion.

My footsteps vibrate along the floor down the hall, but that's not enough to distract Kaylee, who isn't cleaning like she should be but playing with the very toys she's supposed to be putting away.

Not that I can blame her. I have about the same attention span when doing something I don't want to.

Like talking about why I both hate and love music. Why it's important for me not to conform.

I won't compromise myself the way my father did.

Not only for me but for my mom. It's the one promise I made to her before I left Fresno for college. I told her I wouldn't let the industry change me.

I think the only reason she let me go was because Chord already lived in LA and could keep an eye on his little brother for her.

"Your feet are mad," Kaylee says. She looks up at me with her big green eyes, all innocence and fear like I'm mad at *her*.

I sit next to her, gently taking her doll away. "Shouldn't we be putting Mrs. Silly Face away?"

She yanks the doll back. "She does not have a silly face."

"I thought that was her name!"

She tries to hide her giggle. "It's Mrs. Silence because she's one of my only toys that doesn't make noise."

"Let me guess. Daddy totally named her, didn't he?"

Ryder appears from the hallway. "He sure did. She also has a teddy bear called Mr. Quiet. They're in love."

I gasp. "Scandalous."

I can pretend I'm not annoyed in front of Kaylee. It's not so much that him offering to help is annoying, but it's that he's just like every other person I've met in the industry.

There are the labels who run the music biz and the managers who try to keep both the labels and artists happy, but it's always the artist who has to change, adapt, and become what people want.

When did art become about what sells the most albums?

I know it's been that way for a long time, but I want to be able to express myself with all that I am, not who everyone else wants me to be.

This is probably why after graduating from Almost Famous, I'm floundering.

Ryder probably thinks I'm still the pretentious guy he met on day one, but I have my reasons.

Maybe one day I'll explain them to him, but right now I want to focus on Kaylee and my job here.

Yeah, that doesn't last.

"Bub, can you go wash up for dinner?" Ryder asks.

I jump up. "I'll get started on making it."

Kaylee runs off. Anything to get out of tidying this room.

Ryder follows me.

Damn it.

"I'm sorry," he says.

I side-eye him as I get out chicken breasts and stuff to make batter to cover up the ground-up vegetables in Kaylee's food. "Don't worry about it. Let's drop it."

"I *can't*."

The fridge door slams shut. On its own. Totally wasn't me. "Why not?"

Ryder leans against the kitchen counter. "Do you know why Eleven broke up?"

"Harley Valentine wanted to go solo?"

Ryder huffs. "We were all ready to do our own thing, but do you know what the catalyst was? Despite what the tabloids printed, it wasn't because we constantly fought … Well, we did fight, but it was like brothers. We'd yell, we'd get over it, and then it'd be business as usual, but the main reason we broke up was because of me."

I frown.

"I loved being in the spotlight. I lived for it. But the second Kaylee was born, all that love for the industry was overshadowed by fear. Like you saw when we left the play center, fame and children don't mix."

"I don't … I don't understand what you're getting at."

"I let fear for Kaylee darken my career and fame. Whatever it is you're scared of, you need to—"

"I need to make like Elsa and *let it go*?"

He steps closer. "Don't be too afraid to step into the spotlight. With one song, I know you were born for it."

He moves next to me, and his arm brushes against mine. My body responds in a way it really shouldn't, but it's not like I can help it. Here's this guy, basically telling me what I've wanted to hear from industry professionals ever since I left home, saying I was born to live my dream and encouraging me to take it.

I get the pity stare from most people when I say I'm trying to make it as a musician. There are countless people trying to make it in this business, the majority of whom won't see the inside of a recording studio.

"Think about what I said, and if you want help with anything— anything at all—I'm here." Ryder touches my shoulder and squeezes.

"Thank you," I whisper. "I should …" I point to the ingredients on the counter before I start to read into the simple friendly touch.

When he lets go, I immediately want to feel it again, but he steps away. "I'll go see why Kaylee's taking so long in the bathroom."

"I've noticed she has a new fascination with filling the sink up with bubbly water and giving her toys a bath."

"Oh. Fun."

"At first I thought she might have been having digestion issues, but nope, it's just very important to make sure her Bratz dolls have good hygiene."

"Oh, thank God for that. I was beginning to worry for them."

I crack a smile. "Me too. Maybe that's why her GI Joes are hooking up with each other. The girls are smelly."

Ryder laughs and backs away with an expression I can't quite read, but one I'd love to see on his face time and time again.

CHAPTER 7
RYDER

I CAN'T FIGURE out why Lyric is so adamant about sabotaging himself. I can't get his singing voice out of my head, and I've been dreaming about the scene I walked in on.

My daughter, the light of my life, dancing around this ubertalented man as he sang a hauntingly beautiful song.

I've heard that damn song so many times since the second *Frozen* movie came out, both the Idina Menzel version and Panic! At the Disco's. Neither of them gave me goose bumps the way Lyric's did.

I was ready to call every record label I could think of to tell them to sign Lyric, but I get the feeling if I did that, whatever has been holding him back would refuse the offer.

He's amazing with Kaylee, and it would suck to lose him as a nanny when things are going well so far. I haven't had to worry about Kaylee getting bitten or bullied, and I feel better knowing Lyric's always with her at playgroup to keep an eye out.

But I can't help feeling like he's wasting his talent being a nanny when he could be huge.

His image might need some work, but he has the voice to carry whatever image he wants. Ed Sheeran doesn't fit the mold of what labels look for because he doesn't need to. It's his voice that carries him.

Lyric is objectively hot, *and* he has the voice.

A tapping on the glass between the studio and the control room breaks my Lyric-infused daze.

Cash cocks his head at me.

Oh shit, we're recording.

I hit Stop and press the button for the intercom between the rooms. "Sorry about that. I got distracted. Let's go again."

He hangs up his headphones.

The rock star that is Cash Kingsley stalks toward me like he usually does after we're finished for the day, and I know what he's thinking.

"We're not done yet," I say as soon as he's through the connecting door.

"I think we are. You're not exactly *here*." He leans against my desk, and our legs press against each other. "What's up?"

His hand brushes over mine. It's a small move but an open invitation.

I don't take it. "Nothing's up. It's all good. But if we're done …" I stand to put distance between us.

He follows me out of the control room and into the office.

Now what, Ryder?

"Seriously, what's with you?" Cash steps closer, his deep brown eyes holding confusion.

"Nothing. Just an off day. I'll be okay."

He keeps coming closer, and my body feels the need to back up.

We do this dance until I'm flat against my office wall and Cash is boxing me in.

"Want me to make it better? You know how good it was the last time."

"The *only* time. And my kid is here."

"Her manny is with her."

I don't like the derisive way he says *manny*. Like it's a crime to be a male nanny. It must show in my eyes because he steps back with a laugh.

"Oh, I get it. That's your problem."

"What's my problem?"

"You wanna get with your hired help."

"I don't," I protest. Maybe a little too vehemently.

"Uh-huh. Sure. When we passed him on our way in here, I thought my dream man was brought to life right there. He's hot. Like hotter than hot. He's, like—"

"Lyric's straight." Why did I say that when I know it's not true?

"Damn."

"Yeah, real shame."

"Guess we're rescheduling the session?" Cash asks.

"Yeah, sorry. We'll tell the label we had to cancel this one for whatever reason. We can blame Kaylee. Tell them she was sick. It's the best thing about having kids—they get you out of *a lot*."

"Even a love life, it seems."

Kaylee was the excuse I gave him when I told him I didn't want a repeat, and while it was true then, something has shifted. I don't know what, but blaming Kaylee for my lack of interest in Cash feels like a lie now.

I'm not interested in him because he's not …

Lyric's image flashes through my head, and I groan.

I thought I was getting a hold on this crush thing. We've been working well together. I've been keeping professional distance.

It's been good, damn it.

"What's that face for?" Cash asks.

"What face?"

"You look like you've tasted something sour when all I mentioned was your love life."

I shove him toward the door, and we walk down the hallway to the front of the house. "I don't need a love life. Fuck love."

"Daddy said a bad word."

I sigh at both Lyric and my daughter just inside the front door. They were leaving to go to the park when Cash arrived, and like when he saw Cash earlier, Lyric's eyes widen.

Evidently, I'm a lazy, cliché sellout, but Cash Kingsley is a rock god.

I could point out Eleven has way more VMAs and Kids' Choice Awards than Cash Me Outside, so …

Lyric's kind of frozen, in the middle of taking off his jacket, and Kaylee stands there looking up at him as if it's his job to scold me for swearing.

"You're, uh, him. Uh, Cash … Cash Kingsley."

Cash puts on a charming smile I know from personal experience is hard to resist.

He glances at me out of the corner of his eye before making his move toward my man … ny. My manny. Kaylee's manny, damn it.

"Fan?" he asks and offers his hand to Lyric.

Lyric shakes it with *both* of his hands. "Understatement."

"Oh, sure, he meets me and insults me, but you, he's gaga over." I huff.

Cash looks back at me. "Clearly this guy has taste."

I shoot him the finger.

"Daddy!"

"What?" I ask innocently.

"That's the rude finger."

"Cash deserved it," I mutter.

Finally, Lyric lets Cash go, but it's only to look at me. "Is that two dollars in the swear jar?"

"Nice to meet you, Lyric, but I better be going," Cash says.

Lyric looks confused. "How'd you know—"

Cash turns to me. "You're right, Ry. It's a shame this one is straight."

My heart drops dead.

Ringing in my ears echoes around my brain.

That asshole!

No, I didn't tell him Lyric has no idea about my identity, and no, he didn't technically out me, but because I know Lyric is *not* straight, and I told Cash he was … oh fuck.

There is absolutely no way out of this.

I call after Cash as he moves toward the front door. "I'm burning all your songs in a dumpster fire."

"Look forward to it," he yells back and leaves.

My gaze flicks between Lyric and Kaylee, and they stare back.

There's only one thing I can do. Pretend none of that happened.

Cash's motorcycle roars to life outside, and I pretend that doesn't exist either.

"Hey, who wants dinner?" I turn on my heel.

"It's only four," Lyric says.

I don't look back. "Early dinner." My voice cracks.

"Ryder?" Lyric's voice is both stern and inquisitive.

It makes me pause, and I slump as I turn back around. "Kaylee—"

"Go clean my room. I know."

"I was going to say go play, but sure. If you're offering to clean …"

My daughter's face lights up. "You said play. No backsies." She runs off.

"So, dinner?" I ask again.

His hazel eyes narrow at me. "Why does Cash Kingsley think I'm straight when you know I'm not? Like, definitely not."

"Maybe you give off a super-straight vibe?"

"Bitch, please."

My feet stumble backward as if they think I can get out of this by running away. Yet, my newly found, high, squeaky voice jumps in. "I might've told him you were straight? Okay, bye."

I go to leave but can't.

"Why?" The question comes out sounding hurt with a slight edge of anger thrown in, and there's no way I can leave it at that.

There are so many things I could say: because you're my nanny. Because Cash is not the guy for you. Because I didn't want Cash to think you were available. Because the thought of you and Cash makes me feel angry and gross, and I don't know what that's about. The words that come out, though, are not what I was expecting.

"Because Cash and I had a thing, a very brief thing, and I'd prefer it if he didn't start pawing all over you in front of me. But if you want his number, I'm sure he'd love to take you out."

I hold my breath and wait for Lyric to jump at the chance. All he does is look confused.

"You're … and … I mean, the rumors are true?"

"You might have to be more specific than that. There are rumors that I died, so I hope you're smart enough to know that isn't true."

Yes, a joke. Something to cut the fucking tension growing between us because never has a ten-foot gap felt so small.

"That you're … and Kaylee was—"

I screw up my face. "Okay, I know which rumors you're talking about, and no, Kaylee is not a fucking publicity stunt, she is biologi-cally my daughter, and I've never lied about how she came into this world. But, yes. The other rumors surrounding my sexuality have some merit." I'm rambling, but I can't seem to stop. "I don't like talking about my orientation because I don't even know if there's a label for what I am. I'm mostly gay, but saying that makes me feel dirty and disrespectful to the bi community. Calling myself bisexual when I actually don't want to be with women makes it sound like I hate women. I fit under the bi umbrella, maybe pan, but I've never found the right definition because it often changes. One day I'll be convinced I'm one hundred percent gay, other days I find myself checking out anyone and everyone. And now I realize I've spewed a whole lot of information you didn't ask for, but that's me. In a nutshell. You can see why I don't go around telling everyone I just met."

"Does Kaylee know?"

I blink. That's the first thing he asks?

"Umm. She knows I believe anyone can love anyone, regardless of gender, but it's not like I've come out to my four-year-old or anything."

Lyric nods. "So, you're a label-less queer guy who likes who he likes and those likes change depending on your mood. End of story."

"Pretty much. Though, even the queer label makes me uneasy with the negative connotations it used to come with, but I guess it's the one I'm most comfortable with. So many people put emphasis on labels which is why there are so many, but none of them make me go 'Yes, that's me!'"

"Cool. You said something about dinner?"

I let out a relieved breath. If the whole world reacted the same way Lyric did, there'd be no need for people to fear coming out.

CHAPTER 8
LYRIC

I THINK I handled that wrong.

I figured the best thing to do wouldn't be to make a big deal out of it.

But it is a big deal. Ryder Kennedy was sexy as fuck before I knew he was queer. Now that I know, he's heartbreak-worthy. Because let's face it, he's way out of my league.

He's a celebrity. I've never really bought into that thing where celebrities are above everyone, but it's definitely a different lifestyle. One look at this house tells me that.

He said he had a thing with Cash-fucking-Kingsley like it's nothing notable.

I don't actually know why I decided to play it cool.

I am so not cool.

Not with this.

I want to know more.

I want to know *everything*.

Now it's been days, and I don't know how to bring it up again.

Since it all came out, he's been more relaxed around me. I mean, not that he was ever super uptight, but I don't know. Something has changed.

Or maybe it's my perspective on the whole situation. The very few times I joked about being gay or mentioned Kaylee's GI Joes kissing, he shut down a little. I thought it was because he wasn't entirely comfortable with me being that vocal about my sexuality. But it turns out that wasn't his problem at all. It was his reservations about me finding out.

Which I also get.

I can understand why he doesn't date and why he's kept it from the public.

But damn, that's gotta suck. Especially with a daughter who's probably too young to understand.

It has to be *lonely*.

Don't start fantasizing about making him un-lonely.

I just wish I'd asked more.

"Oh, hey, by the way, please tell me everything about your sex life because I'm unhealthily obsessed with it since I found out you bat for my team."

That would go down so well.

I also can't stop thinking about Ryder and Cash together. It's both hot and a little guilt-inducing because it's objectifying my boss, and I really shouldn't do that. That would be bad.

So bad.

Like he might have to spank me bad.

And there I go again.

Fuck.

Okay, professional mode.

I can do this.

Ryder comes from the direction of his office and over to where I'm tidying the kitchen after making Kaylee lunch.

Damn, he's hot. All spikey brown hair and bright blue eyes.

Shit. I can't do it.

It's like my brain had put Ryder in the *hot but unattainable* part of my mind which allowed me to appreciate him but not go beyond that. Now, he's probably still unattainable but not for the same reasons. Which means my brain has gone into creeper, *check him out every chance I get* mode.

Oh God, I have a crush on a dude who was in a boy band.

Kill me now.

Oops, there I go judging again too.

I'm a mess.

He approaches me with a weird smile on his face that I can't help but return, but when he slips a piece of paper in front of me with Cash's name and number on it, my face falls.

"What's this?" I know what it is, but I don't understand why.

"I was wrong to tell Cash you were straight, so I called him and told him I lied, and he told me to give you this. If you want to go out with him, which it's clear you do, then you should call him."

"I—"

"Although, I should warn you, he's not the relationship type, so if that's what you're after, he's not the guy for you."

I stare at the number. "How is it clear I'd want to go out with him?"

"Oh, I don't know, the way you looked at him? Sorry, gawked is probably a better word."

"I gawked at you like that the day we met. It's how us normal folk stare at celebrities." Totally wasn't checking you out the exact same way. Nope. It's the celebrity thing. Yup. Celebrity thing.

Totally.

For sure.

Ryder's eyes narrow. "Are you seriously telling me if Cash Kingsley asked you out, you'd say no?"

Ask me that a few weeks ago, I would've said "In what world would I ever get the chance to meet Cash Kingsley?" Now, I can't even believe it's an option to go on a date with him.

"I don't know how to feel about dating my boss's ex. That's weird. Especially when said boss is the one setting us up."

"Cash isn't an ex. Just a friend who I happened to have one weak moment with. And I'd like to think I'm more than your boss. I mean, right? We're best friends, aren't we?"

"Oh sure. Now you throw *that* in my face." I laugh.

"Well, all I know is I was never this chatty with any of Kaylee's other nannies."

"Why not?"

Ryder shrugs. "Maybe because when she was a baby, there wasn't much to update me on. 'What did she do today? Oh, drank some formula and took a huge dump.' It's not like we had to talk about her socialization skills or reading level or any of that."

I lean against the kitchen counter and fold my arms. "Did any of them know that you're ... you?"

"That I'm Ryder Kennedy. Yes. Because, you know, they could see."

"You're *hilarious*."

"No, none of them knew they had no chance of hooking up with me, if that's what you were asking."

"We don't have to talk about this if it makes you uncomfortable."

He takes a plate from the drying rack and stacks it in the cupboard. "It's okay. It doesn't. I mean, it does a little, but probably because only a handful of people actually know about me, so I don't talk about it much at all."

"Can I ask about you and Cash?"

He freezes. "What did you want to know?"

"Well, you just gave me his number. Is that not weird for you?"

"It's one hundred percent weird, but it's not like I can tell you what to do with your personal life."

"But, you had a thing with him. No matter how short. Best friends don't do that to best friends."

"It's a simple question. Would you go out with Cash if he asked you?"

"He's Cash Kingsley."

Ryder scoffs.

"I would go out with him, but only if it was okay with you."

Please say I can't. Please say I can't.

Ryder averts his gaze. "Why wouldn't I be okay with it? There were definitely no feelings involved between us."

That disappoints me more than it should. Not the feelings thing. That ... kinda makes me happy. But that he doesn't have a problem if I want to go out with Cash. Then I remind myself about the whole out of my league thing and come crashing back to planet earth. "O-okay. I guess I'll text him, then."

"You do that." Ryder walks away, and my gut churns.

Cash Kingsley wants to go out with me. That sentence doesn't even compute correctly in my brain. Yet, I can't seem to get excited about going on a date with him.

Because, apparently, I'd rather be on a date with someone else.

And that someone else is my boss.

I stare at the empty message box with Cash's number in the address bar. If I don't contact him, Ryder will wonder why. If I do contact him, it's done. Ryder gave me the impression Cash is expecting me to message him. That doesn't mean we have to go out.

Whenever I think that, reality hits me that I'm hesitating over going out with the lead singer of a band I've admired ever since they were discovered a few years ago, and I realize I'm being stupid.

Yet, as I type out a message, doubts still circle in the back of my mind.

Hey. This is Lyric.

I hold my breath, but I don't have to hold it long, which is surprising. I was kinda expecting him to be busy with … I don't know, being a rock star?

Hey. I didn't expect to hear from you.

Awkward.

I reply: *Well this is awks. I was under the impression you wanted Ryder to give me your number.*

I did. I just didn't expect you to use it. We gonna go out or what?

Straight to the point. I guess I can appreciate that.

I can do most nights except weekends when I gig.

Ooh, where you gig at? I could meet you at a show.

Cash Kingsley at … my show?

Uh, really? You don't have to torture your ears like that.

Not to mention I'd freak the fuck out about performing for Cash.

Cash responds immediately. *I'm sold on it now. If you don't tell me where it is, I have other ways of finding out. Then I'll show up anyway.*

I type out my reply and hold my breath as I hit Send.

I play at Cedar Bar on weekends at 9.

Nice! I used to play there back in the day before I found my band. I'll see you tomorrow night.

Oh shit. Am I actually going on a date with him? Is he going to really hear me sing?

I swear I sweat for twenty-four hours straight.

I'm not exactly present with Kaylee all day, but luckily Ryder is busy in his office finishing off songs for the label and doesn't notice.

Plus, she's a pretty autonomous kid, which makes my job easy.

We go pick up Chase from school, and then they play together for a few hours.

By the time Chase and I leave so I can drop him at home before I go to the club, my head is a complete mess. Over someone I'm trying to convince myself I *should* be into.

I'm more focused on Cash seeing me perform than the actual date part.

The small club I gig at has never seemed so daunting.

I'd never experienced stage fright before until I'd started auditioning for label execs. The same crippling pressure I feel when enduring an audition washes over me as the smell of stale alcohol hits my nose.

This is my stage. My safe space. But that's still not enough to settle the nerves.

Music is in my blood. It's what I've always wanted to do.

But the fear of getting it the wrong way, taking a wrong turn, making my father proud while simultaneously disappointing my mother … it bears down on me at the worst times.

I already need a fucking drink, and I just walked through the doors.

Calm the fuck down, Lyric. He's probably not even going to show up.

I go backstage and freak out some more, clicking my fingers like it's a nervous tic. Lucky I'm a solo act or I'm sure my bandmates would want to murder me by now. I'm even annoying myself.

Click, click, click. But I can't stop.

One of the bartenders, Alex, pops his head in the back room. "You will never guess who's here."

"Please don't say Cash Kingsley. Please don't say Cash Kingsley," I mutter.

"Holy shit, how'd you know?"

My gut churns, but it's not in the gentle butterflies kind of way. "He's here for me." For some fucked-up reason.

In what world is the lead singer of *Cash Me Outside* here for *me*?

"And you didn't tell us?"

"I didn't know if he'd turn up!" I pace the small room.

"You need a drink?"

"Make it a triple."

He whistles but disappears, coming back right away.

By the time I down the drink and make my way out onto the stage with my guitar, I'm pretty sure I'm close to losing the contents of my stomach.

If this were a normal date, like going to dinner or whatever, I wouldn't be this rattled. Having the lead singer of one of the biggest acts in the country sitting there waiting to listen to me … This can't be real.

I'm thankful the stage lights are blinding and I can't see Cash. But I know he's out there, and my first song, a cover of the Lumineers's "Sleep on The Floor" is croaky and a little off-key.

My heart pounds.

Fuck.

Shake it off, Lyric.

Alex appears at the side of the stage with another drink.

I cheers him and down it before kicking into my next song which is marginally better.

The stage lights are hot, and I sweat through my shirt.

By the time I'm halfway through my set, I've forgotten all about Cash. Maybe that's because Alex appears every few songs with a new drink for me.

I should be strong enough to turn them down, but yeah, that's not gonna happen with where my head's at.

And then when I finish up my last song, I realize how much of a blur the whole performance was.

I don't know if it's from the alcohol or adrenaline.

I'm wobbly on my legs as I leave the stage and head for my dressing room.

Backstage, the room spins.

It's the alcohol. Definitely the alcohol.

I grip the edge of the counter and squeeze my eyes shut, trying to get the room to stop spinning.

"Hey, man, you were great out there."

I turn to find a blurry Cash standing in the doorway. "Uh, thanks. I was … kinda shaky."

Cash smiles. "Stage fright?"

"Nerves."

His smile widens. "About lil ol' me?"

"Maybe."

"I'm kinda wondering how you're still standing. I've never had that much to drink onstage in my life, and that's saying something because the guys are always telling me to cut back on the scotch. And beer. Tequila. Sometimes vodka."

I nod, but that makes the room extra spinny. "Complete honesty, I don't drink much. Like ever."

My eyes lose focus on Cash as he splits into two people and my vision goes wonky.

The two Cashes step forward. "Hey, are you okay?"

I stand up straighter. "I'm fine. Totally cool. Cool, cool, cool, cool, cool."

Only, I'm not cool.

Nowhere near cool.

I feel it happening. The vomit rising.

My gut churns, and my throat seizes up.

There's nothing I can do to stop it.

And that's how I end up throwing up all over my idol's shoes.

CHAPTER 9
RYDER

I'M the biggest moron on the planet because I know how Cash operates. He's smooth and charming, and he'll use Lyric, then disappear. The only reason he wanted a repeat with me is because I didn't want one with him. He's emotionally stunted.

I feel like my warning to Lyric wasn't loud or emphatic enough.

Lyric says he's looking for a boyfriend, and Cash certainly isn't boyfriend material.

On the other hand, Cash is good about being up-front about that stuff, and Lyric's a grown adult. He's allowed to do whatever he wants.

I'm also a grown-up who's allowed to do whatever I want, and I want to throw a Harley Valentine-inspired hissy fit over Lyric and Cash going on a date. So screw you, smarter, more levelheaded version of me and let me have my moment.

The worst part is, I haven't heard from either of them all weekend, and I've spent the whole time wondering what they got up to on their date.

Cash messaged me on Friday to make sure it was okay, and I couldn't exactly say no. He already suspects I have a thing for Lyric, and no way am I admitting that aloud to anyone. Especially Cash, who'd most likely try to play matchmaker and screw up a really good thing between Kaylee and Lyric.

"Daddy!" Kaylee's voice pulls me off the train of thought I've been on for almost two days. It always leads to imagining Cash on his knees, but not for me. Then it turns to replacing Cash with a vision of me, staring up at Lyric as he stands above me.

Wait, what was I doing?

"You're putting a hole in the paper!" Kaylee yells.

Oh. Right. Coloring.

I glance down and yup, there's a hole where I've colored over the same spot over and over again.

"Sorry," I mumble.

"Why aren't you good at this? You're old."

I laugh. "Thanks, bub." Who knew twenty-seven was old? "Daddy's distracted."

"Are you thinking about ants?"

I screw up my face. "Ants?"

"Yeah, because I told you how blind ants can still smell their food."

"They can?"

My daughter pulls a face that lets me know I'm about to get in trouble. "I told you this!"

She was talking about ants?

"Sorry. Distracted. Still. Uh, again. Anyway, what's this about ants?"

"Do you know some animals eat their babies? How yucky is that?"

"I could eat you." I lean over to nibble her shoulder, but she pushes me away.

"Don't eat me! You're not a fire ant!"

I'm so confused. "Fire ants?"

"They *do* eat their babies. But normal ants don't."

"How do you know so much about ants all of a sudden?"

"Lyric gave me books to read. Said they're on the curr … curwicklium for school."

"Curriculum?"

"That's what I said."

Of course it is.

Speaking of Lyric, I glance at the time on my phone and find he's fifteen minutes late. He's never late.

So, of course, my mind goes to him spending the weekend at Cash's place because he could. He doesn't have a kid stopping him from doing that. He'd be at Cash's disposal.

I'm about to call to check up on him when I hear the front door open and close.

He strolls through, looking a little tired but no more than usual.

"Sorry I'm late. Traffic was backed up because of an accident. I tried to call, but your phone went straight to voicemail."

I glance down at my phone. "What?" The little moon icon is displayed at the top. "Shit. I had it in do not disturb mode."

Sure enough, when I switch that off, my phone lights up like a Christmas tree with messages and missed phone calls.

There are a few from the label and from Cash.

I stand. "I've gotta get to work."

Part of me is thankful I don't have time to ask about his date, because now that I've seen him, it turns out I don't want to know.

The phone calls were to tell me Cash has rescheduled his session for today which means I'm going to see him.

Lyric is going to see him.

I don't know if I'm ready to see them together.

They'll both be in work mode, so surely they won't, like, be unprofessional or anything. Then again, I know firsthand Cash's version of professional mode.

All day, the imagery in my head doesn't stop. It's the same images I've been thinking about all weekend. They always start with imagining Cash and Lyric together and always end with me replacing Cash in the scenario.

I palm my cock through my pants, willing it to *stop*.

I think about going upstairs to jerk off. If I don't, there's a good chance when Cash turns up for his recording session this afternoon, I'll take him up on his insistent offer of a repeat to release all this pent-up sexual frustration. Or I'll punch him for going on a date I told him I was totally okay with.

But the thought of jerking off while Lyric and Kaylee are in the house is just too weird for me.

Good thing I don't because Lyric comes to find me.

"Hey, Kaylee and I are heading to the park."

"I'm going to be busy all afternoon recording with Cash, otherwise I would take a break to come with you guys."

"Oh. Cash is coming over?"

I try not to read into Lyric's voice going all high-pitched and weird.

"Yeah, he should be here any minute."

"Cool. Cool, cool. Kaylee and I will be out of your hair." He turns and moves down the hall faster than his usual pace, and all I can think is he's going to try to meet up with Cash as he arrives.

Ugh. He's *excited* about it.

I guess their date went really well.

Yet, when the buzzer for the front gate sounds ten minutes later, I can only figure they missed each other.

I let Cash in, and he doesn't appear any different than usual. He doesn't act any differently either.

He greets me with a warm hug and a cocky smile. "Are you gonna be distracted today?"

"Are *you*?"

"Your nanny here?" he asks.

"Nope."

"Then I think we're all good."

I turn on my heel and make a break for the studio while continuing to flip-flop between wanting to know every detail and living in denial.

Cash and I get straight to work, and unlike last week where I was too busy thinking about Lyric, this week, I'm glad to focus on anything but him.

Cash and I move through his band's songs quicker than we normally would. Not because we're rushing it, but because I think we're both ignoring the man between us.

When I go into my office to grab a pen for Cash so he can tweak some lyrics, I hear movement in the nanny's quarters. Apparently, Lyric and Kaylee are back from the park.

Cash does his thing and then finishes his millionth take of the session.

He clears his throat. "Can I get another water in here, man?"

I hit the intercom. "Sure thing. I'll go get it."

"I could go get it."

"No, you're good. *I'll* go."

Cash laughs as if he knew that would be my response.

I walk down the hall to where Kaylee and Lyric are, finding Kaylee alone watching TV. Figuring Lyric's in the bathroom or whatever, I keep moving toward the kitchen … where Lyric's blond head appears. He's crouching on the floor, his back to me.

"Uh, hi," I say cautiously behind him.

He startles and turns to look up at me. "Oh. Hey." He jumps to his feet.

"What're you doing?"

"Umm, playing hide-and-seek?"

My eyes narrow. "With who?"

He flusters. "Uh, your daughter. Who else would I be playing with?"

"You mean the daughter watching TV right now?" I point to Kaylee sitting in a trance in front of the screen.

"Kaylee," Lyric says. "You're supposed to be finding me."

She turns her head. "What?"

"Oh sure, when I tell her it's time to practice writing her ABCs, she pretends she can't hear me, but no, this time it's loud and clear," Lyric mutters.

"So, why are you hiding?" I ask.

"Wait, Cash didn't tell you?"

"Tell me what?"

"I'm surprised he didn't. I would've. I would've told every single person I met, even the dude who bags my groceries at the store."

That intrigues me. "What happened?"

"Let's just leave it at our date was a disaster. If I never see Cash again, it will be too soon, and I will die of embarrassment, okay?"

"Disaster how?"

He averts his gaze and stares down at the counter. "I'd kinda rather not say."

"Wait, he didn't, like, hurt you or anything?"

Lyric bursts out laughing. "Hell no. He was really sweet. I was the disaster."

"You're going to have to give me something, or I'm going to go back in there and ask him."

Lyric thinks about it. "I'd be cool with that. Then I won't have to relive it."

"He went to see you play, right?"

"Uh-huh."

"Did you fall off the stage or something?"

"I *wish* that's what I did. Oh God." He closes his eyes. "I'm never drinking again."

"Okay, now I have to know. Last chance to stop me."

He turns to Kaylee. "What's that, sweetheart? You need me?"

"Nope!"

Lyric scowls. "Man, I have to teach her how to be a better wingman." With a sigh, Lyric looks me in the eyes. "I might have gotten nervous about Cash coming to my gig, and I usually don't drink. Like, I'll have one or two after my set. But this time, I had so many I lost count."

"Uh-oh." The thought of a drunk Lyric is kind of cute.

"Yeah …"

"He owes me a pair of shoes." Cash's voice comes from the doorway, and he's got a huge smile on his face as he leans against the doorjamb. "I was wondering what was taking so long."

I side-eye Lyric.

"Oh, you know, just reliving the most embarrassing moment of my life. Which is saying a lot, because I've bombed in auditions countless times."

Which, I still don't understand how with a voice like his.

"I'm guessing you didn't puke all over any of those producers or label execs, though," Cash says.

"Truth."

"You didn't really … did you?" I ask Lyric.

"Oh yeah. Big-time."

I half feel sorry for him, half want to laugh at him.

Red creeps up his neck and onto his cheeks.

Cash comes around the counter and goes to the fridge to get his water. "So I dropped him at home and we agreed to pretend like it never happened."

Lyric must not have gotten that memo considering he was hiding from Cash, but I won't rat him out.

Cash nudges me. "We should get back to it. A few more hours and you won't have to see me until my next album."

That makes me a little sad because I enjoy working with Cash, but I can tell Lyric is relieved.

"Is it all right if you stay late tonight?" I ask him. "Cash is super close to finishing his album."

"It's okay with me," Lyric says.

"Thanks." I follow Cash back down the hallway to the studio, but instead of going into the booth, he spins to face me.

"I want you to know, I had plans for that guy."

I shiver. "I don't want to know."

"Oh, I think you do. Do you realize how much your face lit up when you found out nothing happened between us?"

"That's because him vomiting all over you is hilarious," I argue.

"No, no. It was not that, and don't even try to convince me otherwise. My plan was to be an absolute asshole to him."

"What, why?"

"Because you like him. Friends don't do that to other friends. He told me you encouraged it, but it was obvious he felt the same way I do about it all. Don't push a guy you like toward someone else."

"Thanks for the life lesson, but you really should be getting in that booth."

"Tell me I'm wrong. Tell me you weren't jealous."

"The only thing I was jealous of was you getting to hear him play. He refuses to let me help him get a record deal because he wants to do it on his own."

Cash winces. "I did hear him sing. He's …"

"Phenomenal."

His eyes narrow. "Are you sure you've heard him sing? He's okay, but he's really green."

"Maybe he was green because he was drunk. I've heard him sing with Kaylee. He has an amazing voice."

"I … I didn't hear it. I mean, he's good, don't get me wrong, but I can see why he bombs in auditions."

How is everyone in this industry missing what is right in front of them?

"I've made you mad. I'm sure you're right. I'm sure the guy is talented. I just know what it's like to be put through the wringer when it comes to auditioning for labels and managers. It doesn't matter how much talent you have, if you don't show them everything you've got, they won't sign you. He's not showing everything he has. At least, he wasn't when I saw him."

Cash goes back into the recording booth, and we finish out the rest of his songs, but the whole time I'm thinking about Lyric.

It doesn't make sense to me why others can't see what I can. It's clear something is holding him back, but I don't know what.

We finish the final song that needs to get done, and while I suspect the label will send Cash back my way to fix minor things or redo a song in a different key or what-the-fuck-ever they'll find to complain about, I know this will be it for a while.

Cash comes out of the booth and gives me a big hug, but before pulling away, he says in my ear, "It's obvious you have a thing for the guy. Go for it."

"It's not that simple."

He slaps the back of my head. "Stop complicating it."

I grumble something unintelligible and walk Cash out.

I can't ask my nanny out, but I do want to get to the bottom of why he's getting nowhere with his career.

He said he doesn't want my help, but fuck it, I want to help him. I see potential in him everyone else is clearly blind to. I want to draw that potential out of him and make him the next biggest act to hit the charts.

I just have to figure out how.

CHAPTER 10
LYRIC

I KNOW it's immature of me, but when I hear Ryder and Cash finish up in the studio, I decide I really need to check on Kaylee. I mean, she's been asleep for two hours, but who knows? She might be choking on air or something. Just because it's never happened doesn't mean it won't. I am a very thorough nanny.

When I hear Ryder's voice calling for me, I finally leave Kaylee's room.

"Checking on her," I whisper. "I thought I heard a noise."

"Would that noise happen to be a certain rock star leaving the house?"

Busted.

I ignore him and try to make my move to go back downstairs, but he steps in front of me.

Apparently, Ryder finds my mortification amusing. "Come on, it's the best story ever. How often will you get to tell people you threw up on someone famous? I can see it now. In a few years, you're going to be on some talk show and they'll ask about the time you threw up on Cash Kingsley. It's a great anecdote."

He might have a point.

"Maybe. In a few years. You know, after I've died from embarrassment and can talk about it again."

Ryder's still entertained it seems. His smile is wide on his unfairly gorgeous face. "I want to propose something to you."

My stupid heart hopes he's going to ask me out.

Which I know won't happen, but the hope is there anyway.

Because I like to torture myself with thoughts of things that are impossible.

"I want to produce a demo for you."

Definitely not asking me out, but definitely not what I was expecting either. "A-a demo?"

"Cash told me about your set. You told me about your last audition. I'm failing to see what everyone else is missing. I heard something in you when you were singing with Kaylee."

"To be fair, you heard one song. A *kids'* song at that … Wait, did Cash say my set was shit?"

Do I really want him to answer that?

Thankfully, he doesn't. I don't know if I could handle knowing I not only made a fool of myself in front of Cash by drinking too much but that he thinks my music sucks too.

"There's more to you as an artist than they're seeing. I'm convinced of it. I know you're against me helping you for whatever reason, but please, let me do this? We can do your sound, your voice, your style … I just want to help you get to the bottom of why you're not getting anywhere when you have talent even I'm jealous of."

Ryder Kennedy is jealous of … me.

That can't be right.

I also can't accept this.

"This feels wrong," I say. "It'd be like using my job as your nanny to get a career in music, and I don't want to compromise myself in that way." I can't.

Right?

"That's not what this is," Ryder says.

I *want* to say yes to this. I really, really want to. So why does it feel like saying yes would be selling part of my soul?

"It's just an EP," Ryder says. "You don't even have to use it if you don't want."

Say yes.

I let out a loud breath. "Okay."

"Okay?" Ryder's face lights up.

"Yeah. Okay." A lump gets stuck in my throat, and I wince as I swallow. Nerves settle in my gut.

"Are you all right?" Ryder asks. "You look like you might throw up, and then that'll be two celebrities you've vomited all over in one week."

I rub my stomach. "Maybe let's not talk about puke."

"Do you always get this nervous when it comes to music?"

"Yes," I blurt.

"Hmm. I'm beginning to see where your problem might be."

"It's not … I don't know. I don't think it's nerves exactly. More like, I know if I fuck it up, that I'll fuck it up. And then I'll be a fuckup."

"Which will make you a fuckup? Is that the point you're trying to make? I might've missed it."

"Exactly. Sorry I didn't make that part clear."

Ryder grins. Damn him.

"What I mean is, I don't think performing has ever been my issue. That's not what I'm nervous about. It's the stuff that comes with what happens afterward."

"The pressure to get a record deal?"

"The *right* record deal."

"We can work on that."

He moves into Kaylee's room and grabs a … baby monitor?

"I know she's too old for it now, but this house is so big I'll never hear her if she needs me. Come with me."

Each footstep between her room and the studio seems to get me nowhere, until it takes an entire year to walk that single hallway between the messy quarters of the house and the fancy part.

I belong in the messy part.

Instead of stopping in Ryder's office, he opens the door to the sound room.

He has a small setup, which he'd need being a one-man producer and sound engineer. But if listening to Cash's new song showed me anything, it's that Ryder doesn't need anyone else in here with him.

"Have you ever been in a studio before?"

"Only the ones on campus at Montebello. That's where all my current demos are from. But a professional one? Once. When I was, like, ten. My dad bought me and my siblings an hour so we could lay down a track together and be like him."

"Oh, your dad's an artist?" Ryder asks.

I avert my gaze and stare into the intimidating studio. "Was. And not a very good one. He didn't get far even though he tried. He desperately tried."

"What does he do now?"

I frown. "He, uh, died. On tour. He was playing guitar for some B-list band. He might not have made it huge, but he lived like he had. Mom begged him to give up that lifestyle, but it killed him before he did."

This used to hurt to talk about but not anymore. I carry a lot of reservations around because of it, but I'm no longer angry.

"It's a more common thing than people make it out to be in this industry," Ryder says. "It's why when Eleven was together, we had people whose job it was to make sure we didn't do that shit. Liver failure or overdose?"

"Heart attack, actually. From all the coke. I always remembered him being cool as fuck because he was a rock star. Never mind that we had no money and were living off food stamps. We still saw him as a role model. Someone who worked hard because he was always gone. I wanted to be exactly like him growing up, and then after getting accepted into Montebello and having my heart set on there, Mom sat me down and told me the truth. About everything. How he struggled with drugs and depression. How the industry chewed him up and spat him back out. How each time he came home a different person with a different image until she didn't know who she was married to anymore."

"The rock star life definitely isn't family-friendly."

"Anyway, she doesn't want me to end up just like him. It's why I want to be careful going into this. It's why I rarely drink and don't party. I just want to make music and try not to lose myself along the way."

Ryder nods slowly. "Is that also the reason why you refuse to conform to what labels want?"

May as well lay it all out there now. "My dad was told so many times that he'd get a record deal if he changed his image, his sound, his *everything,* and he was so desperate to hit it big that he did it. And then he still couldn't get signed. He ended up playing for a lot of biggish names, but always in the background as a backup singer or guitarist."

"I know the empty promises well. And everything makes a whole lot more sense to me now."

I crack a smile. "You thought I was pigheaded and stubborn because I'm super pretentious, am I right?"

"Well, yeah."

"Can't blame you. I *am* those things, but only because I have reason to be. I love music, but I also resent it. I'm a complicated guy."

Ryder takes a seat in his producer chair and pulls up a second chair for me. "Then let's try to work through those complications. Before we record anything, I want to get a feel for what your sound is seeing as you're picky about it."

"I'm not picky. I'm …"

"Particular? Fussy? A pain in every label's ass?"

I'm about to get angry when his pouty lips thin out as a smile spreads across his gorgeous face.

"I'm joking. Sort of. The labels will see you like that, but I admire your determination to stick to your principles. We used to complain about our lack of creative freedom a lot but sucked it up in the end and did what the label wanted us to. We figured if we didn't, our songs wouldn't be released and we'd never be famous."

"I want fame, but not like that."

Ryder leans back in his seat. "I'm only going to say this once, and you're not going to like it, but I'm telling you now that while your heart is in the right place, you have to be okay with possibly never getting the recognition you crave. Because if you're not getting heard at all …"

"If a tree falls in the woods but no one's there to hear it, did it really happen? You're going with that bullshit?"

He laughs. "I guess I am."

"I think I can be marketable and there're people out there who'll want to listen to what I have to say, but at the same time, if I never make it as myself, I'll be fine to accept that. Like I said—"

"You want fame as yourself or not at all. Thought you'd say that, but I wanted to be sure." Ryder takes a pen and paper out of a drawer and puts it on his lap. "So what is your sound?"

My mouth feels dry all of a sudden. "Umm …"

"If you can't even tell me what your sound is, we have bigger problems."

"No, I can. It's kinda eclectic."

"Who are your influences?"

I've got nothing. Like, my mind is blank.

"You said you sang Imagine Dragons for your audition, right?"

"Uh, yeah."

"So them. Who else?"

"Sound Garden. Audioslave. Uh, Three Days Grace." I rattle off some more names, and with each one, Ryder's frown grows deeper.

"Any *recent* influences?"

"Are you calling me old?"

"No, but I'm wondering why all the bands you want to be like are older than you. There's a reason the alternative rock scene isn't big lately."

"You're doing the judgy thing again and sounding a hell of a lot like a label exec."

"Sorry." He does not sound sorry.

"If you want me to name popular shit, I guess I could live with bands like the Lumineers. Sheppard. Mumford and Sons."

"That helps. What about Hozier? I bet you could bring the house down with 'Take Me to Church.'"

"*Too* mainstream."

"Too mainstream," Ryder murmurs. "Do you mean that because it lived in the top forty for what felt like forever? Because given the content, it's surprising it did so well for so long. It basically crucifies religion."

"Yeah, but it's so … I don't know. Obvious? Cliché?"

"You really need to relearn the definition of cliché. Truly listen." Ryder starts singing, and I'm taken aback.

Like, seriously, he says he's jealous of my talent?

Who knew that when he's not being drowned out by four other voices, Ryder can actually sing? Logically, I should have known, but it's easy to assume all the wrong things when he's famous for nothing else other than being in Eleven.

I'm mesmerized as he sings the song effortlessly.

I never connected with the sexual undertones of this song before. The whole song is about sexuality and religion, but the full-on vision of Ryder on his knees begging to see God through sex is, umm, inspiring.

I didn't like this song before. Now, I won't be able to hear it without thinking of this moment. Ryder singing with his eyes locked on mine.

My palms sweat, and my mouth dries. I wipe my hands on my jeans, but I realize that draws attention to my lap, and if Ryder were to look down, he'd see exactly how unprofessional his kid's nanny is being right now.

Ryder cuts off his words and stares right into my eyes. "It's not cliché. It's representation. It's a cause. It's expressing the pitfalls of the church through a song about sex."

I clear my throat. "Point taken."

"This is the type of song that's a big fuck-you to an establishment without blatantly telling a label you're not changing who you are."

I know I'm supposed to say something, but I'm lost for words. I'm still stuck in Ryder's voice.

Ryder blinks at me. "Did I break you?"

I shake out of my trance. "Sorry. Why aren't you the one in the recording studio?"

Ryder pulls back. "Hey, whoa, this is not about me. This is about you."

"Hmm, I think it's actually about music in general. Your voice …"

"Not bad for a boy bander, am I right?"

"Why did you never go solo?"

He looks at me with the most derisive look on his face. "Why do you think? The same reason I left to begin with. Kaylee never signed on for this life, and until she's old enough to handle it, I won't subject her to it."

"But …" I lick my lips, trying to think of the best way to say this without freaking him out. "You do know there's no escaping that, don't you? She was born into this life. Hiding isn't the answer. Especially when you have a voice like yours."

"I have to protect her."

"Protect her other ways. You have me now. What are you going to do? Keep her in this mansion forever? Lock her in a tower like some fairy-tale princess and hope the press never sees her?"

"I stepped out of the spotlight so she could have a normal life."

I huff a harsh laugh. "This is not a normal life. You tell me it's a waste for me to be Kaylee's nanny, that I should be out there signing record deals and performing, but what about you?"

"I did seven years of that. I don't need any more. Once Kaylee's grown and an adult—"

"You'll be a has-been who can only get work if you and Eleven get back together. And I beg you on behalf of my ears and everyone else's on the planet, please don't get back together with Eleven." I'm joking. Mostly.

"I have some terrible, no-good news for you." He leans in close and lowers his voice to a whisper. "Harley's trying to get us back together."

"Really? *Harley* is? He's like …"

"A Grammy Award–winning artist without the rest of us? I know."

I frown. "Then why?"

"You might not understand the music behind the group, but what Harley has learned out there on his own is doing it alone sucks. We were like brothers. We fought, we partied, we were bored shitless together on the road. We faced interviews together, we traveled together. We were family. He misses it."

I put my judgmental self away and look at it from his perspective. I remember performing with Chord and Melody when we were younger and loving it. If we had the chance to tour together, I'd probably take it. It sounds like a hell of a lot more fun than doing it on my own. But I seem to be the only one with Dad's artist gene—the do-or-die-trying curse.

Chord went into entertainment law to protect artists from shit like what happened to Dad.

Melody shunned the industry and music altogether like Mom.

"You get it, don't you?" Ryder asks.

"I do. But it sounds like Harley isn't the only one who's missing it."

"I miss recording like fucking crazy, but Kaylee's more important. It's as simple as that."

I want to sit here and argue with him all night because despite having conflicting opinions, I like debating with him.

He's mainstream, and I'm indie.

He thinks he's protecting Kaylee. I think he's hiding her from the world.

We both want to make music, but we both have things standing in our way: my inability to connect when auditioning and his inability to loosen up over his daughter.

"What do you want from life?" I ask.

"This just got deep." Ryder huffs, but I can see him truly thinking about the question. "Reality aside? I want Kaylee to be safe. I want to be a recording artist again." He levels me with a look. "And I want to exploit your potential and make you a star."

I swallow hard.

Ryder's piercing blue eyes lower to my mouth, and a breath gets caught in my throat.

"Lyric …" His hand goes to my thigh, and I flinch. Not because I don't want it but because I'm not expecting it.

Ryder either doesn't notice or doesn't care.

"Uh-huh?" I croak.

"Stop procrastinating and get your ass into the booth." He pulls away with a smile, and I want to both smack him and kiss him at the same time.

No. No kissing.

Bad kissing.

I stand. "What am I recording?"

"As your producer, I guess I should give you a say. So, what's going to be the cover song on your EP?"

I know what he wants me to choose. He wants me to do "Take Me to Church."

Everything in me wants to protest, but if anything, Ryder's shown me I might be protesting a little too hard.

I can't help wondering if I fight everything everyone has ever told me because I think I have to do it my own way or no way at all.

My way might be my stubbornness hating everything remotely marketable. How do I expect to be successful if I'm against that?

There has to be a happy medium between sales and selling your soul. Getting your voice out there and being drowned out by pop.

And if Ryder wants to help me find that medium, I'm going to try to let go of my hang-ups and let him.

"Do I get to borrow a guitar?" I point to the wall where he has a line of guitars that cost more than my car. Then again, that's not hard considering I don't have a car.

He holds out his arm to them. "Whichever one you want."

They're intimidating. I run my hand over them all and pick the one I think is the least expensive. It's older-looking.

Then I freak out about whose guitar it might be and wonder if maybe it's worth more than all the shinier ones in there.

Forget about the guitar, Lyric.

When I open the door to the booth, I breathe in the scent of felt and soundproofing foam.

It's intimidating and exhilarating. It makes me freeze and take it all in.

"The headphones won't bite you," Ryder says through the intercom.

I narrow my eyes. "How fired will I be if I flip you off?"

"Don't think of me as Kaylee's dad right now. Think of me as your producer. We're in this together, okay?"

"Okay."

The lights in Ryder's sound booth dim, but I want to see him.

"Can you leave those up?"

He reappears again. "Scared of the dark?"

"Nope. I want to see your face when I sing the fuck out of this song." I want to try to get him to react the way I did.

"Rolling, so ready when you are."

A loud breath leaves me, echoing into the microphone. "Uh, guess that was picked up, huh?"

A chuckle comes through the speaker. "Relax. I can only guess, but

I'm assuming the reason you bomb in auditions is because of nerves. Make like Tay-Tay and shake them off."

Easy for him to say.

"Have fun," Ryder says. "Ready to go when you are."

Here we go.

CHAPTER 11
RYDER

THERE ARE … no … words.

With just a guitar and his voice, Lyric connects me to the song, to the words, and to his soul.

I'm professional enough to focus on my job and drown out the twanging in the guitar and amplify his rasp to get the perfect sound while trying not to get lost in it all, but I'd be lying if I said I wasn't a tiny bit distracted by him.

I'm distracted by the golden hair around his face, falling loose out of his man bun.

I've never seen Lyric with his hair down, but suddenly I want to.

And now I have a vision of him releasing his hair tie and shaking his head in slow motion while piercing me with his hazel eyes.

Through the glass, he smirks at me as if he can read my mind. Shit, I hope he can't see what's going on in here right now.

It takes me a second to realize the song is over.

I fumble to end the recording and give him a thumbs-up.

"How was that?" he asks.

How was it?

I don't think there are enough words to describe what he's done to me with this one song.

I clear my throat. "Come hear it for yourself." I beckon him into the audio room.

He hangs up the headphones and puts the guitar back on the wall with the others and comes to take his seat once again.

I didn't say anything when he chose it, but that guitar was the one I used on tour with Eleven.

Watching him walk into the booth like a scared little deer caught in headlights was kind of cute, but now I can't tear my gaze away from him as he walks out all confident, biting his lip a little nervously. If he was anyone else besides Kaylee's nanny, I'd probably crawl into his lap and offer myself up as a snack.

But he is Kaylee's nanny, so I won't do that. Think about it, sure, but I can't actually do it.

Nope.

Stop staring at his lap, Ryder.

"Ready?" I ask.

"Yes. No. Maybe?"

I smile and don't give him the option. I hit the playback button.

I've produced for a few newbs the label has sent me over the past few months, and one thing I've noticed is the first time an artist hears the roughest take they'll ever have, they're usually too excited about having a proper recording to really analyze the technical aspects, but as I watch Lyric listen to his voice, to the guitar, and to Hozier's words, I can tell all those nitpicky things are running through his mind.

"It's a bit rough there," he says when he hears a part where he goes a tad off-key.

"No one ever uses their first take. We'll redo it all. But how does it sound? How does it feel?"

"It feels unbelievable. It sounds not as sellout-y as I thought it would."

"You'll be singing boy band songs before you know it."

He scowls.

"That was a joke."

Lyric relaxes. "Better be."

We go back to listening, and at the bridge, something in his face changes. He's no longer scrutinizing every detail, and he's finally hearing what I've heard ever since I walked in on him singing that stupid *Frozen* song.

He locks eyes with me as if he can sense me watching him.

"You're amazing," I say.

"You are," he replies. "You made me sound good."

Oh shit, did I just move closer? "A good producer doesn't take over. They amplify what's already there."

His eyes are so expressive, holding gratitude and a humbleness that the vultures in this industry would take advantage of if Lyric didn't have the inner strength he does.

"I see you for who you're trying to be, and I admire it. We need to get record labels to see you the way I do."

Well, maybe not the exact same way.

Wait, did *he* just move closer? "Why?"

I'm confused. "Why what?"

Oh, Lyric, please don't lick your bottom lip. It's too hard not to—yup, there I go, mirroring his action.

"Why do you see me differently?" he whispers.

The song drowns out, fading into nothing, and all I can hear is my heartbeat pounding in my ears.

I don't think anyone has made me this nervous and full of want at the same time. No one, in all my years as a closeted artist, has ever been so wrong yet so irresistible.

This isn't a weak moment like I experienced with Cash; it's fundamentally deeper.

We may not agree on some things, or a lot of things, actually, but there's no denying I love the way Lyric is always honest with me. He's not afraid to give me his opinion, and he doesn't tiptoe around me just because I'm Ryder Kennedy.

My whole recording career was about that, and even now, while I'm producing, people tell me they trust me and my judgment because of who I am and what I've accomplished.

Lyric doesn't buy into that shit.

He's unapologetically him, and it's the biggest turn-on I've ever experienced.

I don't know which of us moves first, but the next thing I know, we're leaning into each other, so close I can feel his breath on my skin.

"Ryder? You haven't answered me."

I don't think I can. "We should probably, uh, do another take."

Obvious diversion is obvious.

"We should," he croaks.

We don't.

Lyric's long guitar-playing fingers sneak around the back of my head and tangle in my hair.

I want this to happen for reasons I'm not ready to explore, but I don't think I have a choice. My body is making this decision for me, and it's screaming at me to let it happen.

Screw consequences.

The voice of said consequences reaches out from the depths of my soul. "Daddy!"

Lyric freezes, his lips not quite on mine, and it takes a second to realize it's not a voice inside my head at all but my real-life daughter, who I seemed to have momentarily forgotten existed while Lyric's mouth was so close.

"Daddy!" Kaylee's voice comes from the baby monitor.

"Fuck," I grumble.

Lyric pulls away, and I stand. His eyes go straight to where my hard-on is tenting my jeans, and as much as I'd like to explain, I can't right now.

And explain what, exactly? That I've been thinking about kissing him since the day I met him, and now I'm regretting offering to help him because I don't know how to keep my hands off him?

"I'll be right back," I croak.

I rush through the house to Kaylee's bedroom, giving little thought to the man I just left and focusing all my energy on getting my dick to deflate.

Kaylee's in tears when I open her door and get to her side.

I kneel beside her. "Bub, what's wrong?"

"There were explosions."

I pause. "Explosions?" *Please don't say poo explosions. Please don't say poo explosions.* I glance down and let out a relieved breath when I don't see any evidence of an accident.

The joys of parenting.

"Mommy ... Mommy's on fire."

I climb into bed next to her, hugging her so tightly I fear I might be suffocating her. "It's okay. You were having a bad dream. It's okay."

She sobs on my shoulder while gasping between words. "Can … we … call … Mommy?"

I pat her hair and soothe her with shushing noises. "We'll talk about it in the morning."

Hopefully, when you've forgotten about this.

"Try to sleep now," I whisper.

It takes a bit of consoling and rocking, but after about fifteen minutes, she drifts off.

I try not to let my emotions show when it comes to Maggie. Especially in front of Kaylee.

I respect the hell out of Kaylee's mother, but it's hard to explain to Kaylee why she's gone. The times Maggie has been around have been short and confusing for Kaylee. And clearly, my explanations have frightened the poor girl into thinking her mommy is going to explode.

I'm going to have to make some calls in the morning and find out where the fuck Maggie is.

But first, I need to deal with Lyric.

Oh, shit. Lyric.

Now that I've had a chance to cool off, I'm dreading dragging my ass back to the studio because I know I'm going to have to tell him it was a mistake.

Or *almost* a mistake.

Getting that close to him was wrong.

Though, right now, I think my only error wasn't diving in and kissing him before we got interrupted.

I have to go back down there and either pretend we didn't nearly kiss—that I wasn't hard for him before his lips even touched mine—or I have to face it head-on and tell him it can't happen.

We can't have that kind of relationship even if something has never felt so right before.

I don't get to connect with people very often being who I am and doing what I do. When Eleven was together, it was even worse.

Lyric's different.

And he's so fucking talented.

After one song, I know we'd make a great team. Not just as

producer and artist but as something more. Something I've never allowed myself to even contemplate because of Kaylee.

I trudge my way back through the house toward the studio and find Lyric on the couch along the back wall, but when I enter, he doesn't even look up at me. Instead, he jumps to his feet.

"I should go. I was going to, and then I thought it'd be sucky to leave without saying anything, but I didn't know what to write if I left you a note, and—"

"Lyric, please sit down."

His gaze flicks up to mine. "Oh God, I'm fired, aren't I?"

I snort. "Wouldn't it be illegal for me to fire you after almost kissing you? That's a sexual harassment suit the tabloids would love to get their hands on."

"I would never—" Lyric looks like he's freaking out.

"I know. Just, please sit? We can, uh, talk."

Lyric nods and sits but runs his palms over his denim-clad thighs.

I sit on the opposite end of the couch, making sure to put some distance between us.

"Is Kaylee okay?" he asks, and I could kiss him for asking about her first. Not only because it delays the awkwardness that's about to happen but because it shows he really does care about her.

"She had a nightmare. She has them sometimes."

"About her mom."

I cock my head at him.

He points to the baby monitor.

Oh, right. He heard everything.

"You're really good with her," Lyric says. "I know you think you have no idea what you're doing sometimes, but you know what to do when it counts."

"I've never loved anyone more in my whole life, but it's hard. She is my number one priority." I swallow hard as I look at him. "Which is why—"

I swear I see him physically deflate before he puts on a weak smile. "I understand. This was a lapse in judgment on my part." He stands again. "You know, I thought the hardest thing about this job would be working for the hot *straight* guy. Then I found out you were …" He struggles to find a label because he respects me enough not to put one on me. "Well, yeah, anyway, I'm sorry I couldn't control myself, and it will never happen again."

His words feel wrong. They don't sit right with me.

"Besides, I'm sure this happens all the time, right?" Lyric's voice cracks. "I'm guessing bonding over recording is how you and Cash happened, so—"

"I feel like I should be offended, but I'm hoping you didn't mean that the way it came out. That I almost-kiss all the acts I produce."

"No! I mean, yeah, no, I don't mean that at all. I'm trying to find justifiable reasons to chalk this up to a heated moment instead of ..." Hazel eyes pierce mine.

"Instead of what?" I ask, my voice coming out a breathless mess.

Lyric's throat bobs as he swallows. "It doesn't matter. I should go." He makes no move to leave.

I stand slowly and approach him even slower. "Lyric, I ..."

I *hate* this.

Dismissing Cash was easy because I'm not the type of guy who needs someone or needs sex.

So why do I need Lyric to not walk out that door and leave right now?

"You don't want to fuck things up for Kaylee," Lyric says. "I get it."

"She already loves you. If things didn't work out ... That's why we should probably forget tonight ever happened. Well, apart from the kick-ass song."

"Agreed."

Yet, I don't stop moving until my body presses against his. "There's only one problem with that."

"Mm?"

"I don't think I can."

CHAPTER 12
LYRIC

THE WORDS ARE WHISPERED along my skin, and I know I need to be the bigger person here. I need to walk away because Ryder is asking me to.

His number one priority is Kaylee. I need to respect that.

My number one priority should be keeping my professional life, personal life, and my connection to music all separate from Ryder.

Kissing him will mush all of them together, and I won't be that guy.

Because realistically, there's only one way this whole situation ends: badly.

"It's already forgotten," I say.

Disappointment makes me want to put the words back in my mouth and swallow them down, but I know I'm doing the right thing.

Ryder's so close, so tempting.

I want to kiss him because I bet kissing him would be fun. But also, kissing him would be agony.

"I should go," I say.

"Yeah," Ryder breathes.

"Ryder ..."

Something in his heated gaze snaps. He shakes it off and steps back.

Ryder's blue eyes lose their brightness for the first time since I've known him.

I leave the studio and go to get my bag from the nanny's quarters. Ryder's footsteps follow me, but I need him to stop.

"I can walk myself out. Have been doing it for a while now."

"Right. Sorry. Habit. I always walk my artists out, and I guess I'm still in producer mode."

"Goodnight."

"Wait," Ryder says, and I freeze immediately.

My strength snaps with one fucking word.

One.

In that voice I've heard a million times, but he's changed the way I hear it with a single song. I can't stop the visceral reaction, the need to obey whatever comes out of his mouth.

I slowly turn back toward him.

"It's late."

I deflate faster than a balloon.

"You should take my car instead of the bus."

"What if there's an emergency and you need to take Kaylee to the hospital or something? You'll need the Tesla."

"I know. I'm saying you should take one of the others. I have plenty."

My mouth drops open. "You want me to take one of your toys? The toys you haven't even shown me yet because, in your words, they're your babies? And no matter how many times I've said you trust me with your actual baby, you insist it's different?"

"You make it sound like I think my cars are more important than Kaylee."

I cock a brow at him.

"Just follow me before I change my mind," he grumbles.

Ryder leads me out the front and to the warehouse of cars that sits under the house. On the outside, it looks like a usual three-car garage, but open that sucker up, and it's like his very own Batcave.

I practically trip over my own feet. "Ferrari. Definitely taking the Ferrari."

"You're fired," Ryder jokes, but the panic in his tone is very, very real.

"I'm kidding. I'd probably drive it twelve miles an hour because I'd be too scared to crash it." I walk along the squeaky floor. "Mustang at the back looks nice. This little roadster is cute." I run my hand over the hood of the BMW.

Ryder grabs a set of keys off the wall. "Take the Pontiac."

I sigh dramatically. "The GTO? If I must. This job has the worst perks."

"I'm the most terrible boss ever."

"Right? You almost kiss me and then make me drive your fancy-ass car."

Ryder purses his lips. "When you put it that way, it sounds wrong."

"You making sure I get home safe is *so* wrong."

"You know what I mean. From the outside, everything that happened tonight now kind of sounds skeevy and gross. Like I'm trying to pay you off or something."

Our hands touch as I take the keys from him, and I have to remind myself to let him go. "For the record? I'll never think you're skeevy and gross. Nothing actually happened. You just have a hard-on for music, I guess."

"Sure. It was *music* making my dick hard in there. Nothing else."

I burst out laughing. "Exactly. It had nothing to do with my long golden locks or my winning smile. Not to mention my sunny disposition and nonjudgmental attitude."

"You know, you think you're being sarcastic right now, but apart from your stubborn pretentious streak, you're practically a Teletubby."

"Fuck off."

"A Teletubby with a dirty mouth."

I wince. "Swear jar?"

"Yep."

"Back in nanny mode, then." I take out a dollar from my wallet and shove it at him. "Fine. Now, I'm going to go before it gets any worse and I end up having to pay you to employ me."

"We'll record more tomorrow night."

"O-okay. So, the recording thing is still happening?"

"Yes, Lyric, I still want to record your demo. Sex was never a condition of that offer."

"No, I know that. I just … it might be awkward." And I don't know if I'll be strong enough to walk away again.

I need to find a way to work with him without drooling all over him.

That task might be harder than a guy on a double dose of Viagra.

"We can keep professional distance," Ryder says. "I've been doing it since you started working for me."

I pull back. "What?"

"Please. You're gorgeous. I wanted to jump you the day we met even though you insulted me."

I don't know what to say to that, but everything inside me wants to make a joke or reply with something witty. The notion that Ryder wanted me when we met is absurd.

The notion this is even being talked about is weird. And wrong.

We stay, standing close enough to breathe each other in, but there's something more than just a foot of air between us. Feels like finality when it should be a beginning.

"Go home and get some sleep. I'll see you back here at nine."

I hold up the keys to his car. "Thanks again for this."

"You should look at getting a car of your own now that you have income."

"I've been thinking about it."

"Well, until then, if you ever need one …"

My chest warms. Damn him. "You might need to stop being so nice."

"Why?"

"Because that professional distance thing? So not gonna happen if you keep this up."

I walk away from him before we do something we'll both regret.

Only, as soon as I'm in the car, I regret not doing something even more.

I can't help wondering what he tastes like.

If he's sweet and tender or rough and take-charge.

I shiver at the thought. At either of those scenarios.

I should've kissed him.

Ideally, he'd kiss with all tongue and bad breath, and then I'd be so turned off by him I'd be satisfied with ending my curiosity.

Instead, I spend the whole drive home thinking of his big, pouty lips and the smell of his spicy cologne.

I fantasize about how hard he'd kiss. If he'd back me up against a wall or throw me down face-first.

Stop it, Lyric.

I need to forget about Ryder Kennedy.

These blurred lines aren't good for either of us.

And speaking of blurred lines, my dick didn't get the memo about Ryder being off-limits. No, it keeps sending messages to my brain. Clear images of Ryder in his bed right now. Maybe staring up at the ceiling and having the exact same thoughts I am.

Even though it's a fantasy, I can't help wishing it were real. And even though I know I should stop, I don't.

By the time I pull into my brother's driveway and kill the engine, I'm hard as fuck and begging for relief.

My hand unzips my jeans and takes my cock out.

This feels wrong, doing this in Ryder's car, but it also feels so hot.

Images of Ryder tossing and turning, unable to sleep because his thoughts are full of me, my songs, my voice, keep filling my head.

He'd imagine what it would be like to kiss me. Maybe bend me over his control desk in the sound room.

Comically, while he'd be pounding into me, I'd reach out to hold on to something—anything—and accidentally mess with all the settings. Then the next time he uses the studio and one of his artists sounds like a chipmunk, he'd remember how he'd fucked me and be distracted for the rest of his session.

He'd come find me afterward and would tell Kaylee to keep watching TV or to go play by herself, and unlike real life where we know that wouldn't last long, she'd do it no questions asked while Ryder pulled me into the bathroom and got down on his knees for me.

His mouth would move over my hard cock, slowly and teasingly, because this is my fantasy world, and we have no possibility of being interrupted by a tiny human and could take as long as we wanted.

He'd want to take his time, go slow, but with him sucking on my hot skin and my cock nudging the back of his throat, I wouldn't be able to stop myself from fucking into his mouth over and over again until—

My eyes fly open, and shit. I got so lost in my fantasy, I came all over my hand.

So professional, Lyric.

Really.

About my boss, no less.

Not that he has ever felt that way to me. It feels more like we're a team than boss and employee. We clicked instantly that day we met.

It's why I made all the best-friend jokes.

For once in my grown-up life, making friends was as easy as picking a fight and then playing nice.

But essentially, what it comes down to is he's my employer. I work for him. It doesn't matter how comfortable I am around him.

Situations like this rarely work out, and legally, it could be a nightmare for him.

When Chord and Brenna started dating, they worked for the same law firm. They had to disclose they were seeing each other to HR so that it could be all tied in a neat, little legal bow and they wouldn't sue the company if shit went down.

Ryder and I can't do that. Our contract is between the two of us.

Being with me—even contemplating being with me—would bring a lot of legal hurt on Ryder, and that's the last thing I want for him.

As the thrill of orgasm fades, it's replaced with guilt and shame.

Because thinking about Ryder this way is wrong. Jerking off in his car is definitely wrong.

I might need to do the only other thing I can to ensure we keep our distance.

I shouldn't let Ryder produce my demo, but there's a lot of stuff about Ryder I shouldn't do.

Hasn't stopped me yet.

CHAPTER 13
RYDER

AFTER A LONG NIGHT of restless sleep, and not because of Kaylee this time, I'm convinced Lyric and I have screwed everything up even though *nothing happened*.

I dread the moment he's going to walk in the door all morning. I drink three cups of coffee while I wait, and when he finally shows up, I'm a trembling, buzzing mess.

Then he just says good morning in his lazy Cali-boy way with his breathtaking smile, gets Kaylee ready for playgroup, and leaves again.

The first interaction wasn't too bad, but knowing I promised him we'd be in the studio tonight has me still antsy when they get back.

I stare at my computer without actually working. For the entire day.

I decide to stay in the studio and try to get what I wanted done today in the few hours between them getting home and Kaylee's bedtime, but it goes much like how the rest of my day has gone—with me thinking how the hell am I going to be able to resist kissing him if I keep working with him.

Yet, when he knocks on my office door, I'm so eager for it there's no way I can send him away.

I'm excited to make music with him, and it's possible I haven't been this excited since I was on the other side of the glass.

"I brought you leftovers seeing as you didn't make it out of your office for dinner." He puts a plate of his infamous vegetable-filled spaghetti on my desk.

"Okay, I'm gonna need you to not be so perfect. Thanks."

"It's just food." Lyric takes the spare seat next to me. "What are we recording tonight?"

I moan around a bite of pasta, only remembering now that I didn't have lunch, and I'm starving. "I was thinking I'd like to hear one of your originals."

I can't help smiling at Lyric's terrified face. It's adorable that he's nervous, but it's something he'll have to get over before he makes it in this business.

"Remember, everything is fixable. Take Cash's song you love. It was shit before I helped him shape it into what it is now."

His gaze flicks to mine. "Wait, you helped write that?"

"Ended up cowriting it with him. What? Shocked I can actually write a meaningful song? Check your pretention, Lyric."

"Can I hear it again real quick?"

"You know you're still going to have to show off your songs, right? But, sure." I find the single on my computer and load it up.

When it plays back, Lyric's intense stare makes my confidence waver a little bit, but I want him to see I'm more than Eleven.

I could have gone solo if I wanted to. It was my choice to step out of the spotlight, and even if Kaylee wasn't an issue and I were given the chance to do it on my own, I wouldn't take it.

I loved being part of a group. They were like my family for a long time, and although we've lost touch, if any of them turned up on my doorstep and asked for help, I'd give it to them no questions asked. If it weren't for Kaylee, I'd jump at Harley's offer to get Eleven back together.

"You cowrote this," Lyric says, still in disbelief.

"Yup. I'm deeper than you think."

"That's what he said."

I walked right into that one.

Lyric shakes his head. "No way am I showing you my originals."

"Nice try. You're not getting out of it."

"Okay, but can I just say, I respect the hell out of you. I was wrong when I thought the image your label manufactured was the true you, and I think you're an amazing musician."

"Aww, flattery will make me so much nicer when I tear your song apart."

Lyric breathes deep.

I laugh. "You don't need to worry. Unless you don't want to hear constructive criticism. Then we might have issues."

"I'm good with criticism. Though if you call me lazy and cliché, I'll show you how much of a double standard I have."

"Hey, at least you were being honest, but no more stalling." I get one of my guitars from the studio and hand it to him. "Song. Go."

Lyric clears his throat and starts playing a melody on the guitar. He refuses to look at me as he strums and sings words that are so … Lyric. I try to keep my face emotionless as he plays through his song in case he looks up at me and gets disheartened because I'm pulling the look I want to. It's not exactly a positive one.

Lyric has this amazing talent, but he's so focused on sticking it to the man, he's not seeing the potential of what he could be.

Maybe I'm giving off that vibe because he stops halfway through. "You hate it."

"I don't hate it. At all. It's a very *you* song."

"Meaning no one's gonna pick it up?"

"You hate labels so much you're singing directly about them. The public won't resonate with that. But what if you take those feelings and write them into a breakup song? Love is something people always want to hear about."

"A love song? Eww."

"Do you know 'Love Song' by Sara Bareilles is actually a hate song to her label? So is 'Harder to Breathe' by Maroon 5. They take their hatred for the system and write it into a song about love and heartbreak and frustration."

"So you're saying—"

"I'm saying tell them to fuck off in a subtler way." I grab a pen and paper. "What was that first line again?"

"The perfect sound …"

"And then the next one is about image, right? So, the song is clearly about not being good enough or the perception of not being good enough. If we put that in the context of a relationship, what do people want? Are we pronoun-ing this? Are you going to be an out artist right off the bat knowing it could affect debut album sales?"

Lyric looks at me like he's wondering if I actually asked that.

"Okay, okay. Just checking. So something like about being the wrong type of guy. Someone he won't bring home to momma."

Lyric bites his bottom lip. "Are parents really still like that? I mean, my mom didn't even blink when I told her I was gay. When I told her I was going to be a musician on the other hand … If she had assets instead of a mountain of debt, I think I would've been removed from the will that day."

I avert my gaze. "Trust me when I say there are definitely parents out there like that. Unfortunately."

"I think the only time my mother would hate someone I'm dating is if he was a musician."

"Guess I'm out, then," I joke. Though, it's not really a joke. "Lucky we decided the whole kissing thing was a bad idea."

"Ooh." Lyric takes the pen and paper from me and scribbles something down.

> *Kissing you was a bad idea.*
> *I'm not your right type of guy.*
> *You spend your days making music*
> *I spend mine getting high.*

I narrow my eyes at him. "Do you, really?"

"I'm high right now." Then his face falls when he sees I'm not amused. "Dude, it's a joke. Hardly drink and I say no to drugs, remember? I couldn't think of anything else that rhymes with guy."

"We'll work on it."

And it's surprising how easily Lyric and I work together. For the next few hours, we fill our time writing out words and putting them to Lyric's melody. While he jokes around and tries to slip in lyrics that will never work, he's also professional. He takes criticism better than I thought he would, and he only fights me on some of my clichéd preferences.

It's actually *fun* working with him.

Whenever Harley and I sat down to write, we were at each other's throats by the end of the session. With Lyric, time flies by, full of both laughs and productivity, and before we know it, it's two in the morning, and we realize Kaylee's going to be awake in three hours.

At least she's managed to sleep through tonight with no more dreams. So that's a bonus.

"We don't really have time to lay this down tonight," I say.

"We're both going to be dead on our feet tomorrow."

"Are you going to stay the night?"

Lyric's eyes widen.

"In the nanny's quarters," I clarify. "You're more than welcome to."

"Yeah. I'd likely crash your precious car if I tried to drive."

"How about this. We'll go to bed now. I'll get up with Kaylee at five and let you sleep in until you have to go to playgroup at ten, and then I'll nap after you're gone."

Lyric's so adorably tired he acknowledges the plan with a nod and stands. "Sounds fair." He drags his feet through the hallway leading to the nanny's part of the house.

I watch him until I realize I want him to be walking through the other door to my side of the house. Maybe toward my bedroom.

Ugh.

I may be dead tired, but my cock definitely isn't.

Not while watching Lyric walk away in his tight jeans.

Shake it off, Ryder.

I don't have anything planned for the next few days in the recording studio, so I leave our mess of pens and paper all over my desk and go the opposite direction, away from Lyric.

My legs are apparently too tired for stairs and trip their way up half of them. I'm tempted to crawl toward my room.

As soon as I'm behind closed doors, I peel off my clothes and get into bed in my boxer briefs.

Kaylee's going to wake me up in three hours. Four if she sleeps in, which is rare.

Yet all I can think about is Lyric's smile, his eagerness to work, and the way he'd glare at me when I'd suggest something too mainstream.

He thinks he looks mean and threatening or pissed off, but honestly, he looks more attractive when he's mad.

My cock is hard, just like it was last night without him even touching me. I went to bed hard as a rock but was reluctant to do anything about it because it would be a mistake.

For the life of me, I can't remember why right now.

And as I reach into my boxers and try to jerk off to any other image but my nanny, all I keep seeing when I close my eyes is Lyric's long hair in a bun and his hazel eyes that always seem a little bit mischievous even though he's one of the most levelheaded people I know.

The scariest part of it all is how I can be so wrapped up in someone when he's the last person I should be thinking about.

It's his job to be with Kaylee. To protect Kaylee.

Oh fuck. My hand tightens on my cock, and precum dribbles out of the tip. I want to be the guy to give Lyric everything he wants even though I can't be.

I shouldn't be.

Yet the thought of being everything he needs has my muscles tightening, my cock spasming, and cum covering my stomach.

So much for not thinking about him.

CHAPTER 14
LYRIC

RYDER'S SUPPOSED to wake me when it's almost time to go to playgroup, but I wake to the sound of the buzzer for the front gate, and I have to wonder what time it is. Why did we think it was a good idea to stay up so late working on a stupid song? Okay, it's a good song, but right now staying up to work on it until the wee hours of the morning just feels stupid.

Fuck, I'm tired. I don't think I've ever been so tired in my life.

The buzzer doesn't stop, so I climb out of bed and throw on my clothes from yesterday.

Kaylee's playroom is empty, and the large house is quiet.

Maybe Ryder took Kaylee for a walk or something and forgot the clicker for the gate.

Sleepily, I make my way to the intercom near the front door and press the button to talk to whoever is incessantly annoying me.

"Hello?" I croak.

"Ryder?" a feminine voice says.

I glance around the foyer. "I … I don't think he's here right now."

"Who's this?"

"You're the one buzzing my house. Who's this?" Yeah, *my house.* Like, I'm just claiming it right now. I don't think Ryder would mind. Especially if this is some fan who went on some Hollywood tour of stars homes or something. Though, I doubt any of those come out this far.

"It's Maggie. Where's Ryder?"

The name tickles my subconscious.

Maggie.

Oh shit. *Maggie.*

Kaylee's mom.

"Come in." I hit the buzzer to open the gate but immediately wonder if I wasn't supposed to do that.

Maggie who? I might've let in a potentially crazy person because they share the same name as Kaylee's mom.

My phone is still in my pocket from last night, so I get it out and check my messages. My battery's nearly dead, but it's enough to see a message from Ryder saying he called one of the playgroup moms who slipped him their number the other week to find out where playgroup was today.

Wait, he's taken Kaylee to playgroup?

I reread the message, catching the end where he tells me to take the day off.

I can't help wondering if this is his way of saying we should back off. That maybe we should step back.

From recording.

From being friends.

The doorbell sounds, and it breaks my train of thought.

I stare down at myself and know my hair is a mess and I look ratty. For some reason, I want to impress this woman.

She's Kaylee's mom, and I'm … Kaylee's nanny.

Just her nanny.

Remember that, Lyric.

I open the front door and come face-to-face with Kaylee from the future. Her green eyes, dark hair, hell, even her scowl is like Kaylee's when she's mad.

What I'm not expecting?

The military uniform. Or the giant government-issued duffle at her feet.

"Uh, hi. I'm Lyric."

Maggie's eyes narrow. "Friend of Ryder's?"

I don't miss the way she emphasizes *friend.*

"Umm, I'm Kaylee's nanny, actually. Uh, come in."

Okay, so apparently, the idea of Maggie was not as intimidating as the real thing.

I step aside, and she moves through the place like she owns it.

"Umm, Kaylee's not here right now. Neither is Ryder."

She spins on her booted heel. "So, why are you here if they're not? Are you live-in? I thought Ryder didn't have live-ins anymore."

"Oh, uh, no. I don't live here. I, uh …"

She stares at me expectantly.

"We had a late night, so I stayed over. It happens sometimes." Or once. Like, just last night.

"Well, do you know where they are? I kind of came a long way."

"Sorry, yes. They've gone to playgroup. I can tell you the address."

"You got a car? I grabbed an Uber straight from the airport."

"Uh, I don't. But Ryder has let me borrow the Pontiac before. I can call and ask."

"He … Pontiac. You …" She tilts her head. "Are you sure you're just Kaylee's nanny?" She eyes me up and down. "You don't look like a nanny."

"I mean, I guess Ryder and I are kind of friends too."

"Mmhmm."

Could it sound more like we're hooking up? I don't think so.

"I'll, uh, call him."

She goes to stop me. "If you don't mind, could you not tell him it's for me? The reason he doesn't know I'm here is because I wanted to surprise them both. Apparently, he's been trying to get ahold of me. I got the message when I was already halfway home."

"He has. Kaylee's been …" I probably shouldn't go into detail about the nightmares she's been having about Maggie blowing up in explosions, which make so much more sense after seeing the uniform. "… asking for you."

"Aww, my baby girl." For the first time since she walked in here, she has a smile on her face.

"I'll shoot Ryder a text instead asking to borrow the car."

While we wait for him to reply, we fall into an awkward silence, and I get the sense we're both checking each other out and sizing one another up.

"How long have you worked for Ryder?" she asks.

"Not long."

"And you're already staying over?"

"Uh ..."

My phone dings, and Ryder gives me the all clear to take his car.

"He said I can take the Pontiac, so I'll drive you."

Playgroup today is at a rec center that's only about a fifteen-minute drive from Ryder's place, which is good. Any longer in the car with this woman and I might hyperventilate and pass out. I feel like she's even judging the way I breathe, and now I'm conscious of it.

Gah. I shake it off. "How long has it been since you've been home?"

"I just finished up one of my longest deployments. Nine months."

"Oh wow. Long time."

"Yeah. It's the one thing I hate about my job. Being away from Kaylee for that long makes it feel like I miss out on a lot."

"She's growing like a weed. I think she's grown about an inch since I started."

More silence fills the car, and I wonder if I stepped over some sort of line.

Eyes on the road, Lyric. Eyes on the road.

"How much did Ryder tell you about me?" Maggie asks.

"Not much at all. The only reason I let you in is because he told me your name is Maggie. I didn't even know you were military."

"Army. Enlisted straight out of high school."

See, intimidating.

"I'm sure you get this a lot, but, uh, thank you for your service."

She smiles. "I do get it a lot, but thank you. It's been hard, especially since having Kaylee, but I have my reasons for doing it."

"You don't need to explain anything. It's admirable, what you do."

"I know I don't need to justify my career, but ..." She wrings her hands, and I start to see a less confident side of her. "I feel like I'm always needing to defend my choices when it comes to my daughter. I'm not home with her like I should be. I miss out on too much."

"But it's not as if you're out partying or neglecting her. How many men in the military do the exact same thing?"

Maggie's intense stare makes me self-conscious, and it's hard to concentrate on driving. I feel like I'm in driver's ed all over again.

"No one has ever seen it that way before without me having to point it out." Her voice is quieter than it has been. More reserved.

Point for me.

"It seems like a double standard is all," I say.

"Right. Ryder thought so too, which is why we agreed to keep as much about me out of the media as possible. Everyone else sees him as this huge star. To me, he's still Ryder Kennedy, the annoying boy from elementary school who happened to grow up to be famous."

"Who you happen to have a kid with."

"Exactly."

"He's a good dad." I don't know why I feel the need to say that. "Just in case you were worried leaving her with him was a wrong choice. He's sacrificed so much for her and loves her so much."

"I don't ever doubt my decision to give him custody. As crazy as his life is, it's still a more stable life than I could give her."

Yes, Maggie is intimidating as hell, and she's nothing like I was expecting, but with her admission, I know she's a decent person.

We pull into the rec center parking lot, and Maggie takes a deep breath.

"Are you okay?" I ask.

"Is it stupid to be terrified she's forgotten me?"

"She hasn't forgotten you. She talks about you all the time."

Maybe not all the time, but she has mentioned her once or twice.

"Really?"

"She says you call her cute as a button all the time, but she doesn't know why you think buttons are cute."

Maggie bursts out laughing. "She really said that?"

"Yep. She's coming out with the funniest things right now. She's at that age where she loves learning, and it's question after question after question."

"Hmm, is that adorable or annoying?"

"Both, come to think of it."

Maggie settles. "Okay, let's do this."

We get out of the car, and I let her go first.

I've seen countless social media posts, videos, and stories of vets coming home to surprise their families.

I may have even shed a tear over a couple of them.

But as I watch Maggie walk in and every eye turns to her, my vision gets blurry as little Kaylee's eyes widen.

She yells out, "Mommy!" and jumps up from her spot on the floor where they're all playing duck, duck, goose.

As if in slow motion, they move toward each other as fast as they can, but it still feels like minutes instead of seconds for them to meet.

And no video can compare to seeing this kind of reunion in real life. I bawl like a damn baby.

Maggie's long arms embrace Kaylee's small frame.

It's been nine months since Kaylee has seen her mom, and they both cry as they hold each other tight.

They're crying, I'm crying, half the frickin' rec center is crying.

Then I meet Ryder's gaze.

He's not crying. Nope. He looks *pissed*.

CHAPTER 15
RYDER

MAGGIE'S HERE. Like *here* here.

Every time she turns up like this—and it's always by surprise, always blindsiding me—I can't help dreading it.

Not because she's a bad person, because she's really not. She's a great mom when she's present, and she's a wonderful human being.

But I know what's coming because it always does.

She leaves again, and then I have to pick up the pieces with Kaylee. I have to explain to our daughter why Mommy's gone again.

I honestly don't know how army spouses deal with it.

The hardest part of parenting isn't the bed-wetting, the tired tantrums, or the boundary pushing. It's seeing your child hurt without being able to do anything to soothe them.

When Maggie pulls away from Kaylee and our eyes meet, my apprehension is replaced with the warm affection I've always had for Maggie.

She runs for me, throwing her arms around me and sobbing into my shoulder.

"Geez, you're always so emotional," I blubber.

She pulls back to wipe her eyes.

I hug her again. "I have to get the important question out of the way first. How long are you home for?"

Her eyes seem heavy and puffy, but I don't think it's from the crying. "We'll talk, okay? Right now, I want to spend some time with Kaylee and just decompress."

"No problem. Wait …" My gaze goes above her head to where Lyric stands, half his hair falling out of his man bun and his clothes from yesterday disheveled.

"Ah, yeah, your nanny brought me here." Oooh, look, her smug expression hasn't changed from when we were kids.

"He is my nanny. I mean *Kaylee's* nanny. I don't need a nanny. I can look after myself."

"Sure you can. And sure he is." She pats my cheek.

"I want to tell you to eff off right now, but that's probably not the best choice of words to use here."

"Whatever, you love me. Always have."

I roll my eyes. "You know how much I love you turning up and surprising us."

"You pretend to hate it, but you really don't."

No, no, I really do. She just doesn't believe me.

"The only thing I like about it is that it makes Kaylee so happy." I nod in her direction. She's gone over to Lyric to pull him toward us.

"Mommy, this is my Lyric."

Maggie kneels to her level. "Your Lyric, huh? He was nice enough to drive me here so I could see you, so I guess he really is yours."

Something out of the corner of my eye catches my attention. It's someone with a phone. No, it's a lot of someones with a lot of phones. And they're all pointed at us.

"Shit," I mutter.

"Daddy—"

"Not now, bub." Umm, umm, fuck, what to do. I turn to Maggie and hand over my car keys. "Can you take the car and get Kaylee back to the house? Lyric and I will try to get everyone to delete whatever they've taken. Photos, videos."

Maggie goes into tactical mode, whisking our daughter away as fast as possible so Lyric and I can face everyone.

The rec center doesn't only have playgroup people but others as well, so asking everyone to delete their shit is going to be hard.

"How do you want to handle this?" Lyric asks.

"The only way I know how." I step forward and raise my voice so everyone in the hall can hear. "Hey, everyone. I'm happy to have photos taken, sign anything, send a Happy Birthday video to your daughter, mom, sister, whoever, but I'd appreciate it if you could delete anything you've already taken of my daughter or her mom. I don't like when Kaylee's put on social media or her photos hit tabloids. I'm sure you can all respect that. Thanks."

"I was gonna go with low-level threats, but this works," Lyric says under his breath.

"Threats make headlines. I learned a lot from having a PR rep for seven years."

It doesn't take long for people to approach, and by the time I get through everyone, I'm done and fucking exhausted.

My phone is already going off with notifications, and it's probably from people tagging me in social media posts. As long as none of them have Kaylee or Maggie in them, I'm fine with it.

"Let's get out of here," I say to Lyric.

He goes to hand me the keys to the Pontiac, but I stop him.

"Can you drive? I have a lot to process."

I've only had a couple hours of sleep, Maggie's back, and for the first time in a long while, I've had to be *on* for the public.

I'm drained.

"No problem."

Lyric's silent as he drives toward home, and I'm thankful. I'm sure he has a million questions about Maggie turning up.

"Sorry I gave you the day off and then you ended up babysitting me instead."

"I don't mind."

"It's not fair—"

"Ryder, I'm here for you. We're friends. I saw the look on your face when Maggie showed up. I wouldn't have brought her if I'd known."

"No, no. You did the right thing." The frustration I felt when I first saw Maggie is back. It builds in my gut and grows, rising to my throat and making its way out of my mouth in a grunt.

Lyric flicks the blinker and turns into the entrance of one of the many hiking trails up here.

"Where are we going?"

"I can't pull over anywhere else up here."

"Pull over for what?"

He parks the car. "This. Get out."

"Lyric—"

Before I can stop him, he's out and rounding the car. He beckons me to do the same.

I open the door. "I don't really feel like going for a hike."

"We're not hiking."

I approach him. "Then what are we—" I'm engulfed in Lyric's warm arms.

The parking lot is empty, and this trail isn't overly popular, so I melt against him, not caring that someone could come up here at any moment.

"You looked like you needed a hug."

I'm not prepared for this.

His embrace releases all the tension, all the misplaced anger over something that's supposed to be happy, and I end up a heap of dead weight in his arms.

Lyric holds me close and doesn't bring up the fact that I'm trembling as if it's freezing when it's actually eighty degrees out here.

"Wanna talk about it?"

"No," I croak.

He lets out a small laugh. "Okay."

I pull back just enough so I can look up at him while not losing the warmth of his body against mine. It feels right to be here, standing close to him and wrapping myself around him.

"Sorry." Both for my train of thought and for basically holding on to him for dear life. "Maggie coming home always messes me up."

"You said you're friends, though?"

"We are. It's complicated."

"Want to uncomplicate it for me?"

I force myself to step back from him. My ass hits the hood of the car as I lean against it, and he mirrors the position next to me.

"Maggie's a great mom. When she's home. She often can't tell me where she is when she's deployed, so it's basically impossible to get ahold of her, and as you saw the other night, it's hard for Kaylee. So, when she is present, this black cloud of dread hangs over me because

I know she'll be leaving again soon, and I'll be the one who has to pick up the pieces."

"That's rough." Lyric's words are comforting and validating even though sometimes I think I need to suck up my issues with Maggie.

I was the one who wanted to take Kaylee full-time, so I shouldn't complain that I'm the only one Kaylee has. "I don't even think that's the worst part. The worst part is, even though I anticipate Maggie leaving every time, there's a side of me that wants her to stay, and sometimes I wonder if that would be worse."

"Why's that?"

"It's always the same thing. I fear Maggie will regret the time she's missed out on with her child and want to see more of her. Which she has every right to do. But in my mind, it always ends with lawyers and court-ordered custody agreements. What if Maggie sees me with Kaylee and realizes she made a huge mistake letting me raise her on my own? Courts basically always side with mothers, and it's not like I'm giving Kaylee the most stable life. What if—"

"Ryder …" Lyric reaches for my hand. "You're the best dad I know. I know you doubt that a lot, but it's true. There's no way a court wouldn't be able to see that."

"Even if her photo is splashed all over the tabloids because of me?"

"That's not your fault."

"I don't think a judge will see it that way."

He can't say anything to that because he knows it's true. "Do you really think Maggie would take her away from you?"

I sigh. "No, I don't. It's just another one of those fears I've had since becoming a father. You know, some days I wish for it? I know that's horrible and bad to say, but I want a break. Then the thought of Maggie wanting her permanently makes me want to hold on tighter. Shit." I rub my chest. "It makes my heart sore."

"It doesn't have to be all or nothing. What if Maggie took Kaylee for a couple of days? It'll give you the break you need."

"What if a few days turns into more and everyone realizes Kaylee's better off without me?"

"That won't happen. I don't know what I need to say to make you feel better about this, but you're a great dad, and Kaylee belongs with you. I think you're scared because you've been doing this on your own for so long you don't know what you'd do without her. But I promise you, you won't ever have to find out. I've spent a total of maybe twenty minutes with Maggie, and while she's suspicious about who I am to you, she seems like a decent person. She already told me she thinks you're a great dad. She does miss Kaylee, though. Maybe you could see her visit as a positive thing instead of stress-inducing."

"That's easier said than done."

"I know it is. And it'll be hard for you to let go. But I think you should do it."

I look up at the sky. "What would I even do with a few days off?"

Lyric smiles, and nope. Nope, nope, nope. The image that pops into my head as I look at his charming face is not what I should even be thinking about doing on my days off.

Then he leans in and says something I haven't had the privilege of contemplating since Kaylee was born. "You can do anything you want."

Whenever Maggie's home, she either stays with me or I put her up in an Airbnb close by, but she planned ahead this time and got herself a hotel room despite my protests.

"Kind of defeats the purpose of having a break if they're both here with you," Lyric mutters to me when I say it for maybe the hundredth time.

"I know, but …" I try to tuck my controlling side back in, but Maggie can't afford something nice, and now I'm making excuses to keep them with me.

"Are you sure about this?" Maggie asks, sensing my hesitation.

"One hundred percent," I lie. "Unless you're not. You don't have to—"

"I appreciate it. Honestly." Maggie smiles warmly at me. "Maybe tomorrow when we get back, we can talk?" She turns to Lyric. "Are you able to watch Kaylee tomorrow?"

Lyric nods. "That's generally in the job description."

She laughs. "I'm going to go check on Kaylee to make sure she's packing more than her stuffed animals." As she steps past me, she pauses and speaks softly. "I like him."

I agree with her but can't voice it. I'm more focused on why she wants to talk.

Maybe I shouldn't let Kaylee go.

As if reading my mind, Lyric steps forward and cocks his head at me. "This is a good thing."

I rub the back of my neck. "I know."

"Do you?"

"Shut up," I mutter.

Maggie reappears with Kaylee. "Okay, we're ready."

I'm not, but I try not to show it.

I get to my knees and hold my arms out for Kaylee. "You have fun with Mommy, okay?"

She pouts. "You not coming, Daddy?"

Aww, sweet child. *Yes, I will come with you!*

"Not tonight, honey," Lyric says for me.

She looks up at him. "You're not coming either?"

Lyric shakes his head. "Nope. You get to have special time with your mom, who you haven't seen for a really long time. Doesn't that sound fun?"

"Yeah, but then you don't get to have fun with us!"

Maggie smirks. "I think Daddy and Lyric will have their own fun."

Maybe *that's* what we have to talk about. Clearly, she thinks something is going on between us.

Kaylee's green eyes meet mine. "Are you sure you'll be okay?"

Lyric chuckles. "I'll make sure he's okay. Is that all right with you?"

"You're on Daddy duty tonight." She's so serious about it, and it's adorable.

Lyric mock salutes her. "I'll babysit him for you."

"Good work."

We watch them leave, and as soon as the front door closes, Lyric clasps my shoulder. "Enjoy having the afternoon and evening to yourself."

I realize he's leaving and say the only thing I can think of in the moment. "You're not going to babysit me? You promised my daughter."

"Yes, and verbal contracts between adults and children are legally binding," he says dryly. "It's not like we pinkie promised, Ryder. Geez."

Lyric might have a point.

"But …"

"But what?"

"What the hell am I supposed to do with myself?"

He leans against the kitchen counter. "What do you *want* to do? You have the opportunity to do anything and go anywhere. Well, within reason. Flying to Paris for an hour or two wouldn't really be worth it."

I have to really think about it because I haven't had this opportunity in nearly five years. Maggie's never had her overnight before unless she's been staying here and I've been with them.

Without Kaylee, all I have is music.

"You could go clubbing, to dinner, to—"

"I want to record you," I blurt. "I want to do your demo."

"Out of all the possibilities, *that's* what you want to do? Maybe we should have a discussion on the important things in life."

I step forward. "You still don't get it, do you? You are important. Your voice is important. And I want to help get it out there."

"Okay, I don't think it's even possible to say no to that."

I smile. "Good."

"But—"

"No, no buts."

"I was going to say I wouldn't mind going home to shower and get dressed in fresh clothes. I'm still in my stuff from yesterday."

I eye him up and down—as if I haven't already memorized every inch of his body in my mind. "You're my size. Shower here and borrow some clothes."

Lyric looks a little uncomfortable with that idea, but he agrees to it. "If you're okay with that."

"It'll give us more time in the studio. You think you're ready for a full recording session? Endless hours of singing the same thing over and over again until we get it perfect? Once you make it big, that will be your life."

"I'm so ready."

"I'll go get you some clothes." I would invite him upstairs to my room to pick out something for himself, but I don't trust myself in the same room with Lyric and a bed. Hell, I don't entirely trust us in the studio together. But there's nothing else I'd rather be doing. If we were to go out somewhere or do something in public, I run the risk of being recognized and stalked by paparazzi, and I've already hit my peopling limit for the day. Not only that, but I wouldn't be able to stop thinking about Kaylee.

As it is, I know thoughts of her will be distracting, but I'll be able to mostly block them out if I'm focused on something I'm passionate about.

And Lyric is definitely something I'm passionate about.

His demo, I mean. Of course. Just his demo.

I grab him a pair of sweats and a T-shirt, but then something in my shirt drawer catches my eye, and I can't resist. I switch out the shirts and run back downstairs, only to find him tidying Kaylee's playroom.

"I told you to take the day off. You're not Lyric the nanny today. You're my artist. And if any of my artists were cleaning my house, I'd be mortified."

"I don't mind. Honestly."

"Here." I throw him the clothes.

The glare he sends my way is expected. "I can't record wearing this."

"Aww, come on. It's not like you're going to be filmed. It's important to be comfortable when you're recording. It's long, long, long hours."

He holds up the offending shirt. It's from the Eleven touring days, and it has a giant picture of my face with my name underneath it in neon font. "An Eleven shirt? Really? No. I'll record shirtless if I have to."

Yeah, that's not a great idea. "I don't know how many tracks we'll lay down if you do that."

Lyric's glare doesn't let up.

"For me?" I give him the same pout Kaylee does when she wants something.

"You get off on people wearing your face on their chest?"

"Okay, wow, way to make it creepy, dude."

Lyric laughs. "I'm not the one making it creepy! It's a shirt with your face on it. Like, a giant face." He holds it up next to me. "It's not even proportionate."

"I'm offended you won't wear it. Aren't we friends? Best friends if I recall."

"No, right now you're my producer. How am I supposed to work under these conditions?"

"Okay, fine. Want me to go get you another shirt, diva?"

He looks contemplative. "The shirt is fine." He sounds defeated, and I might be a little evil because I kind of love it.

"Great. You go shower while I get everything set up in the studio."

He wanders off in the direction of the bathroom in the nanny's quarters, grumbling something about not wanting to become famous because of a song he recorded while wearing a boy band shirt.

"Just think, it's another perfect anecdote for late-night talk shows," I call after him.

Lyric flips me the bird.

We're already having fun. I can't think of a better way to spend my day off.

CHAPTER 16
LYRIC

I CAN'T BELIEVE I'm wearing a Ryder shirt. Like, for real. What's worse is it smells like him. That's not helping me focus. Especially because that means he's worn it. It doesn't smell like detergent. It smells like Ryder—a mixture of lavender laundry soap and spicy cologne.

Wearing his scent and trying to concentrate on getting these first two songs for my demo recorded do not mix well.

Ryder keeps up the lights in the control room so I can watch him work as I sing, and while that was a good idea the first time we did this, I'm wondering if it's making my lack of focus worse.

Ryder is patient with me. He tells me when to start again and offers suggestions to tweak the arrangement to best show off my voice and talent.

He's *professional.*

And here I am wearing Eleven merch and wondering how self-indulgent he'd have to be to wear a shirt with his own face on it.

His warm voice comes through the intercom. "You okay? You need a break?"

We've only been at it a couple of hours. I can't take a break yet. I want to get this original song done so we can move on to the second attempt of "Take Me to Church."

"I'm good."

"Are you sure? You seem distracted." Ryder tries not to smile. "It's the shirt, isn't it?"

I throw up my hands. "Yes, it's the damn shirt."

"I'm that distracting? I'll take that as a compliment."

"No." Well, yes, but that's not the only thing. "It smells like you, which means you've worn it, and I can't help thinking about you wearing your own merch and how weird that is. I'm wondering if you need therapy."

Ryder throws his head back and bursts out laughing, but I can't hear it because he hasn't hit the intercom button. His face is beautiful when he's carefree.

I mean, he's always beautiful, but there's something about the relaxed version of him that's so damn alluring.

"I have never worn that shirt in my life." He's still laughing as his voice comes through the speaker.

I narrow my eyes. "Then why does it smell like you?"

"Maybe it's the sweatpants? Or maybe you're having a stroke. Or maybe you've memorized what I smell like, and that might be creepier than you wearing my face."

"Come in here if you don't believe me. It smells like you."

"All right then."

Oh shit. I didn't think he'd actually do it.

Ryder comes through the connecting door and stalks toward me, and I don't think I've ever regretted taunting someone more.

Because as he steps up to me and leans in, dipping his head to smell his shirt at my shoulder, the urge to wrap my arms around him is almost overpowering.

"Hmm, it does smell a bit like my cologne." Ryder smells me again, and fuck, my cock likes that more than it should. "Maybe a worn shirt of mine got put away with my clean clothes."

"Or maybe you're egotistical and like to wear your own shirt around the house. Maybe you jerk off in the mirror while looking at your face."

He's standing so close I can feel his breath on my skin. "That doesn't sound right. I love my Eleven days but not that much." Ryder pulls back and looks into my eyes. "Have to say, you look good in my shirt, though." His gaze travels down. "More than my shirt, actually. Just my clothes in general."

"I look good in anything." My voice goes up at the end like I'm actually asking a question.

"Mmm. That's the problem I'm having." Ryder wraps his arm around my back and pulls me against him.

He can no doubt feel my erection digging into him.

Seriously, he hadn't even touched me, and I was already hard.

Now I'm pushing against him, shamelessly moving my hips slowly and subtly. As if that'll hide that I'm trying to grind up on him.

"I'm starting to think we can't have a recording session without getting inappropriately close," I say.

"It's your fault."

"For taunting you to come in here?"

Ryder's focus travels down to my lips. "For being so fucking irresistible when you sing."

He reaches for the headphones on my head and removes them for me. They drop to the ground, and Ryder doesn't even flinch.

And then—

Oh, holy mother of … everything holy.

Ryder's mouth comes down on mine for the type of sweet torture I've only ever fantasized about.

Ryder Kennedy is kissing me.

Pop sensation Ryder Kennedy has his lips on mine, his arms wrapped around me, and his tongue in my mouth.

My brain can't process it.

My mind may not be on board, but my body is.

I'm not sure if he pulls me to him or if I take the lead, but his lips feel familiar. Like I've kissed him a million times over a hundred lifetimes.

My tongue meets his, and I swallow his moan.

We stand in the recording studio, nipping, kissing … *devouring.* We make out like teenagers, giving it our all like we'll never get the chance to again.

Because if we think about it too hard, we'll realize this really won't happen again.

Ryder's lips are as soft as they look, and his plump bottom lip teases the hell out of me.

His scruffy cheek against mine feels like heaven, and as his hands run down my back, he thrusts his hips, rubbing his cock alongside mine.

It's sensory overload. It's a dream come true.

A dream I never knew I had until I met him, but one I've had frequently since I started working for him.

"Shit." I break away.

Ryder's forehead scrunches. "What?"

"This is …"

He closes the small gap between us again. "Inevitable."

"I-inev—"

"I never should've hired you."

"Ouch."

Ryder laughs. "You're great with Kaylee. Perfect. But ever since you arrived, I've been fighting *this*." His mouth is back on mine, and whatever strength I had to try to stop this no longer exists.

I pull him even closer, groping and groaning. We stumble and manage to knock over the one piece of furniture in here—a lonely stool.

Ryder turns us and backs me up against the padded soundproof wall.

All the while, I don't stop my assault on his mouth, his tongue … his fucking pouty lips.

He presses against me, his cock dragging against mine in slow, torturous thrusts that only seem to increase in pressure as we both rock our hips.

It's going to be over really soon if we don't stop.

I grip his hips and gently separate our lower halves.

Ryder pulls his mouth away. "What now?"

"You feel too good."

The sides of his sexy as sin lips quirk. "Why's that a problem?"

"Because I'll ruin a completely decent pair of your sweatpants."

Ryder teases me by running his finger along the waistband. "I can fix that problem."

I let out a string of harsh curses when he sinks to his knees.

My cock is so hard Ryder's sweats are tented right in front of his face. He glances up at me with a mischievous grin before running his nose and mouth along the outline of my cock over the material.

I groan because I want more, then groan even harder when he pulls the sweatpants down my legs.

The anticipation of his mouth on my cock has a bead of precum slipping out of the tip. But he doesn't put his mouth on me. Instead, he slowly stands.

He looks me in the eye as he leans in to kiss me softly.

My cock is needy and feeling neglected, but the next second, his fingers wrap around my hard length.

I jerk forward and almost lose it.

I have to grab onto him. Anywhere I can grip him. My hands grasp his shoulders while he pumps up and down. He jerks me slowly but firmly.

I gasp and break from his mouth but keep our foreheads together. Our breaths mix, and his grip on my cock tightens, making me weak in the knees.

"Fuck, you're good at that."

"I've had a lot of practice," Ryder murmurs.

"Oh. Right. The no-dating thing. Maybe I should ..." I reach for him.

Together, we get his cock free, and then we're back to making out and jerking each other off. It's sloppy yet controlled at the same time. Ryder definitely knows what he's doing, but there's an urgency to it and a need to get to the finish line that makes it messier.

I want to argue a cum-stained shirt isn't ideal either, but then again, the chance to say I came all over his face isn't an opportunity I can pass up.

Plus, removing it will require me to stop touching him, and I can't when his long, thick cock is pulsing in my hand and leaking for me.

Ryder breaks his mouth from mine despite my whine of protest, but he doesn't go far. He stares down at us as we work each other over, his breaths fast and wispy.

"I need to ..." He doesn't finish his sentence.

I just nod. "Ditto."

He tilts his hips, and our hands bump against each other. It takes a second to realize what he's doing, and when I release his dick, he guides my hand to wrap around both of us.

Pressed against him, I throw my head back as he keeps his hand on top of mine, guiding me to jerk us both at the same time.

"So good," he whispers.

"Mm" is all I can manage.

Ryder's mouth lands on the junction between my neck and shoulder, and he sucks hard.

"Holy fuck."

The hard love bite, the frantic way we're getting each other off, it's rough and consuming, needy yet intimate.

I stroke faster, and he sucks on my neck harder.

"Oh fuck. Oh fuck." I tip over the edge, spilling into both our hands and God knows where else.

Ryder thrusts his hips forward harder. Once. Then twice.

I'm still trying to catch my breath when he shudders in my arms.

More cum goes everywhere.

Ryder holds me to him until he stops convulsing, and even then, he's slow to pull out of my arms.

A heaviness falls between us, like an elephant just walked into the room and neither of us wants to acknowledge it.

My mouth is dry, my throat scratchy. "So, that happened," I croak.

We're covered in our own mess, but we don't move to clean ourselves up.

Ryder doesn't look me in the eye as he laughs. "Yeah. It did."

"I don't think we make a very good team."

His head swivels so fast in my direction, I fear it might fall off his neck. "What do you mean?"

"Surely, this is the least productive you've ever been during a recording session."

"Not by a long shot. But, uh, yeah, sex usually isn't the reason for delays. Wait here."

Sure. I'll just wait with his sweats around my ankles, my dick hanging out, and cum everywhere. No problem. Not awkward at all.

Okay, it's too awkward.

I bend down and at least drag the pants up my legs.

Ryder returns with a box of tissues.

We clean up the best we can, and Ryder zips up his jeans.

The whole thing happened so fast, I never got a good look at the cock I've been fantasizing about.

I'd like to say I'll take advantage of that another time, but I don't know if I will.

I await the inevitable *oops* and *let's forget it*, but neither come.

Nope. It seems this time we're skipping to the *it never happened* part.

Probably because last time nothing actually happened. We can't claim that this time.

"Think you can concentrate now?"

"Is that what we're chalking this up to?" I reluctantly ask. "Getting off to make me concentrate better? Because I gotta tell you, if smelling like your cologne was throwing me off, don't even get me started on smelling like your cum."

Ryder cracks a smile and finally looks at me. "Be a good boy and get these two songs recorded, and maybe I'll let you have more."

I try to hide my surprise but fail. I'm pretty sure my eyebrows live in my hairline now.

Ryder sighs. "I don't know what it is about you, but I'd be naïve and stupid to believe I could resist you. I already tried that, and I've lasted how many days?"

"I don't know, but it's felt like a billion."

He snorts. "Exactly. We could keep playing this game where we try to stay away from each other. We can pretend we're not attracted to each other, or …"

I step closer to him. "Or?"

His finger trails down my neck, rubbing over the spot he sucked on, and I don't need a mirror to know there's a red, angry, claiming mark there. "Or we let this happen."

I want to ask what this is, but maybe we need to take this in baby steps. "I thought you didn't date."

In a flash, his touch is gone. "I don't."

I think I have my answer. "Oh. O-okay. Then this would be what exactly?"

"I … I don't know. I put my whole dating life on hold after Kaylee. Which means no sleepovers. And it's not like I can find someone who's willing to be in a relationship like that. Which is why Cash and I happened in the first place. He didn't want a relationship. Just sex."

"So, you're not going to have a relationship until she's, what, eighteen?"

"No. Maybe?" He runs his hand through his hair. "I don't know."

"Look, I understand the Kaylee thing to a degree. I understand not wanting to tell her anything, especially when we don't know what this actually is. We agreed not to go there, and now we have. But it doesn't feel like this was only about getting off. It's been building for a while."

"It has," Ryder says. "Stay the night?"

"Stay?"

He nods. "I want to see if I can do it. I want to see if it will work. I don't know what tomorrow will bring, but for tonight, I want to see if it's even possible to be something more. And then tomorrow, when Kaylee comes home, I can try to figure out how we could all fit together."

His hesitance is unnerving to say the least. But what's the alternative? I walk away? That's not gonna happen.

"Let's play it by ear," I say.

Ryder's face lights up, and even though this is risking a lot—my job, my demo, and my heart—I think it's a risk worth taking.

Because when Ryder kisses me, everything makes sense.

I don't know how, only that it does.

Ryder's promise of more to come if I manage to get my two songs recorded has the rest of the afternoon flying by.

Maybe getting off together is what we needed to do to be productive, because despite smelling like him and wearing the cum-stained evidence, when dinner rolls around, we've got two finished and polished songs on my demo. Ryder wants at least one more song, possibly two, but we're done for tonight.

When I walk out of the booth, a sense of accomplishment washes over me and makes me smile. It widens when I throw myself into the seat beside Ryder and he leans over to kiss my cheek.

I cock an eyebrow at him, but he shrugs.

"Testing it out."

"And?"

"And I hope I can keep doing it."

I know what he's promised me isn't much, and the thought of this trial date—or whatever tonight is—not working out churns my stomach. But stepping back and pretending something isn't going on between us won't work. We'll end up here again. I'm sure of it.

Ryder leans back in his seat. "What do you feel like for dinner?"

"I could go for some Indian."

"Hmm, spicy food is not really the right choice for what I have planned later."

The cheeky look on his face takes me off guard. Oh, yeah, this could totally work between us.

"I have no idea what you mean? I'm innocent."

Ryder scoffs. "Of course you are, but fine. If you want Indian, we'll get Indian."

I narrow my eyes. "Something else instead?"

Ryder smiles triumphantly. "I know what to order."

I'm not sure if we should take this further tonight because we're in this weird area between dating and not, but I want the possibility.

Being *the* Ryder Kennedy would make dating hard. Being a single father would make it harder. He can't date like a normal person.

It kinda takes the romance out of it a little, but being with him might be worth it.

He orders, and while we wait, Ryder leads me into the fancy, put together part of the house, where he tells me to land my ass on the big, soft sectional couch in front of the big-screen TV.

"You know, I'm under no illusion that you actually have your shit together, so this side of the house doesn't intimidate me like it used to."

"You say such sweet things. I'm totally put together and proper and not at all dysfunctional."

"How many times over the last few hours did you check your phone to see if there was anything from Maggie?"

Ryder scowls. "Just for that, you don't get any popcorn."

I grab my chest. "Hit me where it hurts."

He smiles. "I'll be right back."

Okay, so I might have been bluffing. This part of the house still makes me feel like I don't belong here. Especially when left alone.

I shift on the seat, trying to get comfortable, but the softness reminds me that the reason I don't fit is because I'm not used to being in expensive places.

Which is weird considering my brother's place isn't exactly a hole, and I've never felt out of place there. Though, sometimes when I leave the pool house and venture into the main house, I feel like I'm intruding, even though Chord and Brenna assure me I'm not.

The pool house is more what I'm used to living in. Small, basic, and no-frills.

Ryder eventually comes back with a giant bowl of popcorn and a heap of candy.

"Where have you been hiding this?" I sit up as he splays it all out on the coffee table.

"In the big kitchen. Far away from little eyes who would want to eat it all. You'd be surprised how many artists need a sugar kick while recording."

"Yeah?"

"Harley used to be the worst. Our handlers had to guard him. While they were keeping an eye on our drug use, they also had to make sure Harley wasn't sneaking out and filling up on M&M's."

"Who knew Harley Valentine was such a badass."

Ryder laughs. "Right? He loves the hard stuff."

He takes the spot next to me, and I lean back, resting my arm along the top of the couch.

"What do you want to watch?"

I lick my lips. "Don't care."

Ryder's blue eyes fill with heat. "Is that how it's going to be?"

I reach for a Twizzler and shove it into my mouth. "Yup."

His hand grips my shirt—well, his shirt—to pull me close, but I stop a breath away from his mouth.

"Don't hurt your pretty face."

He tilts his head. "Huh?"

I move his hand from the shirt and smooth it out. "Your pretty face."

"You're an idiot."

"Never claimed not to be."

Next thing I know, I'm on my back with Ryder on top of me, his mouth on mine, his hand in my hair, and I know without a doubt there's no way we can go back to how we were before.

What we have is too pure.

Ryder's hand slips between us, rubbing over my cock.

Okay, so it's not entirely pure, but it's natural.

It's … indescribable.

I don't want to put pressure on him or us or what this could potentially be, but I need him to try, and I'm not sure he's there yet. I'm not sure he ever will be when his focus is one hundred percent on Kaylee.

It's admirable, but he also needs to learn to take something for himself.

I want to be that for him, but it's a tough situation.

If this doesn't work out, it could break all three of us.

CHAPTER 17
RYDER

WITH LYRIC'S lips on mine, it's hard to remember why I have my no-dating rule.

When we're like this, pressed against each other, grinding and feeling each other up, it's easy to forget who I am.

I'm not Ryder Kennedy or someone's father, and I'm not a guy from a boy band.

I'm a man who has absolutely no control over his lust.

In the past, I was never sex-driven. It was always kind of a bonus if I got some, and I can't think of a single time I've ever been desperate for it.

I've never felt the need to jerk someone off in the middle of a recording session.

When Lyric hinted at regret, internal alarm bells went off, telling me to hold on to him as hard as I could because only a fool would let someone like him get away.

But this whole situation scares the shit out of me.

There are too many what-ifs running through my head and too much fear this will blow up.

That's why, even though I'm begging for more right now, I slow down.

My kisses become softer. My touch gentler.

Lyric separates his lips from mine, resting his head against the couch cushion. "Everything okay?"

"Food will be here soon, and if we keep going, one of us is going to have to answer the door naked."

"I'll do it. Just don't stop."

"Thank you for your sacrifice, but the delivery guys know me, and if a naked guy opens the door, I assume tabloids would be all over that."

"Oh, right. You know, sometimes it's easy to forget you're famous."

"You mean, me signing autographs and taking pictures for almost an hour today didn't remind you?"

"It did, but here"—Lyric's hand cups my cheek—"you're just Ryder to me."

Damn. Why do those words affect me so deeply? It's like they're reaching into my soul and giving me something I didn't know I desperately needed.

I'm frozen in awe.

"Did I say something wrong? Do you have, like, a fandom kink or something? Want me to be all"—Lyric raises his voice to go high-pitched—"'Ooh, Ryder Kennedy, I love Eleven, and you're sooooo cute. Will you have my babies and marrrrry me? I'm wearing your shirt and everything!' Does that do it for ya?"

I burst out laughing and climb off him to sit up properly.

"I'll take that as a no." He sits up too and looks at me with a concerned scrunch in his brow. "What happened just now?"

I run a hand through my hair. "I think the only other time someone has seen me as 'just Ryder' was when I was with Maggie. When …" I gesture with my hand for him to come to the conclusion himself.

"When Kaylee was …?"

"Yup. When Kaylee was made. Conceived? I don't know, pick the most unromantic word you can find because that describes it to a tee."

"Will you tell me about it?"

I huff. "You want to know the intimate details about me being with a woman?"

"Yes, that is exactly what I meant," he says. "Give me exact body parts and recreate the whole thing." He rolls his eyes. "You *know* what I mean."

I think about it for a minute. It's obviously not a story Maggie or I share with people. But for some reason, I want to pour my heart out to Lyric. I want to explain how one awkward night changed my life forever. "When it happened, I was home after an Eleven tour visiting my lovely homophobic parents in Texas."

"Wait, you're from Texas? Where's your sexy Southern accent?"

"You think Eleven's vocal coaches didn't practically beat it out of me?" Vocal coaching is a real form of torture. It took months for me to lose my twang and about a year for me to stop naturally returning to it.

"Wow." Lyric looks worried.

"Not that you'd let them anyway, but labels wouldn't change your perfect California-boy accent."

Lyric shakes his head. "Sorry. This industry stuff still surprises me when it shouldn't. What's wrong with a Southern accent? You'd think that would be cute and marketable."

"In Nashville, maybe. Anyway, back in Texas, I wanted out of the house and away from Mom and Pop's views on how the band's stylists enjoyed making us all dress gay."

"Wait, there's a gay dress code? Is this why I can't find a relationship? I dress wrong?"

"It's exactly why. Didn't you get the memo in the monthly newsletter?"

"Maybe I should check my spam folder."

"Maybe. It's kind of crazy how it all happened. The paparazzi hadn't found me at home yet, so for the first time in a few years, I was free to leave the house and do what I wanted without anyone there telling me not to. It was way past dinnertime, and it was dark, but I wanted out. I walked to the local playground and saw a figure on the swings. I pulled my hood up, but she'd already spotted me. There was little Maggie Costa grinning at me. We'd gone to the same schools since first grade, and it was weird to go from my life of fame straight into the past."

"Please tell me your daughter was conceived on a playground. That's so dirty and cool."

Yup. So romantic. "It would've made an awesome rom-com if not for one very glaringly obvious problem."

"The fact you prefer dudes?"

"Exactly. She was the first woman I'd been with since Eleven's first year on tour. Sex with women was always hit-or-miss for me. Should've been a big clue, right? It wasn't until I started messing around with guys in the industry who I knew would be discreet that my sexuality started making sense. Even if I still don't have a label for it, it makes sense to me."

"That's the only thing that matters," Lyric says, and I can hear how genuine he is come through in his soft voice.

"Anyway, Maggie. She was visiting after a deployment. She'd lost someone close to her over there, so she was a mess, and we got to talking about our lives. She dumped her depressing shit on me. I told her she made me feel like a spoiled diva, then she said, 'You're still just Ryder to me.' That was pretty much all it took."

"Ooh, I'm putting this sex weapon in my back pocket for later."

"Sex weapon?"

"Yeah, it's like a magic word. Instead of Abracadabra, it's *Just Ryder.*"

I wish I could say it doesn't do anything for me when he's mocking me, but I'd be lying.

Lyric chuckles. "I still can't believe you got freaky on a playground. You're lucky you weren't arrested or that someone didn't see it and sell photos to the tabloids."

I lean back on the soft cushions and rest my head against the backrest of the couch. "Although, if that'd happened, it might've dispelled some rumors about my sexuality."

"Pretty sure it only would've welcomed more. *Ryder Kennedy, Sex Addict.* I can see the headlines now."

The buzzer for the front gate sounds, so I stand. "I would say you're wrong, but that's probably an accurate depiction of what it would've been like had we been caught."

I collect the food from the front door and tip the guy generously. I've found most places are cool with the celebrity thing and don't run their mouths if they're paid well and know we'll be repeat customers.

When I get back to the formal living room, Lyric's sitting there with a contemplative stare.

"What's up?" I lay the Styrofoam boxes from my favorite café out on the coffee table with two plates and sit on the floor.

Lyric stays on the couch still looking spaced-out.

"Lyric?"

He snaps out of whatever it is and sinks to the floor next to me. "We should play a game while we eat."

"A game?"

"Yeah. All you have to do is say myth or fact to the following tabloid stories."

"Here we go."

We get comfortable, and I eat while Lyric starts with the questions.

He takes a bite of his sandwich and talks around the mouthful. "I know we've already covered this, but I really need to be sure. Did you actually die?"

I laugh hard. "I did. In a plane crash a few years ago. I'm either a ghost or your imagination. Pick one."

"Has to be my hot as fuck imagination because no way are ghosts as attractive as you are."

"Thank … you?"

Lyric ignores me and is ready for his next assault. "Umm, I already know the Kaylee rumor about her being a test tube baby isn't true. Soooo, ooh, hashtag Ryley4Ever. Did you and Harley ever hook up?"

"I almost don't want to deny this because the fandom behind that rumor is awesome. But it's a myth. Harley and I are great friends and that's all."

I don't miss the way Lyric lingers for more information about Harley and the rumors of his sexuality, and while it's pretty well-known in Hollywood circles, it's not my place to say more than that.

"Does your rider really have a sacrificial chicken slaughter before a performance?"

"Nah, that was Denver's."

He eyes me.

"I'm fucking with you. Total myth. Eleven's rider was tame. It had to be because our label didn't want us becoming bratty divas. Those rumors get spread around like crazy and cost gigs and appearances."

"Ugh. The more I hear about labels, the more I wonder if I should go indie."

"That's a legitimate conversation to have if you want to have it."

Lyric takes another bite. "Maybe another time. This is fun. Hmm, what else was there …"

"I'll get some out of the way for you. None of the guys except me have a kid—all those love child claims are fake. Umm, oh, in the early days, we did accidentally leave Blake at a rest stop somewhere in the middle of Ohio. So that one is true."

Lyric almost chokes. "Really?"

"He's so quiet. We didn't know he'd gotten off the tour bus to take a leak."

Lyric laughs. "How mad was he?"

"Not at all. He banged some groupie he met while he waited for us to circle back."

Lyric throws his head back. "That's amazing. Okay, which one of you is the manwhore? You've got Harley, the heartbreaking monogamist. You, the single father. Blake, the quiet token blond. So, it's either Mason or Denver."

"Denver," I say immediately. "Hands down. Mason is … I guess he's a little guarded? Always has been. Of all of us, he's the one who believes in love the least. Even temporary love in the form of hookups. I mean, not that he never did that, but it certainly wasn't as much as Denver."

"Wasn't Mason engaged at, like, nineteen?"

"Yep. The reason he doesn't believe in love. She wanted him for his fame. It's something we've all kind of dealt with at some point." I realize something. "Hang on. How did you know he was engaged at nineteen? I could maybe overlook the fact you knew Harley and I wrote most of Eleven's songs, but Mason's engagement is a pretty obscure piece of Eleven trivia." I gasp. "Are you secretly a boy band fan? Oh my God, this is brill—"

"Calm down. I remember my sister crying over it when it happened."

"Oh, damn. One day I'll get you to admit you love Eleven. Even if

I have to play our songs randomly until they catch on and you start singing. Next step is dancing, and then you'll be completely consumed."

Lyric sits up straighter. "That's the meanest thing you've ever said to me."

"And that's the meanest thing you've ever said to *me*. We're not really that bad, are we?"

Lyric lowers his voice and mumbles, "You might not be entirely horrible."

"Step one complete." I smile at him, and he returns it, but his next question throws me.

"Did you ever do this with Cash?"

I swallow hard. "Cash?"

"Yeah, like, order food and laugh and give each other shit." He looks down at his plate.

"Cash and I never did anything outside of the studio. He has the emotional reach of a vibrating dildo."

"Man, I'm so pissed I threw up on him. Who doesn't want that?" He laughs, but there's really no humor in it. "Sorry, forget I said anything."

I inch closer to him so our thighs touch as we sit cross-legged. "Lyric, I've never done *this* with anyone. You need to understand what Cash and I had was convenience. I hadn't been with anyone since Kaylee was born, and he was … there."

"Just like I'm here? This"—he waves his finger between us—"is convenient."

"If it were that simple, you wouldn't be here now."

I'm not trying to be a dick, but I need him to know this is hard for me—that I'm not taking this lightly.

My hand travels up his thigh, but he refuses to look at me, so I take things into my own hands.

Climbing into his lap, I straddle his hips. He lets me. Then he looks up at me with his expressive hazel eyes, and it makes me want to promise things I probably shouldn't.

"I know I can't promise much, and I know you're not entirely okay with that."

"I've been burned in the past by the casual thing."

"This isn't casual. I don't want it to be, at least. I just don't know how it will work blending with Kaylee."

"I get it," Lyric says. "I think. It's not like I want you to tell Kaylee or the public or hell, even Maggie, but I don't want to be treated like a cheap hookup either."

"I'll never treat you that way. I care too much about you as a friend to do that."

I catch the way he winces slightly at the word friend, but I don't know what else to call him.

Instead of trying to smooth that out, I lean down to kiss him again, and I try to put everything I feel for him into it.

I want to taste him and explore him, and as he runs his hands down my back and grips my ass, I want to give him more of me.

"Had enough dinner?" I murmur against his lips.

"Yup," he breathes.

"Let's go upstairs."

"Is that allowed?"

"It's new for me, so bear with me, okay?"

"We don't have to rush this. I promise. It's a Chase day tomorrow anyway, and I should probably go home tonight so I can drop him at school in the morning."

A million reasons to ask him to stay run through my head, threatening to bubble out of me like a river of rambling words.

"Can you get Brenna to drop Chase off at school? When Maggie brings Kaylee back tomorrow, you can take the Tesla to pick him up."

Lyric smiles. "Funny how it's easy to problem-solve when sex is on the table."

"That's not … Okay, maybe it is a little bit, but we don't have to have sex. I just …"

"Just what?"

"I think if you walk out that door right now, there's a good chance you'll come back tomorrow and we'll pretend like this didn't happen, and I don't want that. I want you to see that this is different."

"Different how?"

I hate that his voice is small, but I still struggle to find an answer. "I don't know that part yet. All I know is I don't want you to leave."

"I'm trying to be the bigger person here, Ryder. We've already crossed a lot of lines we said we wouldn't. Going upstairs with you will only mix everything together more. Kaylee. Recording. *Us*. I want you to be completely sure first. I promise I'm coming back."

He's right. I know he's right.

Reluctantly, I climb off him and land on my ass. "I know I should appreciate this, but honestly, I hate you a little bit."

Lyric leans over to kiss me. I can't help kissing him back.

He chuckles into my mouth. "Oh yeah, you hate me a lot." He stands, and I let out a whine. "We'll see how you feel tomorrow, okay?"

"I can already tell you. Fucking horny. That's how I'll be feeling."

"I hope so." Lyric kisses the top of my head. "I'll see you tomorrow."

I nod. "Tomorrow."

I wonder what the chances are of Maggie wanting Kaylee again overnight.

Turns out, the chances are high.

Really high.

After waking to phantom cries from Kaylee most of the night, only to remember she wasn't in the house, I'm dead tired when Maggie brings her home. After giving me a hug that is in no way long enough, Kaylee says she has to go say hello to all her toys and ask if they missed her.

I'm one sip of coffee in when Maggie drops the bombshell.

"I'm not re-upping."

I almost drop my damn cup. "Couldn't wait for Lyric to show up to drop that on me, huh?"

"Oh, wait, he's not here?" She looks around.

"Subtle, Mags. No, he's not. We hung out a bit last night, and then he went home."

"Hung out or"—she waggles her eyebrows—"*hung out?*"

I don't answer her.

"He gets my approval. Kaylee wouldn't shut up about him last night. She loves him already."

"Mm." I don't know what else to say to that.

"I'm not blind. It's obvious you two have something going on."

"Well, then maybe when you get out of the army, you should become a psychic because nothing was going on … until last night."

"I knew it," she crows. "So are you guys together now or what?"

"It's not that easy."

"Why not?"

"Like you said, Kaylee already loves him. What happens when it doesn't work out?"

"If. *If* it doesn't work out."

"It's not like I have a lot of free time to explore something serious with him."

Maggie leans against the counter. "Well, you could."

"Right. Because you're not re-upping." And my fears from yesterday come rushing back. All the other times Maggie's come home, she has hung around for a few days, maybe a few weeks, and every time she leaves, I've seen it. I've seen the look of longing in her eyes when she says goodbye to Kaylee.

She's not the type of person to cause drama. Maggie's the least dramatic person I know. But there's still that overprotective fear I have when it comes to anything Kaylee.

"You look upset," she says.

"I'm not. I guess I'm …" How do I say this without sounding like an asshole?

"You're worried I'm going to try to take Kaylee from you?"

"It's not like that—"

She smiles. "Isn't it? I'd like to think you'd know deep down that I'd never do that. So far, this co-parenting thing has been easy because I'm never around. I want to keep this easy thing between us going, but I do want more time with Kaylee."

"You deserve that," I say.

"I'd love more overnights or maybe even a few nights a week—"

I suck in a sharp breath.

"But I'm more than happy to work our way up to that. I've basically been gone her entire life, and you've done this while being on tour and being a celebrity and all the other stuff you've got going on. I know it'll be hard for you to let her go, but I hope you're open to it."

"What are you going to do for work?"

She cocks her head. "I'm gonna mooch off your boy band money, duh."

I laugh.

"But in seriousness, I'm not entirely sure. The only reason I re-upped last time was because I felt I owed John some sort of vengeance."

John—the guy she claims was the love of her life who died overseas. The guy she was so desperate to forget about that she slept with me and made a kid.

Tears fill her eyes. "When she was born, all I could think about was John. Even though she's yours, I always saw John in her. Maybe because of the future we were planning. Maybe because I resented the fact she existed and he didn't."

My heart breaks for both Maggie and Kaylee.

"You never told me that," I say quietly.

"I didn't tell anyone. I focused on the military and told myself I wasn't a maternal person."

"H-have you seen someone? Like a professional someone about that."

She sniffs. "I did. I've been working on it for the last few years, and I'm finally in that place where I want to be here for Kaylee. I feel I owe my daughter."

"I'm not going to lie. It scares me, but as long as we agree to have open communication and—"

"Always."

"When do you get out?" I ask.

"Officially? A few more weeks. I've gotta go back to base in six days, and then it's a matter of getting everything in order."

"You got somewhere to stay out here yet?"

She looks down at her feet. "Uh, no. Not yet." Her green eyes peer up at me.

"You're more than welcome to stay here until you find a job. Longer if you want it."

Maggie levels me with her signature judgy face.

"Which clearly you don't want or need."

"I want to show you I can do this. That I can be responsible."

"Is that why you got your own hotel room this time? You know you don't have to be that way. Not with me."

"I want to do this on my own."

"You sound like Lyric when I mention getting him a record deal."

"Lyric's an artist?"

"Yup. And he refuses to let me help."

"Now I like him even more. I remember how hard it was for you and the other Eleven guys to know who was genuine or not. I don't know Lyric at all, but my gut—and Kaylee—tell me he's great."

Yeah, so do I.

I don't have to question his motives when it comes to me. He's the most genuine person I've ever met. And while I fear Hollywood will want to chew him up and spit him out, I also know he has the self-respect and the dignity not to let it happen.

The sound of the front door opening echoes in the house, and I find myself straightening while fidgeting with the hem of my shirt.

"Oh my God, you're adorable," Maggie says.

"Shut up," I mutter.

Lyric saunters in but stops short when both of us look at him. "What did I miss?"

"Maggie's going to be sticking around for a while," I say, my smile tight.

I'm on board with her staying, but there are so many things I need to consider. What if the only job she can get is somewhere else? Like Texas. What if she wants to take Kaylee? What if, what if, what if—

"As you can see, he's freaking out about it." Maggie's her usual bubbly self, and I don't deserve it. I'm being an asshole.

"I'm not freaking out," I say.

Maggie leans in closer to Lyric. "He's freaking out. I want to spend more time with Kaylee, so he's doing his overprotective-dad routine."

"Ah. Makes sense." Lyric turns to me. "Kaylee will be fine."

"I hate you both," I grumble, and they laugh at me. "So funny," I grumble some more.

Maggie touches my upper arm. "You know we're only teasing. You have every right to feel the way you do, and I understand it. I want to reassure you you're still in charge here. I'll go at your pace."

"Sounds familiar," Lyric murmurs.

When my gaze snaps to his, he throws me an innocent "what?" expression.

"On that note, I'll leave you two to it and go check on Kaylee." Maggie walks away, and Lyric watches her leave.

Once she's out of sight, he turns his smile on me.

"Hey." He leans in and kisses my cheek.

"Hi."

"That okay?"

"More than okay." I kiss his lips briefly.

It's not enough, but it has to be because Kaylee could come out here any minute.

"So, she's staying, huh?"

"She will be. She has some things to get straightened out first, but it looks like she'll be moving here permanently."

"Ah. Uh, cool. I guess I'll be looking for a new job soon?"

Oh shit. I didn't even think of that. "We'll still need you."

"Just not as much. It's okay. This was never going to be a long-term thing anyway. Kaylee starts school in a few months."

"Hey, maybe look on the bright side? When we finish your demo, you won't even need this job because you're going to get signed."

Lyric doesn't look convinced.

"Maggie's only here for six more days, and then she'll be back in a few weeks. I was thinking ..."

"She should spend as much time with Kaylee as she can while she's here?"

"Well, yes, but we can use that time to record. I don't have any producing work scheduled for two more days."

If sex had a tone, it just fell out of my mouth, but I didn't mean it to come out that way. Well, not entirely.

"How much work do you think we're really going to get done when you say it like that?"

I throw up my hand and make the Vulcan salute from Star Trek. "Scout's honor." No way I'm actually promising that for real.

Lyric snorts.

"Okay, I promise to be professional while we're recording." When we're done for the day, that's another story. "I figure with Maggie around more, we'll actually have a chance to do this right. I could go on a real date with you."

"A date? Like an actual, go to dinner and sit across from each other and talk about our lives type of date?"

"It might not have PDA, but it's the closest thing to a real date I can offer."

"Do you really think you can be professional until Maggie gets back?" Lyric's doubtful expression mirrors my exact thoughts.

"Probably not."

CHAPTER 18
LYRIC

SURPRISINGLY, Ryder manages to keep it professional. For two days. Minus a sneaky kiss on the cheek here and there, we've mainly been in the studio doing actual work while Maggie has taken Kaylee to playgroup.

Maggie staying is a good thing. It'll be great for Ryder to have a little more freedom and even better for Kaylee to spend quality time with her mom.

But it does feel like my time as her nanny will be cut short.

And I have to wonder how much effort Ryder will put into seeing me if I'm not conveniently there all the time.

He says what we have isn't about convenience, but I'm still not convinced.

Saturday night rolls around, and as I take to the stage at Cedar Bar for my weekend gig, I see a figure in the audience my body automatically knows is Ryder.

It's all the convincing I need.

He came to see me play.

Unlike when Cash was in the audience, I'm not nervous.

Okay, I'm a little nervous, but I've performed in front of Ryder countless times now. I want to show him I'm taking his advice. I'm listening to him. I've tweaked my sets and chosen songs that show off more of my range.

I've taken my song choices to a new level where I don't ask if it's too mainstream or has the perfect amount of obscure to popular ratio.

I don't give a shit what other people think. I'm only taking my own personal opinion into account.

If I'm honest, it's changed the entire way I listen to music.

I may never be a boy band fan, but I've reached a new level of appreciation for them. Thanks to Ryder.

Still ain't gonna fucking sing one of their songs, though.

My eyes meet the shadowy figure in the audience. He's in a denim jacket with a gray hood to try to conceal his identity, and as selfish as it is, I hope he isn't recognized.

He's here for *me*, and I kinda want to keep it that way.

It's hard not to rush through the set so I can go to him, which is ridiculous because we saw each other yesterday.

He had a new act in the studio today—something he usually doesn't do on weekends. I would've worked, but Maggie was able to take Kaylee.

The beginning of the end of my time as Kaylee's nanny.

I thought Ryder was going to be in the studio all day, but I guess they finished up early.

While I perform, my gaze keeps going back to him, even though I can basically only see the outline of him under the stage lights.

After a million hours onstage, I finally get to my last song, but as I put my mouth to the microphone, I hesitate.

I decide to change it up by singing our version of "Take Me to Church."

Though I can't see his expression throughout it, I imagine him staring at me in the hungry way he has been while we've been in the studio.

The heat in his eyes and the tight set of his jaw.

My dick is hard just picturing it. I've never been more grateful to have my guitar onstage with me.

When I get to the bridge and belt out the lyrics, I close my eyes and remember what it felt like to have Ryder's hands on me. His mouth.

I want it again.

Since when does a four-minute song feel like an eternity?

When I get to the final chorus, I try to lock eyes on him again, but he's gone.

I stumble over the last note and am quick to leave the stage before the applause even begins to die down.

Ryder must've left to beat the crowd or perhaps he was recognized. I try to head for the entrance to follow him, but Alex the bartender appears in front of me and stops me with his hand on my chest.

"You might wanna check your dressing room."

I hate that I can't contain my smile.

"How in the hell are you getting all these celebrities to come see you play?"

Cocky is something I can play well when I need to. I definitely don't need to tell Alex neither Cash nor Ryder were here for musical reasons. "Did you not see me up there? I'm on fire."

He doesn't really believe me.

"For real. Ryder wants to get me a record deal."

"Ryder. Sure, because everyone in LA is on a first-name basis with Ryder-fucking-Kennedy."

"Anyone who has talent is." I slap his shoulder. "Sorry."

"Can you at least get one of them to come see my set some time?" he calls after me as I make my way to the back.

"If you're really nice to me," I call back.

"I give you free drinks!"

I want to argue all performers get free drinks, but I'm too far away now and what's waiting for me in my dressing room is more important.

As soon as I'm through the door, I close it behind me. I don't want anyone else knowing who's in here.

Ryder sits on the old, dusty couch against the wall with a small smirk on his lips and his hood still over his head.

My tongue is thick in my mouth, and I can't find words.

I lean against the door and watch as Ryder slowly gets to his feet.

He takes one step and then two, so incredibly slow and teasing. He doesn't say a word.

Only when he's toe to toe with me and reaches behind me to flick the lock does he speak.

"You don't play fair."

I go weak in the knees. "I don't play fair?"

"No," he croaks. "You sang our song. In *public.*"

"I'm never going to hear or sing that song again without getting a hard-on."

Ryder moves in closer. "Why do you think I had to leave halfway through it?"

"So, you liked the set?"

"I fucking loved the set." His breath is on my skin, so close to my lips. "Are there any cameras in here?"

"Nope."

"Thank fuck." His mouth comes crashing down on mine, strong and full of that spark only he seems to draw out of me.

With the door locked, no kid—wait …

I pull back. "Where's Kaylee?"

"I asked Maggie to take her overnight again."

"Aww, look at you being mature about that whole situation."

Ryder's hand lands on my hip. "It has nothing to do with being mature and everything to do with being unable to keep doing what we've been doing for days."

"What's that?"

"Teasing each other."

I act coy. "Teasing? I don't think I've been doing any teasing."

"All you have to do is breathe near me and it's teasing."

"And you came here to …?"

"To fuck you."

"There it is." I laugh. "And here I thought it was because you wanted to see me onstage."

Ryder reaches for my belt. "Mm, that too."

"But mainly the fucking thing?"

"Yup."

My hand goes to his wrist to make him pause for a second.

Ryder's blue eyes pierce me deep. "Unless you don't want to."

"Oh, I want to. I'm ready to turn around and drop trou any second. But I need to make sure you're okay to do this here. You think you can be quiet enough with everyone out there?" I tip my head backward.

"Door's locked. No cameras. I can be quiet if you can."

"Screw it. I can scream into my shirt if I have to." I shuck my shirt off but make sure to hold on to it.

"I like your enthusiasm." Ryder's hand trails around my chest, and he licks his lips. "How have I never seen you without a shirt before?"

"You prefer it when I wear T-shirts with your face on them."

"True. But I think I could like this more."

I shudder as his hands explore me. From my collarbone down to my pecs.

"Turn around," Ryder whispers against my skin.

Instead, I pull him closer. "I want something first."

I don't give him the chance to ask what. I just take it.

His mouth is what I want. His lips on mine. My tongue against his.

Ryder pushes against me so we're pressed against the door, and when he grinds his hard cock along mine, I moan.

"Shh." Ryder laughs.

"Okay, looks like I need this sooner than I thought." I shove my shirt in my mouth and immediately regret it. I screw up my face.

"Sweaty?" Ryder asks.

I make spitting noises. "Yup."

He takes off his jacket, and then his shirt follows. "Here, use mine. I haven't been under stage lights for two hours."

Aw, fuck, it smells like him.

My dick throbs.

"Ready to turn around for me now?"

"I have a better idea." Instead of fucking against the door, I bend over the counter that runs along the wall and brace my hands in front of the mirror lined with Hollywood lights, my ass high in the air.

"Lie flat," Ryder croaks.

I do as he says with no question, pressing my chest against the cool surface and putting his shirt in my mouth.

I should feel vulnerable in this position, but I don't.

I can't get my pants off fast enough. My fingers finish what Ryder started, and I get my belt and button undone.

"You look so hot right now." Ryder's hands travel down my back.

I can't reply, but I can grunt. I rest my head on my hands on the counter beneath me.

Ryder drags my jeans down my legs with my underwear. The cool air hits my bare skin, and I shiver, but then Ryder's there, covering my body with his.

His breath is hot in my ear. "I'm scared this is going to be over super quick."

I release his shirt and turn my head to the side. "It kinda needs to be. I don't think they'll buy that we've been talking about the record deal you're offering me if we take too long."

I feel him smile against my skin.

"That's what you told them I was doing here?" Ryder's finger slips into my crack and teases my hole.

"Uh-huh." I grunt again.

"You know I *could* make that happen for you."

"Not the time, dude," I growl.

"You're probably right about that."

Ryder's presence disappears from my back, but when I look at him over my shoulder, I realize it's to pull out supplies.

"Came prepared, huh?" I ask.

"To be fair, I wasn't planning to do this here, but yeah, I was hoping this would happen tonight. Somewhere. Anywhere."

"Here's good. Just hurry up. I need you touching me again. I need you … I need you inside me."

A second later, a slippery finger is back to teasing me, pushing inside me and expertly working me open.

Ryder breathes hard. "Yup, definitely going to be over so fast. You're so tight."

He adds a finger, and I have to bite down on his shirt again. I welcome the burn.

The muscles in my back tense as I take his fingers deep.

I grit my teeth to hold in the groan I desperately want to let out.

"I love the sounds you're making even though you're supposed to be quiet."

My heart pounds. I turn my head again. "You always this chatty when you fuck someone?"

Ryder laughs. "Nope. Just stalling the inevitable embarrassment of coming as soon as I'm inside you."

"It won't take me long. I've wanted this since the day we met."

"Me too," Ryder murmurs.

"You have a thing for guys who insult you, huh?"

"It's soooo hot." His fingers brush against my prostate, sending shivers down my spine. "Not as hot as watching you while I finger fuck you, but still pretty hot."

"Ryder, I need … need …" My hips cant backward. "Fuck."

He leans over me again. "I think I know what you need."

His fingers leave me, and no, that's not what I need at all. An agonized sound leaves my lips.

"I'm still here," he reassures me. The sound of a condom wrapper opening sounds like angels singing.

My chest is heaving, and my ass tightens and releases, craving the invasion again.

And when it happens, Ryder goes slow so I can feel every inch as he moves inside me.

I have to bite down on his shirt so hard I worry my jaw will break.

A gentle hand runs down my back. My stomach digs into the edge of the counter, but I don't care a single bit.

The way we're connected, his slow and cautious movements, for a brief moment I feel a connection of something more. That thing I've been wanting for as long as I can remember.

During college, I did the hookup thing. I was never any good at it. It's like monogamy and commitment are part of my DNA or some shit.

I know I need to let things develop on Ryder's time and in his way, but it's hard enough to do that when he's kissing me or smiling at me, or hell, even just looking at me through the recording studio window. It's impossible not to think of more when his dick's inside me.

This is just sex, I remind myself. This is weeks of thinking about this. Of fantasizing about what it would be like to be with Ryder.

As he begins to thrust harder and harder, I get my answer to the hypotheticals I've been thinking about since I met him.

Being with Ryder is awesome. And hot.

He moves his hands to grip my hips hard.

His cock hits my prostate, and I can't do anything but lie here and take it.

The room is silent now apart from our hard breathing. The counter is strong enough to hold my weight, even with Ryder pounding into me.

My ass burns but craves more.

Over and over again, Ryder thrusts into me, and over and over again, I'm taken higher and higher.

My cock begs to be touched, but Ryder's unforgiving pace won't allow me to move my hands.

My muscles spasm, my whole body coiling tight and waiting to be released.

"Lyric," Ryder grits out.

His shirt is still silencing me, and I fear if I release it, I'll let out a yell so loud someone out there is sure to hear it.

He pushes inside once more and stills while his cock pulses inside me. My ass clenches as if wanting to hold him in place.

Ryder's body collapses onto mine, his head, wet with sweat, lands between my shoulder blades.

His hands are still gripping my hips, holding me in place.

Ryder's hot breath lands on my skin. "Sorry."

I release his shirt. "Don't be sorry. That was amazing."

"But you didn't … you know …"

I move my hand and clumsily reach behind me to take hold of his and then place it on my hard and aching cock. "So get me there now."

Ryder keeps his softening cock inside me while he works me over. He doesn't bother with teasing or trying to draw it out. This is about getting me across the finish line the fastest way possible.

He trails his lips along my shoulder blade and brings his mouth next to my ear. "I love having my hands on you. Being inside you."

I shudder. With him boxing me in, my body moves the only way it can. I writhe against him.

He nips my earlobe. "Come, Lyric."

Oh, fuck.

My orgasm takes hold, my body rocking as it washes over me, but Ryder's right there holding me in place while my cum spills into his hand.

He holds me while I catch my breath and become dead weight in his arms.

Ryder's lips kiss the back of my head and my sweaty neck. His tenderness comes through in the way he doesn't pull away immediately.

Eventually, we part, and I slowly stand.

Ryder strips the condom off and pulls up his pants.

"Bathroom's through there." I point.

He doesn't say anything, just leaves to the adjoining room.

My body aches as I move to fix my underwear and jeans and prepare myself to come face-to-face with the possibility of Ryder running.

He hasn't done it yet, but it always feels like he's got one foot out the door.

That he'll change his mind.

I fear he'll realize I'm not worth risking his daughter's happiness for.

I wait for the "We probably shouldn't have done that." Or even the "I still don't know if I can give you what you want."

Instead, when Ryder comes back, he's all casual smiles as he grabs his shirt off the table and throws it over his head.

His blue eyes are constantly on me, and when he's completely redressed, he finds my shirt on the floor and tosses it my way.

I put on the gross shirt, still unable to find the right words to say.

Our lives are intertwined in more ways than one right now, which is why it would've been smart not to kiss him that day in his recording studio.

I should've stepped back then.

Now we're here, and—

Ryder steps into my space. "Lyric, breathe. You look like you're about to pass out."

I suck in a sharp breath.

Ryder presses against me, his arms going around my back. "Come home with me tonight?"

Not what I was expecting. Not at all. "Really?"

"Yeah ..."

"Am I imagining that tone of doubt?"

"No. I'm just new to this. And the last time I asked someone to stay, he left to give me respectful time to think it over."

"What. An. Asshole."

"Right?"

I press my lips together. "Are you sure?"

"So sure. When I'm with you, all I want is more. More of your time. More of your touch. More … of everything. But as soon as those thoughts are there, so are questions about where it could really go, and that's when a million things pop into my head about Kaylee, and you recording, and being an out artist, and being yourself without my closet door in your way, and leaving to go on tour, and I left that life for Kaylee, and it's a big never-ending cycle that freaks me out, and—"

I know I shouldn't laugh, but it slips out. My hands reach for Ryder's shoulders. "It's your turn to breathe."

He does.

"It's okay to have doubts. Fuck, I have a million voices in my head telling me why I shouldn't be attracted to you. Why I shouldn't have sex with my boss or the guy producing my demo. There are a thousand reasons to leave and only one to keep chasing the high you give me."

"What's the reason?"

I bite my lip. "I like you."

Ryder's eyes soften, and he leans forward, capturing my mouth with his.

I let it happen.

I let him take control and enjoy the softness of his lips and the gentle caress of his tongue against mine.

All my reasons for not doing this are drowned out when Ryder kisses me.

"Let's get out of here," Ryder murmurs.

"Definitely."

"Did you drive here?"

"Brenna dropped me off. I was gonna Uber home."

"Perfect. You can come with me."

On the way out, I nod to Alex behind the bar, and when he'd

usually wave me off, he kind of stands there with a stupid stunned expression on his face.

"Who's that?" Ryder yells over the loud music.

"Alex. He's a bartender here, but he performs during the week. He wanted me to put in a good word."

Ryder waves politely at Alex, but then we move fast toward the door. He expertly ducks his head in a way that means the people lined up outside the club can't see or recognize him, and he turns left to go down an alley.

The bright red of the Ferrari is the first thing I notice when we turn the corner.

"No way."

Ryder laughs. "I thought you'd like it."

"You left your Ferrari in an alley? Are you crazy?"

"You want me to park it on the street? It's fine. It's still here, isn't it?"

"It won't be for long. Let's go."

"Here I was thinking you'd fawn all over me and jump at the chance to drive it."

"I'll leave the driving to you. I'm just here for the ride."

We get into the car, and Ryder turns to me without putting the key in the ignition. "Was that innuendo, or are we actually talking about cars?"

"What do you think?"

"I'm kinda hoping we're talking about cars." Ryder smiles.

"Meaning …"

"Meaning, after refueling with some food, I was hoping you might jump in the driver's seat later tonight."

I frown. "Wait, now are you talking about cars or sex?"

Ryder grunts. "Okay, this metaphor thing isn't working. I want you to fuck me later. If you're into that. If not, that's cool too."

"Oh, I definitely want a turn at your ass later."

"Good to know." He turns the car on, and the headlights light up the dark alley. "So, food break?"

I reach across the console and grip his thigh. "I don't need food."

Ryder revs his car and tears down the street. "Neither do I."

I wish Calabasas was closer.

CHAPTER 19
RYDER

I CAN'T GET HOME FAST ENOUGH, but even at the late hour, LA traffic wants to kick my ass.

It's a race against my mind as I head for home. I'm scared my brain is either going to catch up to tonight's events and try to get me to slow down and be smart about this whole thing or run away with this crazy notion that Lyric and I could have something real.

It wasn't my exact plan to have sex with him backstage at his own show, but I'm relieved my prepared side made me come ready for it. Fucking him wasn't just amazing. It was different. It was more than physical. More than sex.

It still scares the shit out of me, but as long as I'm not thinking about all the obstacles, I'm more than prepared to lose myself in him again.

And again.

And then maybe again in the morning before Kaylee comes home.

"So, you really liked my set?" Lyric asks.

"I'm sorry, did fucking you in your dressing room give you a different impression?"

"Maybe you were doing it so you wouldn't have to tell me it was horrible. You know, like when someone asks, 'Does this make me look fat?' and you say 'Oh, wow, your eye makeup is to die for.' That kind of thing."

When I side-eye him, he shrugs.

"I have a sister and currently live with my sister-in-law. You don't think they ask their gay brother for fashion advice?"

I laugh. "No, this isn't one of those situations. This is definitely a 'You looked so hot up there all I could think about was throwing myself at you' type thing. Especially when you sing that song. All I can think about is being in the studio at home with you. Then I think of the amazing handjobs and heated kisses, and—fuck, I'm already hard again."

"Better drive faster," Lyric taunts.

"Mm."

Considering I'm in a sports car, it still feels like we're getting nowhere.

"Why did I decide to move all the way out here?"

"I don't know, but you suck."

"Not yet, I haven't." I take my eyes off the road for a split second to watch Lyric's eyes fill with heat.

By the time we pull up to my gate, and it takes about six years to open, Lyric is running his hands all over me.

From my thighs to my chest and back down to my hard cock fighting against my zipper.

I somehow manage to navigate the car into the garage, but I'm so not getting it into its spot.

Yeah, my babies have designated spots. Like their own little bedrooms.

It's not weird.

Lyric leans over in the small confines of the car and kisses his way down my neck while his hand reaches inside my jacket and moves over my chest.

I throw my head back on the headrest. "Fuck, Lyric. How can you …"

He looks up at me. "How can I what?"

"You drive me crazy." I capture his lips.

The leather seats squeak as we grope and try to get closer, but there is absolutely no room in here.

Why do I love this car again? Right now, I can't remember.

"Why can't I stay away?" I groan.

"Do you want to stay away?"

"No. I just *should*."

"You really shouldn't. And I'm gonna show you why." Lyric opens the butterfly door and gets out of the car.

I try to go after him, but there's one little tiny detail I might be forgetting.

The seat belt practically chokes me as I try to get out of the car without unbuckling it.

Smooth, Ryder. So fucking smooth.

Lyric laughs at me when I manage to free myself and climb out of the car. "In a rush?"

"You know it." I grab his hand and drag him toward the house. "Why's it so far to the damn front door?"

"Rich people problems. My ten-car garage is too far from the door to my mansion."

"Exactly. My life is hard."

"Not as hard as this." Lyric takes our joined hands and rubs it over the bulge in the front of his pants.

"Subtle."

"My dick is offended you think it's subtle."

Taking out my key, I try to open the door, but Lyric plasters himself to my back.

"I'm totally prepared to show you how unsubtle it can be," he says against my neck.

My ass pushes against him. "Fuck."

"Here, let me." Lyric takes the keys from my shaking hands.

I reach behind me and bury my hand in his messy bun.

Lyric somehow gets the door open while grinding against me and kissing my neck and shoulder.

We stumble inside, and I turn to kiss him while I close the door with my foot.

He moans into my mouth, and the sound is so delectable I can't help mimicking him.

As much as I'm in a rush to get upstairs and horizontal, I can't tear my mouth away long enough to see where we're going. So blindly, we move our way through the foyer of my stupidly large house.

Lyric's hands work my jacket off while I reach for his belt.

I want all the clothes gone this time. I want to take the opportunity to worship every inch of his skin.

We leave a trail of shoes and jackets leading to the stairs when we finally have to pull away from each other.

My shirt drops to the carpet as I climb the steps, and his follows.

By the time we reach my bedroom door, we're both completely naked.

Lyric pauses inside the room and glances around, taking it all in.

I only see him, and I don't know what he's finding so fascinating.

I crook my finger at him.

He doesn't move. "This whole bedroom is bigger than the pool house I'm currently squatting in."

I glance around the room, trying to see it from his perspective. I have some rumpled clothes on my bed, and the shoes I wore yesterday are in the middle of the floor, but apart from that, I can't deny my room looks barely lived-in.

The only furniture in here is a chest of drawers right near the door and a king bed with a black leather headboard and side tables.

"Are you judging my room right now? It's not like I've ever had a guest up here to impress."

"It's really depressing that no one's ever broken in this bed with you."

"There are a lot of depressing things about my sex life."

Lyric wears a small smile. "Don't oversell yourself or anything."

"The only way to make a good impression is to make sure the bar for expectation is set low."

"Mm, mediocrity is such a turn-on, but there's one problem with that." Lyric steps closer to me, and my eyes take the opportunity to roam over him again.

From his long blond hair in that permanent messy bun to his tight and lithe body, I could stand here and watch him move all night if it weren't for my dick's neediness.

Lyric's cock looks just as ready for more.

I lick my lips. "What problem is that?"

"You've yet to disappoint me when it comes to sex."

"There's still time."

Lyric laughs.

The happiness he exudes is admirable. The confidence I see as he moves toward me is intoxicating, but I'm fixated on his hair. His golden, shiny hair I both want to stroke and fist in my hand.

"What do you look like with your hair down?" I blurt.

Lyric stops short of me, leaving a few feet between us. "Random question is random." But he doesn't wait for an explanation. He reaches back and pulls out his hair tie, securing the tie to his wrist.

His hair naturally falls on either side of his face in loose curls.

I step forward, but he seems frozen to his spot.

"You're gorgeous." I twine a finger into one of his curls.

"I'm smart too," Lyric says quietly.

"I've noticed."

His hazel eyes bore into me. "Umm, that was a joke to cover up that I don't take compliments well."

"I've complimented you heaps before."

"Not like this. Not like ..." He steps forward, pressing his bare skin against mine.

I shudder against him. "Just so you know, I think you're super smart."

Lyric's voice comes out low. "You also think Pop-Tarts are a suitable breakfast food, so I don't trust your judgment."

I pull back and look him in the eye. "More deflection with humor?"

"No, I really do worry for your sugar levels. Not to mention Kaylee's."

I snort.

I love how things are between us. Downstairs, we couldn't get enough of each other. There was no tearing me away. We needed to be touching, kissing, finding an outlet for the tension that's been building and building, but right now, we can be us. I like that it's easy and hot, yet there's a level of comfort between us since we were friends first.

Being with him once tonight was never going to be enough.

I don't know when or if I could ever get enough of Lyric.

Here, now, I have him in a different way. He's more vulnerable and softer, but he's still full of the light he brought into my life.

"Kiss me," I say.

"I insult you, and you tell me to kiss you. I'd accuse you of having issues, but instead, I'm going to chalk it up to being so adorably cute you forgive me when I say mean things."

"It's something like that." I cup the back of his head, my hand weaving into his hair, and lean in to fuse our mouths together.

We take our time now, the urgency from downstairs dissolving into something deeper.

I turn us and walk him back toward the bed, pushing him down while I climb on top of him.

Lyric feels so damn good underneath me, all pliant and willing.

But it isn't about him this time.

I sit up and straddle him so I can reach for supplies in my top drawer. I usually keep them in my studio where I know little, snooping eyes won't find them, but like going to Lyric's show tonight prepared, I wanted some close by in case my loose plan to bring Lyric back here came to fruition.

Lyric's hands roam all over me, but there's a tenderness there.

I throw a condom on the bed and grab the lube. I go to squirt some onto my fingers, but Lyric holds out his hand.

"Let me." He takes it from me and covers his fingers. "You want to ride my fingers first?"

I nod. It's been a while since I tried this, but I don't really want to admit that.

Either Lyric can sense I'm not used to it or he's overly cautious, because he takes his time teasing my hole while softly stroking my cock. It's not enough to get me off, just enough to keep me hard while I focus on taking his fingers.

When one finally pushes inside me, I remember what it's like to have a cock in my ass, splitting me apart. I crave the ache and the sense of fullness.

I sink down on his finger, taking him easily, and beg him to add more.

Lyric stares up at me with hooded eyes, his long hair framing his face.

This is different than when I fucked him in his dressing room. This is more intimate, and I can make out every expressive emotion on his face. From the want to the doubt.

I want to reassure him. He has to know how he's affecting me too, and not just his fingers in my ass but him as a person.

Leaning down, I take his mouth with mine while I continue to ride his fingers.

With his free hand, he cups the back of my head as if holding me in place to keep my lips on his, my tongue teasing.

I'm so ready.

I roll off him, his fingers slipping from my ass, and I already miss the intrusion.

My ass clenches as I beckon for him to get on top of me, but he only leans up on his elbow.

"You okay?"

"Perfect. I need your cock inside me, though."

Lyric maneuvers himself in between my legs, reaching for the condom as he does.

I can't do anything but watch while he rolls it down his long and impressive cock.

"Are you sure you're ready?"

I pull him down on top of me and wrap my legs around his waist. The head of his cock lines up with my hole.

"Do it."

Still, he pushes in slowly. I'm thankful but needy at the same time. I'm battling between wanting to go slow and needing more.

Lyric hovers above me, his skin flushed. His hair falls around his face, and I reach up to tuck it behind his ear. He grits his teeth as if he's trying to hold on to control.

"Let go," I encourage. "I promise I'm okay."

Apparently, those are the words he needed to hear because he pushes in as far as he can go.

We're both loud, moaning and cursing as I run my hand down his back and feel the ripples of his muscles tensing.

He rolls his hips, but his movements are slow and languid.

I feel all of him, but it's still not enough.

I want him to surround me and consume all of me.

"Kiss me," I beg him.

He takes my mouth as softly as he's taking my body.

Warmth fills my stomach while my heart thuds.

We're connected in a way I've never been to another person. Not physically but inside.

It's like every thought about this not working out gets dimmer and dimmer with every thrust Lyric makes. Every time he moves inside me, it's like we're giving each other another piece of ourselves.

It's intense and something that would usually freak me out, but when I break my lips away from his and look up into his eyes, all that's inside me is the feeling of being complete.

Whole.

It drives my need and fuels my lust.

With his eyes on mine, Lyric increases his pace.

"Harder." I grunt.

He does as I say.

Heat pools in my gut, and I've never known sex to be an emotional act before.

This is new to me, but as Lyric takes me—claims me—all I can do is let it ride.

His mouth drops open, and I know he's getting close.

I try to reach between us to jerk off and get to where he is, but as if sensing my need, Lyric does it for me.

His fingers wrap around my dick and pump hard. "I've got you."

The sincerity in his voice and everything about the gesture has nothing to do with sex and everything to do with us. It's heavy, yet it doesn't feel like I can't handle it.

He takes my mouth with his once more, and my orgasm rocks through my entire body. He continues to pump into me, continues to claim my body, and when he shudders and stills on top of me, I realize it's over.

I don't want it to be.

I want to hold on to us for as long as I can.

CHAPTER 20
LYRIC

TONIGHT HAS BEEN CRAZY.

After collapsing on top of Ryder to catch my breath, I only manage to roll off him when he taps my shoulder to get me to move.

From his messy light brown hair that's usually sticking straight up to his puffy well-kissed lips, he's like this perfect package of a guy I've only ever dreamed about before.

And he's next to me.

Naked.

Ryder rolls onto his side, and I follow him so we're facing each other.

We're both sweaty, both spent, but he still leans over and nips my bottom lip while he reaches for the condom under the sheet to ditch it beside the bed for now.

"You're a fucking tease," I grumble.

"I'd so go another round if I could, but I think you broke me. My dick is insistent on sleeping."

I laugh. "Mine too." I open my arms for him to come to me, but he stares at me weird. "Oh. Are you not a cuddler? That might be a deal breaker for me."

Ryder wiggles his way into my side, and I wrap myself around him. "I'm not used to this. Being affectionate after sex. This whole thing is weird. Only made weirder by the fact we have to pretend nothing happened when we wake up tomorrow."

It's like a slap to the face, and I must flinch or show it.

"In front of Kaylee, I mean."

I relax at that, but he doesn't stop.

"I didn't mean we had to forget it. I don't want to forget it. But Kaylee …"

"Kaylee can't know yet. I understand that one hundred percent."

"Not until I know what this even is. Right now, it's experiencing something more than I ever have for the first time. I don't know what that means."

I want to argue that it means he might be ready to open his heart to someone fully, but I don't want to throw that revelation at him. He has to get there in his own time.

Being with him tonight has reassured me that it's me he wants, and that's enough for me for now.

I feared I might be another Cash to him—that he was lonely, and I was an option because of our proximity.

But something changed tonight. For both of us.

Ryder may still be unsure about how this will work and exactly what he wants, but it's obvious he's trying.

I know what I want from him. I want to do more of this. I want to build something from the ground up and form an actual relationship because that's who I am. Every guy I meet, every date I've had, I try to imagine what we'd be like as a couple.

I learned in college that you don't actually say that shit aloud, though. That stuff tends to scare guys off. It's why I've become so wary about dating apps. They're really *fucking* apps and nothing more.

Ryder's eyes are now closed, and I assume he's going to sleep, but the next minute, one eye pops open. "How do you sleep next to someone?"

"What do you mean?"

"I'm too conscious of your body. And your breathing."

"Sorry, I'll stop breathing."

Ryder laughs. "Thank you. Problem solved."

"I still don't know how you've never done this before."

"I've legit only spent one night cuddled up with someone, and it was because they were going through some shit. I didn't sleep, though."

"With Maggie?"

He huffs. "No, actually. With someone from Eleven."

"Ryley4Ever is real!" I get maybe a little too excited about that possibility.

"Not one bit, but it was Harley. We're like brothers."

"Damn." I kiss the top of his head. "The image of you and Harley together is hot as fuck."

"Really? But we're so lame and lazy and—"

"God, I hate you," I mutter. "Besides, admitting Harley is gorgeous is not exactly complimenting you on your music."

"Who's hotter? Me or Harley?"

"Hands down no contest." I hold him close. "Definitely Harley."

Ryder swats my chest.

"I'm kidding. I'd choose you any day of the week."

Ryder yawns.

"You should try to sleep. Stick to your side of the bed if you have to."

"No, let's do this. I can totally cuddle."

He says that, and then he proceeds to wiggle and get more and more frustrated.

"Roll over," I eventually grumble because now *I* can't sleep.

Ryder rolls away from me, and I lay my arm over his waist.

He settles almost immediately.

"Finally," I murmur into the back of his hair.

He releases a long breath and whispers, "Yeah, this isn't so bad."

When I wake, I'm surprised to find us still tangled together. We moved during the night, but I'm still spooning him. Ryder's partially on his stomach, and my leg sits between his.

I breathe in the scent of sex and hold him a little closer. "I have bad news for you," I mutter.

"Mm?" he says, still half-asleep.

"I think you like cuddling."

"Eww. I'm gross."

I laugh. "When is Kaylee coming home?"

"We didn't set a time." Ryder disentangles himself from me and sits on the edge of the bed. "But I guess we'd better get washed up and clean before Maggie brings her home."

"Shower?"

For a split second I'm worried he's going to ask me to shower in the nanny's quarters, but when he stands, he stares over his shoulder at me and smiles.

"Coming?"

I can't get out of bed faster.

As much as I want to play in the shower, Ryder's all business. Apparently, getting last night's dried cum off us is more important.

"How are you feeling this morning?" he asks as he passes me the soap.

"Sore."

He winces. "Me too, a little."

"Sorry," we say at the same time.

"Totally worth it, though," I point out.

"Definitely. My muscles are all achy."

"Isn't that a bad thing?"

"Not when every time I feel a twinge, I think of how I got it." Ryder wraps his arm around me and pulls me against him.

The water beats down on us, and when he leans in to kiss me, his lips are soft, warm, and wet.

He backs us up so I'm against the cool tiles, but he doesn't box me in. We're both hard, but this isn't about sex.

I break away and run my hands down his back to keep him close. "You know, I thought maybe you'd have second thoughts today."

"Oh, I'm having second, third, fourth, and fifth thoughts, but I know I want to keep doing this."

He kisses me again, and as much as I'd love to stay here doing this until the water runs cold, we have to be careful.

Kaylee and Maggie could come home at any minute, and I want to respect Ryder's wishes to keep this from his daughter.

It makes sense to keep it between us for now because, if I'm being honest, I'm preparing myself for Ryder to freak out or walk away at any moment.

I can't let myself get in over my head unless I want major heartache, and who the fuck wants that?

"We should get out," he says.

"Can I borrow some clothes again? Best thing about dating someone the same size …" *Shit.* "I mean, not dating." That's probably too much of a label for Ryder.

"It's okay. It's what we're doing, I guess." He turns the water off, conveniently needing to move away from me to do it.

"It was a slip of the tongue," I say.

He turns back to me. "I decided to come see you play, to sleep with you, to do everything we did last night, the least I can do is give you a label to define it. You told me what you want, and I don't want to fuck with that, okay? I'm sorry if I suck at all this. I'm not good at …" He struggles to label it again.

"You're not good at taking something for yourself every now and again?"

His bright blue eyes fill with guilt. "I don't want you to think that's all you are to me."

"I don't," I reassure him. "I know this is hard for you."

"Mm, that's not all that's hard." Ryder smirks.

"Still haven't had enough?"

"Nope."

"Too bad we need to get out of the shower, then." I leave him standing there wanting more. Isn't that the advice they give single people? Leave them wanting more. Or something? I don't know. Just like Ryder sucks at having something more, I suck at playing it cool.

We dry off and go back into his bedroom. I can still smell sex, though I don't know if it's the sheets or my memory recalling the smell.

I don't miss the way Ryder looks disappointed when I put my hair up into its usual messy bun, and I put that detail in my back pocket for later.

I have a list of things Ryder likes. So far it's being treated as a person and not a celebrity. And my long hair. I wish I could put my stunning personality on there too, but I'm not entirely sure how much he likes my smart-assery and how much he's humoring me.

Ryder throws me a pair of jeans and a plain Henley.

"What, no shirt with your face this time?"

"Sorry to disappoint you."

"I'm so, so disappointed," I say dryly.

"You will have to return that shirt one day. I know you love it, but it's the only one I have."

"Love, love, love it. I think it got mixed up in the wash at home. I'll find it. Chase probably stole it seeing as he's such a big fan of yours."

"At least someone in your family has taste."

Just as we reach downstairs and start picking up all the clothes we threw around the place in our rush last night, the front door opens, and Ryder and I pause in our steps.

"Lucky we cut that shower short." Ryder shoves his pile of clothes at me. "Go throw them upstairs."

"Maybe next time we should ask her for a specific time she's coming back."

"Sounds like a plan." Ryder's too distracted trying to get to his daughter to notice he just agreed to a next time.

One night without her and he already misses her.

I take the stairs while he flies into her arms and Maggie watches with a smile on her face.

In her civilian clothes, she's a lot less intimidating, but damn, they make a pretty family.

I kinda feel like I'd be intruding on that if I went down there, so I hang back at the top of the stairs.

Maggie spots me while Kaylee tells Ryder all about what she did with her mom last night. "You're here. On a Sunday."

Kaylee turns to see who Maggie's talking to, and her little face lights up.

I walk down the steps to meet them in the foyer. "Silly me. I thought it was Monday!"

Maggie laughs like she doesn't believe me.

Kaylee eyes me skeptically.

Ryder steps in. "Daddy is helping Lyric record some music. He's here to use the studio."

Kaylee looks like she believes him.

Maybe she's figured out I've been hiding vegetables in her food and now all trust between us is gone. Or maybe she's smart enough to know people generally don't mix up days.

"Can I watch?" Kaylee asks.

"I wouldn't mind watching," Maggie says.

Ryder's bluff is being called, and I've got nothing. I look at him, waiting for him to shut it down.

"Uh, sure."

Okay, that's not shutting it down.

"Umm, I don't know how I feel about an audience," I say.

"Didn't you perform at a bar last night?" Maggie asks.

"That's different," I argue.

"How?"

"I, uh, don't know."

Ryder smiles. "Lyric gets nervous around people who intimidate him. You should take it as a compliment."

Maggie seems happy about that.

"And now I'm going to do a magic trick and disappear. 'Kay?" I go to walk away, but Kaylee looks up at me with her big green eyes.

"Pwease, Lyric?"

Aww, fuck. No one can say no to that face. I think it's physically impossible.

"Fine. Let's do this."

Ryder kneels to Kaylee's level. "I have a super-brilliant idea. What if you and Lyric record together?"

Her gorgeous face lights up. "Really, Daddy? But I'm not allowed in there."

"I want to be able to hear you two sing 'Into the Unknown' whenever I want. And if you record it, I won't have to beg you guys to sing it for me." He turns to Maggie. "If that's okay with you."

"As long as it doesn't end up in a label's hands, I'm cool with it."

Ryder gives her a derisive look. "Never."

Kaylee jumps up and down and turns to me. "Can we, can we, can we?"

I smile. "I'd love to."

"I'm so not missing this," Maggie says while eyeing me in challenge.

It's like I can read her mind, and she's saying, "Show me what you've got."

And now I'm back to being intimidated again.

CHAPTER 21
RYDER

LYRIC PULLS me aside on our way into the studio. "I know I usually like the lights up when I record, but can you kill the light in the sound booth? Thanks."

I can't help the chuckle that falls from my mouth. "Are you really that intimidated by Maggie? I don't get it."

Lyric bites his lip.

"Is it the military thing, or—"

"No. She's your daughter's mother, and if she hates me, there's no way you and I ever have a chance."

"You *want* her to like you. Oh, that is so fucking adorable."

"Shut up," he mutters.

"Get in the booth." I shove him.

We get a stool for Kaylee to stand on so she can reach the microphone, but she's glancing around the room with a panicked look in her eye.

"You okay, bub?" I ask.

She nods, but I know she's not okay.

"Want Lyric to show you how it's done first? You can stand here next to him and watch."

She nods again.

I smile at Lyric. "She might have your nerves. Gonna show her how to overcome it?"

Lyric feigns confidence I can tell he doesn't actually feel. "For sure." He holds up his hand for her to fist-bump. "We got this."

The way she listens to Lyric and trusts him is amazing, and the way he pushes through his own issues to reassure her warms my gut. I have to pull myself away before I lean in and kiss him after the big deal I made about keeping this from Kaylee for now.

Maggie's smiling when I take the seat next to her, but I ignore her. She stares at me as if awaiting an explanation while I get everything set up.

I dim the lights and hit the intercom. "Ready to give me something a cappella to play with before doing it properly?"

Lyric throws me a thumbs-up even though he can no longer see us.

"Rolling."

Lyric starts at the soft verse but is animated and makes sure to keep glancing at Kaylee.

As it builds toward the chorus, he slows and tries to encourage Kaylee to take over, but she shakes her head.

When he belts out the chorus, hitting every note flawlessly, Kaylee watches him in awe, and out of the corner of my eye, I notice Maggie's attention is no longer on me.

He stops after the chorus. "How was that?"

"Wow," Maggie breathes.

"Told you. And you ain't seen nothing yet. That was him goofing around." I hit the intercom. "It was great. We'll be good to go in five."

"You think you're ready to give it a try?" Lyric asks Kaylee, and she nods. "We're not even recording right now, so it's just practice. Pretend we're in your playroom watching *Frozen* and singing along."

"Okay." She takes a deep breath and begins to sing.

Her voice is soft and angelic. The day I found out she had a natural voice, the kind that I knew could be exploited for fame, was probably the most proud and dreaded day I've ever had as a parent.

She sings the first verse with Lyric harmonizing, and together, they're … There are no words to describe it.

When they hit the chorus, goose bumps break out over my skin.

Maggie hears it too. "What if she wants to grow up to be famous?"

"Then we're fucking screwed. It's not like I can tell her no. That'd be hypocritical."

"Haven't you learned yet? Ninety percent of parenting is being hypocritical."

"Truth. I don't want her to do the Hollywood thing."

"But if she chooses it, I don't think we get a say."

"We can at least protect her until she's eighteen."

"Or try to. Oh God, she's going to be a teenager in eight years. What the hell are we supposed to do then?"

I shrug. "Pray."

We both laugh.

"But speaking of which, are you going to be back in time for her birthday?"

"My official end date is three days before it, so as long as everything goes to plan, I'll be here. I've missed too many birthdays already."

I reach over to grip her hand. "You're here now. That's all that matters to her."

She smiles. "If I don't say it enough, thank you for being cool about me coming and going from her life the last few years."

I squeeze her hand. "I know it's something you felt you needed to do."

Maggie's eyes fill. She averts her gaze to watch our daughter, and I pretend not to see her emotion.

If Maggie wanted to talk about it, she would. That's who she is. She says what she's feeling and keeps to herself when she doesn't want to talk. So I won't push.

Lyric and Kaylee make it through their practice go, and Lyric praises her for doing a good job.

"He's *so* good with her," Maggie says.

"I know."

And that's why it's so hard to think about a future. Both Kaylee and I would have to be okay with him being on the road for most of the year because there's no doubt in my mind he's going to make it big.

Relationships are hard enough without the added pressure of fame, and I won't make Lyric choose.

He was born to be in the spotlight.

I know this is a future problem for us to deal with because Lyric doesn't even have a manager let alone a record deal, but I know it's only a matter of time. With his talent, the only way he won't get picked up is if his pretentious and stubborn side holds him back.

If all we have is the here and now, I'm going to take it. I just hope when it all comes to an end, I'm the one who's heartbroken, not my daughter.

As I watch them in the booth together, I fear that ship may have already sailed.

Kaylee's already in love with him.

Maybe instead of fighting what we have, I should embrace it fully. I would never make him choose, but I will fight to give him a reason to take us into consideration when he does get that deal.

I hit the speaker button. "Ready to lay it down for real?"

It's funny how a simple thought can make me see how insignificant everything I've been scared of really is.

Don't get in too deep.

Don't let Kaylee love him.

Since I realized during their recording session that it was way too late for that, I've been seeing everything in a different light.

When Lyric builds Kaylee up, I see someone I could co-parent with, when he and Maggie make lunch together, I can see a blended family, and when he looks at me and smiles in a way that's our own private little joke, I see someone I want to spend my nights with.

I want to wake up next to him—hell, I want to cuddle him to sleep.

"Oh God," I mutter, though I don't mean for anyone to hear.

"What's wrong?" Kaylee asks.

"Nothing, bub." I'm realizing I want my first ever grown-up relationship. Nothing to see here.

I'm falling, and I'm falling hard.

"Come on, Kaylee. Let's wash up for lunch," Lyric says and leads her toward the bathroom. "Maybe without giving your toys a bath for a change."

Maggie sidles up next to me. "Our daughter's not dumb, you know."

"Huh?"

"If she sees you looking at Lyric like that, she's gonna know y'all are together."

"No, she won't. She's observant but not *that* observant."

"Have you been paying attention? She picks up on *everything*."

I hope Maggie's wrong. It's way too early to tell Kaylee about us. Hell, up until an hour ago, I wasn't even sure if I could see a future with Lyric.

Just because I acknowledge I want that future doesn't mean it'll magically work out.

All through lunch, I try to avoid eye contact with Lyric. Kaylee can't pick up on something that's not there.

"Hey, kiddo, how about we go to the playground when you're done with lunch," Maggie says.

Kaylee shoves the last of her sandwich in her mouth at once. "I'm full."

Maggie turns to us. "I'll have her back in an hour? That good?"

"That's fine," I mumble. "But just so you know, when you move back, you're gonna have to find a job. You know, give you something to do to fill your time."

She laughs, but Lyric looks at me weird.

As soon as they're out the front door, I shake my head.

"We should get these dishes in the dishwasher." I stand and carry them over to the kitchen counter, but Lyric's right behind me.

"What was that about?"

I turn to him. "Apparently, we're not being subtle. Maggie knows about us."

"Oh." Lyric looks worried.

I reach for him and pull him against me. "You have no reason to be scared. Maggie already approves."

"Uh-huh." He still looks freaked-out.

"We have an hour to ourselves ..."

That snaps him out of whatever's going on in his head and brings a wicked smile to his lips. "What about the dishes?"

"Fuck the dishes."

"Hmm, I'd rather not, but I mean, I guess if you're into that …"

I shove him. "Not what I meant."

"Mmhmm. Sure."

I grip his—er, my—shirt and pull him close, but I don't seal my mouth over his yet. I let us linger an inch apart.

"Tease," he mumbles.

I lick my lips.

He closes the gap, and I breathe him in. His mouth is warm and intoxicating. I don't know how I'm going to keep my distance in front of Kaylee. Especially with Maggie leaving again soon to finalize her military crap.

"I'll never get enough of kissing you," I say against his lips.

"I'm totally okay with that."

He pulls me off the counter, and we wander through the house, too engrossed in each other to watch for furniture.

I hit the doorframe and break away from kissing him even though I don't want to. "We're going to get bruises if we keep this up."

"Maybe if you didn't have such a big house, we'd be close to a bedroom."

"Screw it." I turn and push Lyric against the wall. "Here's good enough for what I want to do."

"What do you want to do?" Lyric's hazel eyes hold amusement in them.

"The first day we ever met, you basically said I suck. I still haven't proven to you how accurate that statement is."

Lyric groans as I drop to my knees, and his hand immediately goes into my hair.

I work open the jeans he's wearing and stare up at him. I like him in my clothes more than I should. It's like he's wearing a little piece of me. Like he belongs to me as much as the clothing does.

It makes that possessive instinct kick in and fills my chest with pride.

I love even more that I didn't throw him underwear and he's going commando.

His hard cock springs free, and I bite my cheek to stop from moaning.

I can't resist a little taste and run my tongue along the hard, velvety length.

"I've wanted to do this for so long," I murmur.

Lyric shudders above me, his hips thrusting forward. His cock runs along my cheek, and I feel the wetness of precum on my skin.

I want to ask him how he feels about his boss being on his knees for him, but I don't want to complicate things between us any more than they already are.

Now that I'm in this, Lyric and I need to be equals in everything. Though, there isn't really anything equal about the vulnerable position I'm in right now, and I'm loving it.

"I want to watch you touch yourself while you suck me off." Lyric's commanding voice is gruff, and my cock is definitely on board. It fights the confines of my pants, eager to give Lyric anything he asks for.

While I undo my jeans, I tease his head by running my tongue under the ridge of his tip.

His cock twitches, and I need my hand to steady it.

As soon as I have my aching dick free, I wrap my fingers around my hard shaft and use my other hand to guide his cock to my waiting lips.

"Holy fuck, Ryder. You've never looked hotter."

I want to dispute that to be a smart-ass, but honestly, I'm enjoying this too much.

Lyric leans back against the wall, thrusting his cock farther into my mouth.

My eyes water the tiniest bit, but I can take it.

What I can't take is the blissed-out expression on Lyric's face as I stare up at him.

His eyes are locked on mine, hooded and intense as he watches his cock continually disappear between my lips.

My hand works frantically at my own neediness. I want to come the second Lyric spills into my mouth.

As he tests out how far he can push me, he gains some confidence.

And when I manage to get him all the way in, I swallow hard and my throat constricts around his cock.

He lets out a curse as if taken off guard and trembles above me. His cum slides down the back of my throat, and I moan around his dick as it empties.

The hand in my hair tightens to the point of pain, and that's all it takes for me to fill my hand.

I'm trying to milk everything he has with my mouth while riding out my orgasm, but something gives, and I have to pull away from him so I can breathe.

Spit and cum drip down my chin, but I don't even care.

I sit back on my heels and wipe my face while Lyric stands there breathing hard but not moving.

When I glance up at him, I can't help smiling at his shocked expression.

"Did I suck you brainless? You're looking a little dopey."

"That was …" His words sound as dazed as he looks.

I get to my feet. "Need some water or something?"

"Or something," he mutters and pulls me close.

Our pants are around our ankles, my hands are covered in cum—same with my face, probably—but he still presses his lips to mine and kisses me as if my mouth was as fresh as having just brushed my teeth.

His tongue laps at mine, no doubt tasting himself on me.

I have no idea how long has passed, which is the only reason I pull away. "We should get cleaned up before the girls get back."

He nods blankly, and I laugh again.

"Noted."

Lyric finally snaps out of his orgasm trance. "What?"

"All I have to do to make you speechless and compliant is suck you off. It's handy to know."

A big smile breaks across his face. "I have tricks too, you know."

"Oh, do you?"

"Yup." Lyric reaches for his hair tie and lets down his long golden hair. After he shakes his soft curls free, he stares at me with a cocked eyebrow.

"Touché."

CHAPTER 22
LYRIC

ALL THOSE LITTLE ESCAPES, those brief moments of alone time with Ryder, they disappear when Maggie reports back to … wherever she needed to report back to before getting discharged.

Ryder's been busy in the studio with a new act he's producing, and I've been busy with playgroup and the usual nanny activities.

I've wanted to drop hints about staying the night and setting an alarm so I can sneak out of his bed before Kaylee wakes up, but with her sleep schedule as unpredictable as her bladder, I know Ryder won't want to risk it.

And I don't trust myself to stay in the nanny's quarters without venturing upstairs in the middle of the night because I miss him.

I long for him.

Ryder's basically given me his Pontiac for the time being while he's working late, and in the brief time after Kaylee goes to bed and his musicians leave, we catch up on the day's events and share good-night kisses.

I want to push for more, but this needs to be done on Ryder's time.

Kaylee will find out when he feels comfortable enough to tell her.

Today is a Chase day, and I have to admit they're my favorite days. He and Kaylee get along so well, and it makes my job ten times easier.

I think Chase might be infatuated with Kaylee. Or maybe it's the other way around.

Either way, it's adorable, and as I send them off to play whatever game they want to play, I leave them in the playroom and flop onto the large sectional couch in the formal living room adjacent. It's the first break I've had since arriving this morning. I throw my head back on the couch and will myself not to fall asleep.

Between staying late here and my gigs on the weekend, I'm a little wiped.

And that, of course, is when Ryder strolls in from the main part of the house. "Hard at work, I see."

I spin to glare at him but relax when I see him smiling. "Your daughter has been …" *Never tell a parent their child is anything less than perfect.* "Uh, let's just say, today she showed great leadership skills and will no doubt grow up to be a boss of some kind. Maybe CEO of a big corporation."

Ryder lets out a small laugh. "She was being a spoiled brat, then?"

"No matter how many times I told her to use her manners, I think they fell out of her head today."

"Do you need me to talk to her?"

"No. It's usual kid stuff. It's just been exhausting."

Ryder takes the spot next to me. "Those days suck." His arm wraps around my shoulders, and then he leans in to kiss my cheek.

I eye the sliding doors I left open so I could still hear the kids if there was an issue.

"Maggie needs to hurry up and come back," Ryder murmurs. His lips touch my neck.

I stay seated where I am, my hands on top of my legs, and try not to cross any lines. "You're either being brave right now or don't care your daughter's in the next room." I keep my voice low.

Ryder groans. "I miss you."

"You see me every day."

"For like a second. It's not enough."

I swallow hard. "I agree."

"Stay tonight?" he whispers. "We can work something out."

"I have Chase today and tomorrow, and then I've got my gig tomorrow and Saturday night."

Ryder blinks. "Shit. It's Thursday already?"

"You've been working hard."

He slumps. "I have. This new kid. He has an attitude on him already. Doesn't like the way he's been paired with a producer who used to be in a boy band."

I fuse my lips together, trying not to smile. "Sounds … familiar."

Ryder shuffles so he can face me. "Oh, no. This is different. When you do it, I find it cute. On this kid, it's infuriating. You're at least respectful. This kid thinks I know nothing about real music."

"And yet he has a record deal with that attitude, and I'm still—"

Kaylee squeals.

I wince. "In charge of dealing with that."

I stand.

"This guy has a record deal because he probably played the game and told them he couldn't wait to work with me and kissed their asses. That's not your style."

"Not at all." I turn to leave, but Ryder stands.

"Tomorrow night, after your gig, I'll pay for an Uber or whatever to get you out here, and we can spend Saturday together."

"Together, together? With Kaylee?"

"We could go to Disneyland or something. Just the three of us."

I try to cover my smile. This is huge.

Kaylee screams again, louder this time.

"You should get that. And I should get back to work."

"You just left the guy in the studio?"

"Yep. He needed a time-out."

"By the sound of it, either Chase or Kaylee do too," I say.

Ryder kisses my cheek. "I'll try to finish up early tonight so you can get Chase home at a decent time."

"Thanks, or Brenna and Chord might hurt me. Or you."

When I go back into the playroom, it turns out Kaylee's screaming with glee because she and Chase are throwing her toys at the fan, whipping them around the room.

I sigh.

Sneaking into Ryder's house in the middle of the night feels weird, but there was no way I was going to pass up the opportunity to fall asleep next to him. And maybe grope him a little.

Or a lot.

He sent me a text earlier telling me to let myself in because he was going to nap and to wake him when I got here.

But when I reach his room, he doesn't even stir as I move about his space.

I strip down to my boxer briefs and slide into bed beside him.

He smells like shampoo and cologne, and his hair is sticking up at all angles like he went to bed with it wet.

As tempting as it is to wake him and kiss him and take his body, I'm not that mean. Or desperate.

I mean, I'm pretty desperate for him, but if he's as exhausted as I have been lately, it really would be cruel to wake him.

And when I curl up behind him and pull him against me, all he does is let out a sweet moan before his breathing evens back out.

I kiss the back of his head and crash hard.

It feels like I only blink when the sun cracks through Ryder's window.

I reach for him, but the bed beside me is cold and empty. I didn't even wake when he slipped out of bed, much like he didn't notice when I got in it.

This is what a relationship with him will be like. It's what any relationship with kids is like, I'm assuming.

Between each other's jobs, me gigging at night, and Kaylee waking early, there are going to be a lot of missed opportunities and mornings apart.

I think I'd be okay with that, but if I'm signed to a label it'll be ten times worse.

I can't help wondering what it would be like to have him with me through all that when it happens.

If it happens.

It's obvious he misses the business. He misses singing. He misses being in the spotlight.

I wish I could give him everything or make him see he deserves to have it all, but he's as stubborn as I am when he gets something in his head.

His number one priority is protecting Kaylee.

I just think he can have his career and protect her at the same time. It might take some compromise and help from Maggie, but it's not as impossible as he thinks it is.

I slowly rise and reach for my jeans on the floor to fish out my phone.

Almost dead. Of course.

Because instead of getting my charger from the overnight bag I brought last night, I jumped straight into bed.

There's a message from Ryder to come downstairs whenever I want. He has Kaylee in her playroom, so she won't know I haven't come from the front door.

I move about Ryder's room and plug in my charger and phone and then change into the clothes I packed for today.

The shirt with Ryder's face mocks me from the bag, and as tempting as it is to wear it to Disneyland to taunt him all day, it'll only draw attention, and the last thing we need is for him to be recognized while we're there.

When I reach the playroom, they're at the small table eating breakfast.

"Who's ready for—" I start, but Ryder makes a slashing movement at his throat.

"For?" Kaylee asks, her big green eyes looking up at me.

"For breakfast!"

She frowns. "I'm already eating it."

"Oh. Well, where's mine?"

Ryder laughs. "Would you like what she's having?"

I look at the bowl of mush in front of her. "Not really."

"See, Daddy. Even Lyric won't eat it. Yucky."

Ugh. Mush it is. "Of course I'll eat it. If you eat the healthy stuff, you get a treat. That's, like, the law of the world."

"What kind of treat?"

"A hug?"

She screws up her face.

"Hmm, candy?"

Her face smooths. "I'm listening …"

"Tell you what. If you finish that whole bowl before I finish mine, you get to pick which candy I'll buy you later."

She starts shoveling the food into her mouth while Ryder gives me an appreciative smile.

After our disgustingly healthy plain bowls of oatmeal, I silently beg him to put his daughter out of her misery.

"Hey, bub? You know what I was thinking we could do today?"

"You working? Is that why Lyric's here?"

"Nope. I thought he might like to come with us when we go to …"

The suspense is even killing me, and I know where we're going.

"Disneyland!"

Her adorable little face lights up, and she does that excited squeal thing again I wish would die a horrible, horrible death.

But she's still cute, and it takes me less than ten minutes to get her ready to go even with all the squirming she does while we try to put her shoes on.

Ryder fills a backpack full of water and snacks, and on our way out, he dons his famous-guy disguise.

I don't know how many people are fooled by a hat and sunglasses, but it's not like they can do much else, I guess.

"Don't celebrities get, like, special entrance and things at Disneyland?" I ask.

"Ugh, we can do that if you want, but they have a staff member follow you around, and it just draws more attention to you. The only good thing about it is we get to skip lines, but I don't know if it's worth it. I want this to be as normal an experience as possible for her."

Kaylee is an excited ball of energy during the long-ass drive, and I don't think she's taken a breath the whole time.

It doesn't stop while we park or walk a million miles to the gates either.

"She's going to exhaust herself before we even get in," Ryder says only loud enough so I can hear.

"It's cute you think that. Really. True fact about kids: they drain their parents of all their energy much like the witches in *Hocus Pocus.* It's why they never stop and why you're so exhausted you don't even wake up to someone climbing into bed with you."

"That so wasn't the plan."

I smile. "I know. It wasn't my plan to sleep through you getting up this morning either."

I want to reach for his hand or do any sort of normal coupley crap with him but know I can't.

"I'll make it up to you," he promises.

I step closer and press against him but not in an overly obvious way. "Can't wait."

Once we're through security and the gates of California Adventure, I turn to Kaylee.

"Where to first?"

Little Miss Precocious looks at me with disappointment. "Mickey ears, Lyric."

"Duh, *Lyric,*" Ryder taunts.

"Oh, silly me. How could I not have known that?"

Okay, so I've only been to Disney once as a kid. We never had the money, and as an adult, it never appealed to me all that much.

Seeing it all from my grown-up perspective, this place is insane.

Who the hell knew how much Mickey merch there was?

We go through a few stalls before Kaylee drags us to a bigger store. There's a whole section of Pride ears, and I am so here for it.

Kaylee picks the black Minnie ears with a rainbow bow.

"Good choice," I tell her.

"What are you going to get?"

"Hmm ..." I tap my chin. "I don't know. What do you think I should get?"

"This!" She takes a red hat with rainbow ears off the stand.

"Ooh, I like it. But I think this would look better on Daddy." I'm probably lucky Ryder's wearing dark glasses and I can't see what I presume is a glare.

Ryder doesn't hesitate. He ditches his current hat and dons the red Mickey one.

I turn back to the wall of possibilities. "I think I want one with a bow."

"They're Minnie's ears," Kaylee says.

"So?"

"So they're for gi—"

Ryder glares at his daughter. "Finish that sentence, bub. I dare you."

She turns to Ryder. "You mean boys can wear Minnie ears?"

"Anyone can wear whatever the hell they want." I put on a fully sequined rainbow pair of ears with a bow.

"You look very pretty." Kaylee's serious voice makes me smile, and I pat her head.

"So do you."

The cashier doesn't even blink at my chosen ears, but she does do a double take when she hands Ryder's credit card back.

We're quick to move on and hope the look she got of him was too quick to make a definite identification.

"What ride are we hitting up first?" Ryder asks.

"Ariel ride! Ariel ride!"

"And she's off," I say.

Her little legs work overtime toward the Ariel ride.

"Just so you know," Ryder says, "we're gonna spend most of today on this damn ride."

I start singing "Part of Your World" from *The Little Mermaid.*

Ryder shakes his head at me, but he's so fighting a smile.

Even though I fight it all day, I can't help the overwhelming feeling of family I get when I'm with Ryder and Kaylee.

It makes me see a future with both of them in ways I've never pictured with anyone before.

And despite Ryder being recognized a handful of times, everyone is surprisingly respectful.

He does his trick of being nice and voluntarily taking selfies so they're less inclined to post candids on social media of the three of us hanging out.

When I ask him if he's worried they'll post photos of me and people will speculate who I am, he waves me off.

"You are her nanny. They can't dispute that."

And I realize that in any sort of relationship with Ryder, I will always be Kaylee's nanny to everyone else. Nothing more.

It's not something I'm entirely comfortable with even though I understand it. It's hiding a part of me I promised myself I wouldn't when trying to make it big in Hollywood.

Ryder does everything to protect his daughter, sometimes too much, but Ryder coming out would put Kaylee in the spotlight. Not only her, but questions about her paternity, about Maggie, and about the whole dynamic they've managed to keep close to the vest. There's no denying that.

And when Kaylee starts to lag by midafternoon and she asks me to carry her on my back, not her dad, my own overwhelming sense of protectiveness for this little girl makes me realize I would willingly do anything for her too.

Even step back into a closet.

Ryder checks the rearview mirror and smiles. "She's out cold."

I turn, and my heart melts a little. She's still got her Minnie ears on. Her face has been painted with blue and white snowflakes—Elsa inspired, of course—and she looks so tiny and small in her big booster seat. "She's adorable. Today was a good day."

He reaches over and squeezes my thigh. "It was a great day. Thank you for coming with us."

"Thanks for letting me hang out with you guys. I know why you don't want to tell her about us yet, but I appreciate you still including me."

"Do you think …" Ryder purses his lips.

My heart thuds a little harder. "Do I think what?"

"Never mind. I was going to ask if you wanted to come back to my place after your gig again tonight, but Calabasas is out of the way, and I'll probably be asleep again."

"I can do one better."

I take out my phone and shoot off a text, knowing the answer will be yes.

"What'd you just do?"

"I gave my set time away to Alex, the bartender guy. He'd jump at the chance to take a weekend slot."

"You gave up your gig for me?"

"Honestly, after today, having dinner and chilling with you in front of the TV sounds a hell of a lot better than singing in a rowdy bar. Who knew Disneyland was so exhausting? And we didn't even stay for the fireworks."

Ryder laughs. "You loved it. I swear you were more excited than Kaylee when you saw *the real Mickey Mouse*!"

I take off my Minnie ears and mutter a half-hearted "Shut up."

"It was adorable and cute."

"Wrong. It was charismatic and manly."

"Especially with the sequined ears."

I grin. "Exactly."

My phone pings, and it's a message from Alex.

"All set. I can stay."

Ryder's gaze turns heated, and I swear he puts his foot on the accelerator a tiny bit heavier. "If we can transfer Kaylee to bed when we get home without her waking up, I'll be able to make it up to you for being asleep last night."

"Challenge accepted."

It's a team effort, but we manage to get a very tired little girl into bed, only waking her enough to go to the bathroom before she falls asleep again as soon as her head hits the pillow.

"Silent high five," I whisper, and we lift our hands without actually touching.

On the way out of her room, Ryder intertwines his fingers with mine and shoots me a smile.

He takes me into the fancy part of the house he hardly uses and tells me to take a seat on a stool at the fancy marble kitchen counter. "Wine?"

"Ooh, this is, like, a real date."

"Yep. I'm going to ply you with alcohol so my cooking tastes edible."

Ryder pours each of us a glass of red wine and then goes to get ingredients from the other kitchen.

I sip the expensive wine while sitting in a mansion and watching the guy I'm sleeping with move around the kitchen like he's a chef and wasn't one-fifth of the most famous boy band ever. It's surreal.

"When did you learn how to cook? I figured you'd have people to do that kind of thing for you."

He smiles. "My momma taught me before I moved to LA to make it big."

"Your mom. In Texas."

His smile dims a little. "Yep."

"Do you ever see your parents?"

"Not since Maggie and I caused big neighborhood drama by deciding to have a child out of wedlock because, in Maggie's words, she's not in love with me, and my words, I'm gay as fuck."

Red wine shoots out of my nose.

Ryder laughs and passes me a napkin. "Turns out I have no trouble with labels when used to make a statement."

"I bet that was the statement to end all statements."

"Yeah. That was basically the end of *everything* with us."

"I'm sorry."

"I'm not. I don't want their toxic views anywhere near Kaylee."

I spin the wineglass stem between my fingers. "Has Kaylee ever met them?"

"Once. When she was a baby." Ryder doesn't stop prepping our dinner as he keeps talking. "As a favor to Maggie. She told me if I was going to do this parenting thing on my own, I'd need a good support system. We didn't even make it through a meal."

"So you did it all on your own?"

He scoffs. "Not really. I had a support system. They just happened to be on my payroll."

"You did the last two years on your own."

"Yep, and look how long I lasted before I needed help."

"Ryder ..." I slip off my stool and walk around the island.

He's chopping vegetables, so I press myself against his back. He puts the knife down and leans into me.

"Even the best parents need help every now and then. Kids are hard. And Kaylee—"

"I know, I know. I spoil her, and she's entitled, and—"

"Not what I was going to say at all. She's smart and precocious and amazing. She's artistic and talented, and she might look like her mother, but her creative side is all you. You, of all people, know how difficult it is to keep creative people focused. She's a handful, but she's perfect."

Ryder's hand reaches up and cups the back of my neck. "How do you do that?"

"Do what?"

"Reassure me that I'm not fucking up her entire life."

My lips ghost along his neck. "Far from it."

He rolls his hips, rubbing his ass against my hardening cock, and moans. "Do you always do this to your dates?"

"What's that?"

"Distract them with your body before you've eaten dinner?"

I laugh, my hot breath landing on his skin, and he shudders.

I step back. "Sorry. I'll let you get back to it."

Ryder picks up the knife and points it at me. "After dinner, your body is mine."

I go back to my seat and take a sip of my wine. "All yours."

In more ways than one.

Now's not the time to freak him out with that, though. I have to give him at least a month to get used to the idea of having something serious with me.

CHAPTER 23
RYDER

IT TAKES weeks of waking up next to Lyric as many times as possible, wrapped around him and practically smothering him, to realize I really am a cuddler.

I can't get enough of him, and when he's gone, his side of the bed is too cold and empty.

Right now, his golden hair is splayed over his pillow, and he's smiling even while he's sleeping.

He's been staying over more often than going to his own place, and I think half my wardrobe is now sitting on the floor of his brother's pool house.

He's terrible at returning the clothes he borrows, but I couldn't care less.

That'll probably change when I run out of clothes, but for now, I have him in my bed at least three nights a week, sometimes four.

It's a miracle we haven't been caught by my very inquisitive daughter, but with Maggie coming home permanently, Kaylee's no longer having nightmares, and I think she's finally—*finally*—moving out of the bed-wetting stage as it's becoming a rare occurrence.

I have no idea what time it is, but I know we won't have time to fool around before Kaylee wakes up, so I slip out of bed to let Lyric sleep a bit more.

Today's going to be a hectic day because I'm now officially the father of a five-year-old.

When the fuck did that happen?

I swear it was yesterday she was crawling around backstage and sucking on microphone cables.

Parent of the year, right here.

I wander through the house slowly, trying to wake up for the day. Kaylee's bedroom is quiet as I walk by, so I assume she must be sleeping.

Only, when I get downstairs and go into the playroom, I realize I was wrong because Kaylee is sitting in the middle of the floor watching cartoons on TV.

"How long have you been awake?"

"Since it was dark out!" She's way too excited about that.

Great. We're going to be filling up a tired five-year-old with sugar all day. That's not a recipe for disaster or anything.

"Excited about your birthday?"

Her face splits with a big smile. "It's my first birthday with friends. And Mommy!"

Ugh, how she's gone five years without any kid friends is a little sad. *Hello guilt, we meet again.*

Over the last five years, Maggie has always managed to see Kaylee *around* her birthday, but she's never been here for the actual day. It's not like she had a choice in that, though. Even her discharge is taking longer than expected, but I know her flight arrives early this morning, and she'll be here before we leave for Kaylee's party.

"I guess I should start making some food to take to the playground today."

Lyric and I got a lot of it done last night, but we have to do last-minute things.

"Yes, you should."

I know I shouldn't laugh at her tone, but I can't stop it. "Okay, Miss Bossy Pants. Why don't you go pick out what you're going to wear?"

"I already know." She gets up and runs over to her dress-up box, and I know she's going to pull out an Elsa dress.

I get most of the stuff done for the party before Lyric even wakes. When he does make his way downstairs, he's in another shirt and jeans of mine, and I have to remind myself I'm determined to keep our relationship from Kaylee. I'm sure there's a good reason for her not to find out, but I really can't remember when all I want to do is kiss him good morning.

As if sensing my thoughts, he approaches, glances over my head at Kaylee, and then plants a kiss on my cheek.

"She isn't watching," he whispers.

It's as quick as that. He steps back and looks around at everything I've already accomplished.

"You should've woken me. I could've helped."

"You deserved to sleep in after last night."

He waggles his eyebrows.

"Because we were up late getting the rest ready, not because of what you did when we were done. Although, that was a good effort too."

"Just good? I need to up my game."

"It was amazing, phenomenal—"

"I'm ready!"

We turn to Kaylee, and I have to bite back another laugh.

Lyric is quick to whip out his phone and take a photo.

She has on her Elsa dress, as suspected, but I wasn't expecting the army helmet and Nerf guns.

"You look super cute, bub, but, uh, are the guns and helmet really necessary?"

"Yes," she says simply.

"Of course they are," Lyric says. "What's a birthday party *without* war games?"

The buzzer for the gate sounds.

Lyric heads for the front of the house. "That'll be Brenna with Chase."

I hit the button on the wall to let them in.

As he reaches the sliding doors leading to the less messy part of the house, Lyric looks at me over his shoulder. "Did you want to … I mean, you haven't met her yet …"

I should meet her. If not as the guy seeing her brother-in-law, then at least as his boss.

"Too much?" he asks.

I realize I haven't moved. "No. It's, uh, yeah, let's do that."

"I'm not leading you to the firing squad," Lyric says. "You might want to try smiling."

"I am smiling. I'm thinking of three different ways to murder you for being a condescending jerk."

"What's a con-sed-ending jerk?" Kaylee asks.

I turn to Kaylee. "Sweetie, if someone tells you that you should smile, what do you say?"

"*Give me a reason to.*"

I turn back to Lyric. "See, I've taught her valuable feminist lessons and shit."

"Swear jar," Kaylee sings.

"And then she betrays me like that," I mutter.

The three of us go out to meet Chase and Brenna, but when the car pulls around, three people get out.

"Chase!" Kaylee calls, and they both run into the house.

I'm still too busy looking at the man in a pristine blue suit with meticulously styled dirty-blond hair and a smile I'd recognize anywhere. He makes my stomach flip, but only because he's familiar.

"Holy shi—vers, you and your brother could be twins," I say to Lyric. "You know, if you cut your hair."

"And aged seven years. Do I really look as old as him?"

"Heard that, little brother," Chord says. He extends his hand to me. "Chord Jones. Nice to finally meet you."

Brenna steps forward. "Yes, I've been dying to meet the boy bander who's been keeping our Lyric busy with all those overnighters."

My hand freezes in Chord's grip, and I try to wipe any guilt from my face. I don't know if Lyric's told them about us. I guess I assumed he didn't even though I technically only asked him to keep it from Kaylee. Well, and the general public, but I wouldn't classify his brother and sister-in-law that way.

"Subtle, Brenna," Lyric says. "Really subtle. Thank you for dropping Chase off. You've done your duty. You can go have date day now."

"Aww, we thought we'd stay for the party." Chord smiles. "Get to know the girl Chase tells us he's going to marry one day. Family is important."

Brenna snickers.

"Oh, dear God. They're doing this to torture me," Lyric mutters.

"Hey, then I'm all for it." I smile. "By all means. Please come in. We're just waiting for Kaylee's mom to arrive, and then we can leave for the playground."

They both look confused, and I'm guessing Lyric hasn't told them anything about Maggie, which I respect. I'm sure Maggie appreciates it too.

Lyric and I lead the way, and as we keep walking, I lean in and lower my voice.

"Do they know?"

"No. They know how much I'm crushing on you and are giving me shit."

"Good to know."

"I wouldn't tell anyone without letting you know."

"It's okay if you do tell them. I just wanted to know what I'm working with."

Lyric lets out a breath of relief, and it's only now that he's relaxed I realize how tense he was about it.

The gate buzzes again as we reach the foyer.

"That'll be Maggie." I duck back outside to greet her, and when we head inside, we find everyone in the playroom.

Lyric's given Chord and Brenna some drinks, and they're chatting while Kaylee and Chase dig through her dress-up chest.

"You can borrow my clothes," Kaylee says. "Lyric wears Daddy's clothes all the time. They're going to get married like us!"

I've never once experienced the expression *so silent you could hear a pin drop*, but right now, everyone in the damn room can probably hear my heart hammering. It's on a mission to break free from my rib cage.

Chord's and Brenna's gazes go to Lyric, sizing up him and his clothes, which are my clothes.

Maggie tries to hold back her laughter.

Lyric looks as dumbfounded as I feel.

"Did she just say ..." I start.

"Getting married, huh?" Maggie asks. "Congrats?"

"Smart-ass," I mumble.

Lyric walks over to where Kaylee and Chase stand by the dress-up box, looking nervous like they think they've done something wrong. They may not understand what's happening, but with this much tension in the room, I'd be scared too.

Hell, I *am* scared. I'm scared about what she's going to say next in front of all these people.

Lyric lowers himself to their level. "Kaylee, honey, why do you think your daddy and I are going to get married?"

She glances around the room as if her answer might get her in trouble. "Because … because …" She looks at me.

"It's okay, bub."

"Because you kiss and sleep in the same bed, and you always wear his clothes."

Yeah, that whole thing where I thought my daughter was oblivious? Turns out we were the ones who were so blinded by each other we didn't know she was watching and listening to every. Damn. Thing.

"And that's what married people do?" Lyric asks.

"Chase says that's what his parents do."

A whispered voice comes from across the room. "I kind of feel like we should leave, but I really want to watch." It's Brenna.

I can't help it. I snort so loud I think I startle myself.

Everyone looks at me, but I can't explain it.

Everything in this moment feels so ridiculous.

"I spent seven years hiding who I was from the public, pretending … so many things that aren't me. I've taught Kaylee anyone can love anyone regardless of identity or gender, but I never actually told her the truth." I laugh hard. "And then she outs me like she's known the whole fucking time."

"Swear jar," Lyric says with a smile.

I laugh more. Maggie and Lyric's family join in half-heartedly as if they feel they need to humor the crazy man who's realizing I've gone to stupid lengths to keep something from my daughter when there has absolutely been no reason to.

Both Chase and Kaylee look confused at my outburst, but as I go over to them and sink to my knees beside Lyric, I hold out my arms for my daughter, and she doesn't hesitate to step into my embrace.

"Marriage might be a long time away," I say into her hair as she hugs me.

Next to me, Lyric's eyes widen. "Long, long, long, long, long, long, long time away."

"Good to know where you're at." I pull back so I can look Kaylee in the eyes. "But would you be okay with Lyric being here more?"

She nods vehemently.

"You're all right with Daddy having a boyfriend?"

Lyric sucks in a sharp breath, and yeah, maybe I should've had this discussion with him first instead of my daughter.

Though, when he smiles and reaches for my hand that's not wrapped around Kaylee, I figure it'll be a short conversation.

"You always tell me boys can like other boys," Kaylee says. "And boys can wear dresses! Chase wants to wear one of my other Elsa dresses to my party."

Lyric and I turn our heads toward Chord and Brenna, who appear to have no issues with that, so I take the one she's holding.

"Then let's find him one that isn't completely stained or torn because you've worn it everywhere."

As we sort through Kaylee's thousands of costumes, I hear Maggie mutter behind me. "If only the rest of the world reacted to coming out like a five-year-old does."

Amen.

Oh God. The rest of the world.

"Hey, Kaylee?" I say.

She looks at me with her big green eyes, and I hate, hate, hate what I have to say next.

"You know how those bad men with cameras follow us when we go out sometimes?"

"Yeah."

"If they find out about Daddy and Lyric, they're going to follow us even more, so we can't tell anyone."

It's not that I want to keep it from the world. I know what's going to happen when it all comes out, and I'd like Kaylee to be at a less vulnerable age when it happens.

"Why?" she asks.

That's a loaded question. One I can't answer in a way a five-year-old will understand.

"Because he's famous," Chase says. "Famous people are followed all the time."

The wisdom of kids.

Kaylee hugs me. "You're just Daddy to me, but I promise I won't tell anyone."

Oh, shit. I might cry.

The best part about not having to hide our relationship from Kaylee anymore is being able to give in to the urge to give Lyric more of me. All of me.

To have an actual real relationship for the first time in my life.

It's amazingly easier than I expected it to be.

Whether it's thanking him properly for helping me at Kaylee's party by having him stay the night or randomly being able to pop in whenever I want to give him a kiss while he's looking after her, it's so much easier now that Kaylee knows.

Maggie has officially moved in and has been sleeping in the nanny's quarters while she looks for a job, and the three of us have this family unit thing going on.

It's weird when I think about it from an outside perspective, but it works for us.

Anyone else would think it'd be awkward for me to be lying on the couch, my feet in my boyfriend's lap, my one-night-stand baby momma on the other couch while we watch a kids' movie with our daughter and my boyfriend's nephew on the floor.

But there's a peacefulness to it, and we're content.

This peace scares the shit out of me even more than getting involved with Lyric to begin with, because the only way to go from here is down.

I've asked Lyric about any upcoming auditions, but he said he hasn't been looking. I wanted to push, but he shut it down pretty fast.

The niggly feeling in my gut that tells me he's holding back because of me is pushed down by my selfishness, wanting him not to get signed to a label.

I'd never block his chances at a record deal, and I know it's inevitable because of his talent, but I'm not ready to let go of what we're developing. I'm not ready for long distance and lonely nights. It's why I never tried the relationship thing when I was with Eleven.

Lyric's hand finds my foot, his thumb running from my arch up to my toes, and I almost have a full-body-gasm. Damn, that feels good.

"You okay? You look like you're thinking pretty hard over there."

I throw my head back on the armrest of the couch. "Whatever I was thinking, it's gone now. Keep doing that."

"This is why I need a boyfriend," Maggie mumbles.

"Back off. This one's mine."

I feel him pause—a little stall in Lyric's hand on my foot—but then he moves again.

Maybe I should stop bringing up auditions and instead focus on having a conversation about finally labeling this thing between us. I mean, I figured he knew I wanted to be boyfriends the other day at Kaylee's party when I told her that's what we are, but explaining it on a basic level to a five-year-old and putting it into serious terms by adult standards are completely different.

He knows how I feel about him, doesn't he?

Yes, because he's so good at mind reading, my conscience tells me.

Yep, we're definitely going to have to have a conversation about that.

When the buzzer goes off for the front gate, the three of us glance at each other.

"Anyone expecting a visitor?" I ask.

"Maybe the universe heard my pleas for a boyfriend and is delivering one to our doorstep?" Maggie says.

I get off the couch and go to the monitor, letting out a little laugh. "Sorry, Mags. This one's taken too." *And gay*. But I don't say that bit out loud.

I do wonder why Harley Valentine is at my house, though.

I groan. "Harley's tour has ended, hasn't it?" I ask no one in particular.

"Why?" Lyric asks.

"He said once his tour was over, I couldn't hide from him."

He buzzes again—typical Harley, impatient and persistent as always—so I reluctantly let him in.

I haven't seen him face-to-face in what feels like forever, but we've kept in touch over the last two years. I'm kind of eager to meet the man Harley's been bragging about.

I don't realize how much I've missed him until I greet him in the driveway.

He gets out of the car and flashes his multimillion-dollar smile my way. "Ryder."

"*Ride her*? I barely even know her!"

He rolls his eyes at me. "You haven't changed a bit. Although, you are looking older." He turns to the wall of muscle beside him who I assume is his boyfriend, Brix. "Note for our future selves, let's not have kids. I'm too beautiful to start looking old."

"Oh, hey!" I feign enthusiasm. "It's actually lucky you came by, because I have something to give you." I reach into my pocket and pull out my middle finger.

"Aww, you're the sweetest." He finally wraps me in a hug, and we perhaps hold on a little bit too tight.

It's funny when a boy band breaks up. Everyone wants to know the reasons why, who hates who, and what the big blowup was that ended it all. But with us, there was none of that. It was the most boring and amicable split ever.

Well, apart from maybe Mason, whose debut solo album tanked and then he disappeared. I don't think he's spoken to anyone from the group for a while.

"I've missed you," I murmur.

Harley pulls back. "Why are you so obsessed with me?"

I laugh. "Fuck you."

"Nah, that's this guy's job. Brix, this is Ryder. Ryder, this is Brix. As in dumb as bricks."

Brix smiles and shakes his head. "He loves telling people that. My name is Brixton."

"Come in."

They follow me inside where I find both Lyric and Maggie peering around the corner trying to get a glimpse. I assume the kids are still watching TV.

"Hey, is that …" Harley starts. "Maggie?"

In the early days, when Kaylee was first born and Maggie had time off from the military, she was around for a while and hung out with all the Eleven guys.

She pops around the corner. "Hi, Harley. I wasn't sure you'd remember me."

"Any woman who manages to sleep with Ryder is memorable."

"Nice, asshole. Real nice."

While they hug and catch up, I go to find my boyfriend. He's still hiding around the corner.

"You wouldn't be intimidated by little ol' lazy and cliché Harley Valentine, would you?"

He looks mortified. "Oh God, you didn't tell him what I said, did you?"

"No. At least, I don't think I did." I grab his hand and pull him toward the foyer. "Harley, this is Lyric. Lyric, Harley Valentine and his bodyguard, Brix."

Harley glances at our joined hands and then back up to Lyric's gorgeous face. "Right. Lyric. The *nanny*." He looks up at his giant boyfriend. "Come on, I'm so right. Am I right?"

Brix nods. "Definitely."

"Right about what?" Lyric asks.

I sigh. "When I wanted to hire you, Harley accused me of wanting to sleep with you. Crazy, huh?"

Lyric grins. "Insanity."

I lean in and kiss his cheek.

"Aww, you guys are so cute, and now knowing this revelation, this totally isn't my bodyguard either. I mean, well, he is. But he's also my partner."

Lyric turns to me. "Did you lie? You told me Harley wasn't gay."

"Did I say that? Or did I say the Ryley4Ever rumors weren't true?"

"Oooh, sneaky."

"So where's your rug rat?" Harley asks. "I haven't seen her since she was, what, two?"

"Three." I call out for Kaylee, and she and Chase come running.

"Whoa. Did you have another one and not tell me?" Harley asks.

I laugh. "This is Chase, Lyric's nephew."

"Are you, like, collecting children or something?"

I cock my head. "You know how you said you shouldn't have kids because they will age you? I think you shouldn't have kids for other reasons. Just a thought."

"Not even going to dispute that." Harley kneels to Kaylee's level. "Hey, kiddo. Do you remember me?"

"You're Harley Valentine," Chase says for her.

"Ooh, a fan? Nice to meet you, buddy." Harley shakes Chase's hand much like I did the first day I met him.

Harley talks with the kids for a while and pretends to listen to their rambling until he can't take it anymore. Which takes about three full minutes before he's giving me a *please help me* stare.

"As fun as this is," I say, "why are you here?"

His gaze turns all glimmery and cocky. Shit. "You know why I'm here. I told you once I was done with my tour—"

"Yep, thought so. Let's go to the studio to talk."

"Hey, kids," Harley says. "You know what's super fun? Trying to get my bodyguard here on the ground. It's impossible because he's a tank. Have at it!"

Brix mutters something about paying for that later before he's engulfed by the two kids trying to climb his sides.

I turn to Lyric. "You all good here?"

"Yup. Go."

With every step toward the studio, butterflies and dread fill my stomach. Harley wants to get Eleven back together, and even though I'm longing to be an artist and perform again, it breaks my heart because I have to say no.

As soon as the door is closed to my office and we take our seats, the room goes quiet. Harley sits there and blinks at me as if he's waiting for me to fall at his feet and give him whatever he wants.

"I expected a bigger sales pitch," I say.

Harley looks smug. "I figure I don't have to say much because I know you want to do this."

"I do, but I can't."

"Why not? You have a nanny and Maggie out there. How long is she home for?"

I hesitate. "She didn't re-up."

His glee is evident. "Perfect."

"No, it's not perfect. I can't leave Kaylee on her own."

"You can leave her with her *mom*."

I glare. "Seriously. Don't have kids."

Harley laughs. "There's something else, and I want you to be a part of it."

I narrow my eyes. "Oh God, you're not coming out publicly and getting married or some shit, are you? I'm calling *not it* on being your best man."

"Ha, ha, and no. Although, I have an idea about the whole coming out thing if you're interested and want do it with me?"

"That would be a hell no."

"Thought so." Harley shrugs. "It's not gonna happen for a while anyway. We figure if I come out, it won't be long before everyone realizes the big guy is more than my bodyguard, and we're enjoying being us right now."

"That's really good. Keep hold of that for as long as you can. What's the news, then?"

"I'm starting my own label."

I perk up. "Really?"

"I got out of that ugly contract mess with Joystar, and I really don't want to go through that again. So I figure ..."

"You figure you'd bankrupt yourself? Smart."

"I'm serious. I want Eleven to get back together and do new music on my label. We can do our own sound, and you can produce. We'll find some new talent and build a fucking empire from the ground up."

"Sounds like a lot of work."

"But how much fun will it be?"

I can't deny that.

He turns big puppy dog eyes on me. "Please, Ry? Please? I'll be your best friend forever."

"Are we twelve?"

"Yes."

"I don't know why you're coming to me first. You really think you can get the other guys to come back? Blake doesn't even sing anymore. Mason could be dead for all we know."

"I came to you first because even though the others will be a hard sell, you're the one I want to do this with most. We were like brothers on the road, and I fucking miss you, okay?"

"Why are you so obsessed with me?" I throw his words from earlier back at him.

"You're going to say yes. I can feel it."

I groan. "I want to. You know I want to. But … I can't."

There's a knock on the door, and then Lyric pushes his way through. "Hey, sorry to interrupt, but Ryder, can I talk to you for a second?"

How long has he been standing outside that door?

"It's about Kaylee," he adds, and I'm out of my seat as fast as humanly possible.

But when he pulls me through the house, past where Kaylee is still playing with Brix and being watched by Maggie, I realize he's lying.

"You were eavesdropping."

He leads me to our—er, my—bedroom. "Guilty." He spins to face me. "You have to do it."

"I have to do it? Says who?"

"Me."

"Last I checked, you weren't the boss of me."

His hands find my shoulders. "You deserve this. You want this. You can't keep Kaylee locked in a tower her whole life."

"She can't come on tour with us. Which would mean leaving her for months. I'm not okay with that."

"From the sound of it, Harley wants you two to make your own rules. Set up tours for the summer when she's out of school, and pay me to go with you as her nanny. Or hell, pay Maggie to be her nanny … Wait, is it technically being a nanny if it's her mom?" He shakes his head. "Either way, this is doable. You just have to let go of that protective streak and take the leap."

"I never thought I'd see the day where you, of all people, want Eleven to get back together."

"I don't. Well, I mean, your own sound could be cool. You're better than all that *your love fits like a glove* crap."

"Those lyrics are not in any of Eleven's songs."

"You know what I mean. You're so much better than that, and this is an opportunity to show off your amazing song writing skills and produce. I already know you can perform the shit out of anything."

"It's too selfish of me. I owe the next few years to Kaylee."

Lyric grunts. "You're so frustrating sometimes. You call me stubborn, but fuck, being happy doesn't make you selfish, Ryder. I would kill for what you have offered to you, and you're turning it down for a reason that doesn't make sense anymore. I'm here. Maggie's here. Kaylee won't be alone."

He's making so much sense it hurts. It hurts that I'm holding myself back, and it hurts that this could affect Kaylee, but what hurts the most is knowing if I don't take this opportunity, I will regret it.

"If you really don't want to go back to Eleven, fine. But at least be a part of Harley's new label. You could do so many good things with it. You brought me out of my head and made me put the music first. This is your chance to do it."

"What about you?"

"This isn't about me."

"Why haven't you been going to auditions?"

Lyric leans against the chest of drawers by my bed. "I figure Kaylee starts school in a few months. I can hold off until then."

"I don't want to hold you back." But I also don't want him to go out there and get a record deal either. If I were to take Harley up on his offer, and then Lyric got signed, we would literally never see each other.

"You're not. It's my choice to take a few months off so I can be with you and Kaylee."

But he shouldn't have to do that!

He shouldn't have to put us first.

The idea of it makes my stomach queasy yet warm at the same time. It makes me anxious yet content. Emotions I don't understand bubble to the surface until I'm overrun by the urge to throw myself at him while simultaneously yelling at him for sacrificing anything for me.

"Why are you doing that?"

"If I really have to tell you, you're not only a pretty boy bander with cliché and lazy lyrics, you're also a dumbass."

"How … romantic?"

"I'm doing it because I want to be with you! Properly. I mean, you said I was your boyfriend, and you didn't hide it from Harley that we're together, or at least sleeping together. I know you hate labels, but I want one, okay? I want one with you. I want you and Kaylee to be my family, and I want to do these things together. I want to make decisions *together*. I want to be included. I don't think I've pushed, and maybe this is too much, but fuck, Ryd—"

I wrap my arms around him and cup the back of his head, sliding my fingers into his man bun as I pull him to me.

Our mouths crash together in an ungraceful mash of teeth and tongues and lips.

He tries to laugh, but I don't let him.

I need to show him how much I need him and how much I want to claim him.

But I'm also scared to give him all of me, because if he leaves, he'll take a huge chunk of me with him. I don't want to hold him back, but he wants us to work it out together.

As a couple.

I kiss him until my lips hurt and his face is splotchy from my unshaven face.

When I pull away, we're both breathing heavy, and we're both hard. As much as I would love to take advantage of that right now, I need to go back downstairs and give Harley my answer.

"There's one label I'm okay with having."

"Yeah?" he breathes.

"*Yours.* I'm more than okay with being yours."

The smile that lights up Lyric's face should be on the cover of his first album.

He leans in, and my stomach flips in anticipation of his lips on mine again. Only, our mouths don't meet.

Instead, he smacks my ass. "Good. Then let's get downstairs and tell Harley you're in."

I hold his hand all the way back to the studio where Harley is waiting. I want Lyric with me because we're in this together.

"According to *my boyfriend*"—I glance at Lyric and smile—"I'm not allowed to turn this opportunity down."

Harley either doesn't register my words or he's having a stroke.

"Harley?"

He turns slowly toward us. "Who's singing on this track?" He hits Play on my computer, and I'd be pissed if it wasn't for the fact Lyric's voice flows from the speakers along with Kaylee's. "I assume that's Kaylee, but unless your voice has gotten some serious rasp to it in the last two years, that's not you."

Lyric's cheeks fill with color as I smile.

"Funny you should ask."

"Ryder, don't," Lyric warns.

I ignore him. If he's making me do this, he has to do it with me. "You should hear Lyric's demo. You'll want him to be *our* first new act on the label."

Harley's face lights up, but Lyric looks like he wants to murder me.

CHAPTER 24
LYRIC

MY MOUTH DRIES.

"This is you?" Harley points to the computer.

"It is. But, uh … I—"

"Lyric is so talented he makes me jealous," Ryder says.

I try to hold my anger in because, logically, I know he's trying to do a nice thing. But that nice thing is making me feel two feet tall.

"Did you really do that?" I mutter to Ryder.

He squares his shoulders. "Yes, I did. Because if you think you're going to put your career on hold so I can chase a dream I voluntarily gave up two years ago, you're sorely mistaken. I know you don't want my help getting a record deal, but if Harley doesn't think you have it in you, he won't sign you. That won't be an issue, though." He gestures to Harley. "He's already half in love with you because of one song."

"That's not the point!" I finally blow. "Are you forgetting my rules?" I hold up a finger. "I want to do this on my own." I put up a second. "I want to do it as myself." A third finger goes up. "And I want to do my music, my way. You really think signing on a boy band label will allow me to do the songs I want?"

"Ooh, harsh," Harley mumbles.

I turn to him. "Sorry. This is nothing against you. Or your label. Or the idea of getting Eleven back together. I just …"

"I get it," Harley says.

I lift my head. "What?"

"Want to know why I'm eager to start my own label?"

"Money?"

Harley laughs. "Hardly. What I'm doing is a risk. I want to make albums of real sounds. Of real songs. Songs from the heart. It's why I left Joystar to begin with. They were trying to censor me. My songs were getting too political and weren't peppy enough. They weren't about love and happy, mushy bullshit. And don't get me wrong, I will expect to have one or two chart-toppers on every album, but my plan is to work with my artists to find the best sound they have."

"That … actually sounds amazing. But, I'm sorry. I can't. I won't accept an offer from you."

"Because of me?" Ryder asks.

"I don't want a record deal on a favor."

Harley stands. "Look, I've only heard one song, but I'm impressed. If you want to send me a demo, I'll happily listen to it and remain unbiased. I'm interested in signing you, but like Ryder says, I won't do it if I don't think you can make it big. I love him but not that much."

I don't believe him. This deal will always be tainted by Ryder's connection. "I'll think about it."

"Well, uh, it looks like you two have some stuff to discuss. I'm gonna get out of this awkwardness as fast as possible." Harley slaps Ryder on the back. "Have fun getting yelled at, and I can't wait until we can work together again."

Ryder smiles. "Who you working on next?"

Harley taps his chin. "I figure Denver. He should be the easiest sell out of all of you."

"Shouldn't you start with the hardest?" Ryder asks.

"Do you even know where Mason is?"

"Nope."

"Neither do I."

I watch their exchange, willing it to hurry up and be over because I need to yell. Or throw things.

Upstairs, we were literally making big declarations, and now, suddenly, he's going back on the only promise he's ever made me.

As soon as Harley's gone, Ryder turns to me.

I hold up my hand. "Don't. This isn't going to be a *thing*. I'm not sending him my demo. End of story."

"Why are you so fucking keen on sabotaging your career?"

"I'm not!"

"I call bullshit."

"Oh, you're calling bullshit? The fact you brought me into this at all, *that's* bullshit."

"I didn't bring you into this! Harley heard your song and is interested. That makes your career fair game. I'm so sorry I want you to achieve your dream even at the expense of my own heart." He mock gasps. "The nerve."

I pull back. "What do you mean?"

"I would love for you to forget about music and stay with me and Kaylee. I'd love to hold you back so you can be part of us, follow me while I explore this new venture with Harley, and live *my* life. But that would be selfish. The side of me that wants you to be happy won't allow me to sit back and let you skip auditions and put off your career for us."

"I'm not doing that. I'm taking a break from feeling like I'm not good enough. And I get to spend my time with two people I'm falling in love with even though I know I probably shouldn't."

Ryder's eyes widen.

"And that look right there"—I point at him—"is why I shouldn't be getting attached. I say that I'm falling for you, and you freak out."

"I'm not." He so is.

"You're lying."

"Okay, fine, I am, but not because I don't want that. I don't know how to handle it because I've never done this before. Not, like, a real relationship. I simultaneously want you to succeed while not wanting you to leave me. I want to lift you up and hold you back at the same time, and I don't understand it. I don't know how to process it in my head."

"So you push me away by doing the one thing I asked you not to?" How can he not see that?

"I didn't mean to push you away. I was trying to support you."

I shake my head. "I don't want to use your connections to get ahead. You *know* that."

"All I did was ask Harley to hear your demo."

"Yeah, and in return he gets you to sign on his new label."

"That wasn't a condition attached."

I fold my arms. "Fucking sounded like it."

"He was listening to your song when we came back in!"

The more he argues, the more frustrated I become.

I let out a loud breath. "Let's move on. Even if Harley wasn't doing it as a favor to you, I will always wonder. I don't need those thoughts stifling my voice."

"Lyric—"

I grunt. "I don't want to sign with Harley, okay? He's Harley Valentine, and the complete opposite of the image and sound I want."

"Usher signed Justin Bieber and they're nothing alike. Harley wants different sounds and voices."

"I can't do this right now." I need to get out of here.

Ryder and I have disagreed before. A lot. About many different things.

But my music is sacred, and I thought he understood that. He worked with me to create a demo I'm actually proud of, and he respected my hang-ups and demands. He might've found them exasperating, but he never pushed.

This, though … this is too much.

"I need to take Chase home."

Ryder stands between me and the doorway. "Don't leave like this. Not in the middle of an argument."

"It's not an argument. It's a difference of opinion."

"A difference that is obviously getting to you. I want to make this right. Tell me how I can make this right."

"Let me make my own career decisions."

His lips purse. He really doesn't want to do it. His bright blue eyes are locked on mine, his jaw set. "Fine."

"Wait, what?" I didn't expect him to give in that fast.

He steps closer. "You're right. You should be able to make your own decisions when it comes to your career."

"Umm, thank you."

"I'm not done."

Of course he's not.

"Your career is yours, and your sound is yours, but I think you're so blinded by the issues you have over your dad's death and how the industry treated him that you can't see what's right in front of you. You're fighting this *too* hard, and the only person you're punishing is yourself."

"I …" I try to dispute that, but I can't.

"You're so scared of repeating your father's mistakes you won't take any opportunity given to you. You always claim you want to be yourself, but I'm not entirely sure you know who that is—musically, anyway. You fight anything remotely mainstream on principle instead of preference. There will always be an excuse not to do something."

"It's not that simple."

"It is that simple. I'm not the one fucking this up for you. Remember that when you find yourself in the exact same position in a few years. Remember it when the bitterness creeps in because I can tell you from experience, you can love someone with your whole fucking heart and still resent them."

I know Ryder has those kinds of issues with Kaylee, and I also know he hates himself for it. I want to reassure him and tell him to let go of those feelings, but I can't make my mouth work.

His words hit me as if he's physically assaulting me, and the punches keep coming. The truth hits harder than anything else he could throw at me, and it stings.

"Don't let your *fear* hold you back, and that's all I have left to say. You get your wish. Your career's all yours to ruin." Ryder turns on his heel and storms out.

It's hard to ruin something that doesn't exist.

Defeat and guilt overshadow the frustration, and I slump.

Because he's right.

I'm holding on to these deep-seated issues over my dad and his death. Any offer from the music industry will always feel like I'm selling out.

But how am I supposed to let go of that?

What Harley was offering sounded perfect—maybe too good to be true. I want to know more, find out if there's a catch. Yet, I already wrote off the idea before I could ask more questions because of Ryder.

I didn't lie when I said I've been avoiding auditions lately because I'm sick of the rejection, but it's more than that.

I'm falling so fucking hard for Ryder. I've possibly already fallen completely. If I were to sign with a label now, I'm not sure we're in a strong enough place to survive it.

He's flighty and never had a relationship. I freeze every time he refers to me as his boyfriend because I'm sure he's going to take it back.

I wanted to hold on to what we are building and postpone looking for representation, at least for a few months, then reassess when Kaylee starts school.

Except, now I'm wondering if that was an easy out. Was I using them as another excuse to hide behind?

Probably. But the problem is I have no idea how to stop hiding.

When Ryder said he was going to leave my career alone, I thought maybe he was saying it to calm an elevated situation, that he didn't really mean it.

I didn't expect him to stay true to his word.

Come Monday, while in the kitchen making Kaylee some lunch, Ryder slides my demo over to me. "Harley's been calling me all weekend and all morning trying to get his hands on this. Take it from me before I'm too tempted. Do what you want with it. Set it on fire if you want. Just take it so I can respect your wishes."

I swallow hard and take it from him with a nod.

He turns on his heel and walks out again.

I'm thankful for the gesture, but this whole situation has put strain on our relationship.

It's not like we're back at square one, but it's definitely driven a wedge between us.

I figure it's only been a couple of days, and maybe we both need time to cool off, but it's just the start.

For the rest of the week, Ryder's busy in the studio with the artist he thinks is a brat, and Maggie is out looking for a job, so I have Kaylee as usual.

We don't spend the following weekend together because I tell him I'm utterly exhausted and want to go home after I gig.

I haven't stayed over, and he hasn't asked me to, but when we've been in each other's presence, he's still affectionate. He still kisses me hello and goodbye, and he still has the ability to make my brain short-circuit by simply pressing his lips to mine.

Things are … okay.

I think.

I've avoided talking to him about music since our fight, and I think he's been biting his tongue. We're going to have to face it eventually, but I'm scared things will blow up again.

We've disagreed before, but I guess this was our first real fight.

And I'm not delusional; I know couples fight.

But I'm worried Ryder will run instead of facing it if I bring it up again. I don't want to give him that excuse.

We are both so passionate about music that when we stop talking about it, all that's left to talk about is Kaylee.

And, I mean, that's not a hardship. Kaylee is amazing. But she's not all I want to talk about.

Part of me wants his opinion and thoughts on what I should do next in terms of my career, but I still fear the unknown, and now I worry bringing up my career will lead to a heated discussion.

I think that's Ryder's point, though.

Being with Ryder and Kaylee is safe and familiar, and they feel like home. Stepping out of that box and going for something I've been chasing since I was a kid and Dad first taught me to play the guitar is terrifying.

What if I fuck up?

What if I go back on my word and disappoint my mother?

What if I go for it and become the man I don't want to be?

I want to learn from Dad's mistakes, not repeat them.

And that's what I'm truly scared of.

It's not singing pop songs or changing my image or becoming a different person. It's becoming someone I don't want to be if I don't have the nerve to say no.

So instead, I say no to everything.

Healthy.

After Kaylee goes to bed on Monday evening, I wait until I see the brat and his entourage leave before I go into Ryder's studio.

I find him slumped over the desk in the control room. "Rough day?"

He startles, but when he turns to look at me, his face immediately relaxes. "It just got a million times better."

"Because the brat left?" I step closer.

Ryder reaches for me. "Because you're here."

He pulls me on top of him, and I straddle his thighs awkwardly on the chair. He cups the back of my head and then leans up to meld his mouth with mine.

With the need I have for his lips, his touch, and his kisses, I'm able to ignore the fact I'm almost falling off his lap, the armrest is digging into my side, and my leg is almost cramping from trying to hold me up.

Ryder's tongue moves slowly against mine.

When he moans, it's almost enough to make me forget what I came in here to say.

Almost.

Still, it's hard to find the right words. Swallowing my pride is hard.

Ryder pulls back and stares up at me like he knows I'm struggling. "Everything okay?"

I bury my head in his neck and kiss his skin as I murmur, "You're right."

His hand freezes in the middle of my back. "In general, or about something in particular?"

I laugh. "Oh, definitely something in particular. You're wrong about almost everything else."

He pinches my side, and I climb off his lap.

Ryder leans back in his chair as I pull over another seat.

I look him in his knowing blue eyes. "I fight everything mainstream because of my father, not because I don't like it."

He at least has the respect to try to hold back his smile. Even if he fails miserably.

I sigh. "I'm going to send my demo to a few labels."

His face lights up until he realizes, while this is a move in the right direction, it's still not going his way. "You're still not giving it to Harley." Ryder's pouty lips thin into a flat line.

"I understand everything you were getting at with him, but with us being … *us*, it makes me uncomfortable."

"Okay then, I'm breaking up with you."

My heart sinks. Did he really just say that? "W-what?"

He puts his hand on my thigh. "Oh my God, I'm so sorry. I thought you'd know I was joking."

I shove him. "Asshole."

"I really am sorry," he says softly. "I support you no matter what you do, and I'm proud of you for putting yourself out there."

I narrow my eyes. "But …"

"But what?"

"Sounds like there was going to be a but coming."

Ryder grits his teeth. "Do not make a joke about coming in butts," he mutters to himself.

"So glad we can have this completely serious, grown-up conversation about something as important as my career."

"You're welcome." He beams. "But fine. What I was going to say was that I know Harley. I know how much he complained about Joystar and how they made us write all those shallow songs. He worked like hell to get out of his contract with them for the same reason. When he says he's building a label where his artists get to sing and do what they want, I know he'll be fair. Try those other labels, sure, but don't write Harley off because of me."

"I-I'll think about it." I don't see myself going in that direction, but he's right. I shouldn't write him off without exploring it first.

He leans in and kisses my cheek. "That's all I'm asking."

I let out a loud breath, not realizing how relieved I am that this conversation didn't end in another fight.

Ryder must sense it because his brow scrunches. "Did you think that was going to go differently?"

"Maybe?" I slump. "I'm sorry. I … I don't know if we're cool. Things have been weird, and—"

"If this is going to work between us, we have to accept the fact we're going to have disagreements."

I nod. "A lot of them."

"Yeah, a lot of them. But as long as we know we're both in this, and we talk, and we're respectful, everything will be okay between us. Always."

"Okay."

"Can you stay tonight?" Ryder asks.

"I really want to, but I should go. I have Chase tomorrow."

"Tomorrow's Tuesday."

"I know." I smile. "I did tell you Chord and Brenna had an event coming up where I'd have Chase an extra day, but it's okay if you forgot."

"Can we just adopt that kid so you can stay over every night?"

"As much as I love that idea, I don't think Chord and Brenna will sign off on it. Weirdly enough, they love their child."

Ryder looks contemplative. "Are you sure?"

"Pretty sure."

"Damn."

"I may have to go home, but I can leave you with something before I go." I slide off the chair and sink to my knees.

He stares down at me and reaches for his belt buckle. "Fuck yes."

CHAPTER 25
RYDER

I WATCH as Lyric takes out my cock, slips it between his lips, and sucks on the head. Ripples of need travel down my shaft and into my balls. Tingles break across my skin, making me shudder.

Lyric smirks up at me with hooded hazel eyes. I never knew it was possible to only smile with your eyes until this moment.

While he sucks me down, he reaches back and pulls out his hair tie, letting the loose waves cascade over his shoulders.

This fucker doesn't play fair.

I play with the long blond locks, twining them in my fingers and gripping the back of his head.

Fuck, he's good with his mouth.

Kissing me.

Sucking me.

The wet heat on my cock makes my thoughts fuzzy before my mind goes blank.

He's on a mission to get me off, opening his throat and taking me all the way so he can go home to his brother's house, but I want to make it last. I don't want him to leave.

Holy shit.

I don't *ever* want him to leave.

The pressure surrounding my cock is too much. My thoughts are too much.

My entire body tenses, as I release into his mouth, pushing my dick between his lips over and over again until there's nothing left.

The high gives me loose lips.

"Move in with me," I blurt out.

His gaze shoots to my face so fast my softening cock falls from his mouth. "What?" His voice is thick from having a dick down his throat.

"Shit, sorry. I didn't mean to blurt that out." We can't be there already, can we?

Lyric leans back on his heels and wipes his mouth. "Did you mean it?"

"I ..." Shit, I don't know. On one hand, everything with us is easy, and I already feel like he's part of my family, and Kaylee loves him, and I ... I think I could love him.

But on the other hand, that's a lot. That's a big step. And we haven't been together long.

He stares up at me expectantly, my cock is still out, and I think I've fucked everything up.

"Okay, so ..." I try to explain.

"It was said in the heat of the moment. Got it."

"No. I mean, well yes, it was, but I want it. I really, really, really want it even if it scares me."

Lyric smiles. "We can work out our fears together. My daddy issues and your commitment issues."

"We'd be a therapist's wet dream."

"We could fund their round-the-world vacations." He stands. "I should go."

I move to tuck myself away.

Lyric's uncertainty radiates from him as he stands and holds his head low, and I want to reassure him somehow, but I don't know how to do that.

Blurting out major life changes after a blowjob is not the way to do it.

We reach the front door, and I squeeze his hand to get him to turn to me. "I know things are weird right now, and I shouldn't have asked you like that. Maybe it's too soon to talk about you moving in, but I want you to know I did mean it. If you want to make it happen, I'm on board."

Lyric leans in and kisses me sweetly. "How about we talk about it when your dick isn't in my mouth and we're not in this weird place?"

I can't help feeling a teeny tiny bit disappointed he's not jumping at the chance, even if it makes complete sense not to rush this or use this to put a Band-Aid on our situation.

He huffs. "And here I thought you were ready to run."

"Not running. The thought might've crossed my mind a few times when you haven't been here or I've tried to visualize what a future even looks like with you, but when you're with me, we fit together and everything's good. It feels right, and I'm never letting go of that."

Lyric leaves with a smile, and while his future in music is uncertain, his future with me is a little bit closer to being exactly the type of relationship I never thought I'd have.

Not since having Kaylee.

I'm in my office, deep in concentration, trying to figure out why I hate the brat's singles.

I listen for every twinge in his voice, every imperfection, and wonder if I'm picking it apart because I hate him or if I'm being my usual pedantic self.

My phone lights up, and the caller ID is a welcome surprise.

Since Eleven broke up, our old manager Cameron Verikas has gone on to manage some amazing acts. When we split in different directions, he said he didn't want to represent any one of us. It was all or none because he said it would feel like picking between his children.

I hit Answer on the phone. "Hey, Cameron. Long time no hear."

"What's happening, kid?" His voice is warm like it always was.

Cameron was our go-between when it came to the label. He fought for us and was a great manager, even though the label won out the majority of the time.

He's like a father figure to all of us.

"Can you still call me kid when I'm almost thirty?"

"Yes. Yes, I can."

I lean back in my seat. "What can I do for you?"

"I've heard of this new guy on the scene. Lyric Jones."

I almost drop my damn phone. Did Lyric finally send feelers out? "And you're calling me because ..."

"Rumor has it you produced his demo."

My eyes narrow, my suspicion tingling. "Uh-huh." I drag out the word.

"I was hoping to get my hands on it."

I let out a loud breath. "Harley, you dirty fucker. Are you on the line too?"

Silence.

"Harley?"

"Okay, fine. I'm here." His tone is defeated yet whiny at the same time.

"There's the whiny diva I used to be besties with."

"Used to be?" he exclaims.

"Yeah. I already told you. If you want Lyric's demo, you need to track him down. I'm out. I like getting laid, thank you very much."

"I think that's my cue to tap out," Cameron says, and we both laugh as he disconnects.

"Ballsy move, Harley."

"I want that demo."

"Yeah, and now Cameron will too. If my boyfriend were to choose anyone to help his career, it'd be him. Not you."

"I don't know about that." His voice is pure cockiness. I wouldn't expect anything different from him. "I have something he wants."

"Oh, yeah? What's that?"

"Well, if I love his music as much as I think I will, he'll have an amazing producer he trusts and an opening set for the relaunch of Eleven."

My mouth drops open.

"Thought that would get your attention," Harley says down the line.

"I can't give you his demo. I'm fucking dying to, but I can't. He won't sign with you if I have anything to do with the deal, and I promised I'd butt out."

"I need him. Honestly, if he's even half as good as what I've heard already, it beats going through a slush pile of demos trying to find a diamond. Lyric is my diamond. I can feel it in my gut."

It makes sense that Harley heard the same thing in Lyric's voice that I did. We've spent so much time together working on songs, on lyrics and melodies, that we'd pick up on the same talent.

It's convincing Lyric that Harley saw it on his own that's the issue.

"I won't give you his demo, but you might want to go for a drink on Friday night at Cedar Bar. Randomly, of course."

Harley huffs. "Randomly it is. Any random time?"

"After eight."

"Thanks, man."

"Later."

I end the call and stare down at my phone, hoping I haven't crossed another line.

AT THE BEGINNING of my set, everything feels normal. I open with my usual song—a song I'm comfortable with. It eases my nerves and the adrenaline from being onstage so I can sink into my own little musical world.

But a few songs in, the energy in the audience changes.

Alex glares at me from behind the bar.

I push through the shift and the weirdness, but then I see him. Well, technically, I see his bodyguard-slash-boyfriend-slash-Goliath first.

Harley Valentine is in the audience.

My fingers stumble over the chords like they always do in front of label execs or anyone important in the industry.

Letting out a loud breath, I tell myself to calm down. I don't want Harley's contract anyway.

Keep telling yourself that.

I've been trying to force myself to send my demo to some labels, but whenever I've gone to do it, I've chickened out.

It turns out admitting your issues isn't the same as fixing them, and that kind of sucks.

I may or may not have been holding out for a miracle cure.

Even though I can't see Harley, I know he's out there. Watching me. Listening to me choke.

Sweat drops off my brow.

Make like Taylor Swift and shake it off, Lyric.

For some reason, my conscience sounds like Ryder.

It eases me.

I think about him telling me to stop fighting everything and do what I enjoy.

After fumbling my way through the last of the original I'm singing, I pull over the stool from the corner of the stage and take a seat.

When I try to get out of my head, I imagine the last time I was truly excited about a song. Not singing a song because I thought it represented who I am and what I want. Not a song that has a meaningful message that I don't connect with.

My fingers start plucking at the strings as if they have a mind of their own. It's a melody I wrote, but when I start singing, it's the words Ryder gave me.

It's the original on my demo we wrote together.

I hadn't let it out into the world yet. Not at any of my gigs.

I've been holding on to it tighter than I should have.

But as I release the angst and my fears about how I want to make it in this industry through a song disguised as a love ballad, my confidence builds.

The audience reacts, but I can't tell if it's positive or negative.

I only hear my guitar and my voice.

I thought that would be a good sign. Usually, there's bar noise in the background, the steady low hum of a large crowd. Hell, some nights I feel like I'm being completely ignored up here.

Right now, there's nothing.

It's as if everyone in the room is collectively holding their breaths.

And when I finish out the song, the silence doesn't stop.

For a beat or two, I think I've walked onto the set of some weird-ass movie where everyone's gone mute because of some random gas leak or bioweapon attack.

It stretches forever, but in reality it's probably only seconds before the bar erupts in cheers, whistles, and clapping.

The smile that pulls at my lips is probably boyish and not at all professional. It feels like my face is screaming, "You like me! You really like me!"

I clear my throat and tell myself to act like I'm used to this kind of praise from an audience.

I finish out the rest of my set with the songs from my demo and tell myself to ignore the giant bodyguard man and Harley as I exit the stage and head for my dressing room.

They're not far behind, though.

I'm pacing the room with my hands on my head trying to dispel the leftover adrenaline from being out there when they enter the room without knocking.

My feet stall when a third person enters the room.

Brix closes the door behind them and stands guard. I guess he's in bodyguard mode not boyfriend mode.

"Lyric Jones, this is Cameron Verikas," Harley says.

My mouth dries. My palms fucking sweat.

Cameron Verikas is here. Like, right in front of me. He's responsible for five of the biggest acts of the last twenty years.

"And judging by the look on your face, I'm guessing you already know who he is," Harley says.

Cameron … *The* Cameron Verikas smiles at me. *Me!* "I'm gonna cut to the chase, kid. I want to sign you and find you a label."

Harley steps in front of him. "I want to sign you to my label."

"Together?"

Harley's pouty bottom lip flattens.

Cameron scoffs. "This guy has no money to give you. And ten percent of nothing is nothing. So no. Not together."

"I don't have *no* money," Harley says. "I have … little money, which, okay, is next to nothing."

"I don't understand."

"Cameron could get your name in front of some big labels who could write you a big fat check for your first album, that's true. But I can give you what you want. A label who wants to produce you as you."

"But you're both connected to Ryder, so I can't—"

Harley smiles. "Ryder said you'd say that. I love that man like a brother, but no way would I risk a brand-new label on a favor."

"I'm looking for a new act," Cameron says. "I don't go around throwing offers at mediocre artists because an old client tells me to.

We're businessmen first and foremost. Remember that whenever you believe someone is doing you a favor in this industry, okay? Favors are easy to repay with very little effort. I've already done more for you than any favor that's been asked of me. I sat through an entire set just to hear you sing."

"People like Cameron Verikas don't do that," Harley points out.

They're right. Both Harley's and Cameron's time is valuable. And even if Ryder asked them to come hear me play—which I don't think he did because we've talked about that—they didn't have to come backstage and offer me anything.

Harley steps forward. "What we're offering is genuine. He can make you big, but I can make your dreams come true."

"Hear us both out, and then make your decision," Cameron says.

"O-okay."

If someone had told me I would have the chance to sit down with Cameron Verikas and Harley Valentine and that I'd even be contemplating picking Harley over Cameron, I would've told them their crystal ball was broken.

Yet, here I am, wanting to hear both of them out.

Cameron could have me shooting to the top of the Billboards in weeks. Months, tops. He's the type of manager a guy like me could only dream of. Yeah, he managed Eleven, but he's also been responsible for some Grammy Award–winning acts who aren't so boy bandy.

Harley, on the other hand, is all boy band. But he wants to change that image, and he wants to give not only me but Ryder his own voice as well.

"The original out there," Harley says. "Did you write it?"

"Yes. Uh, well, with Ryder's help. The melody is mine. He helped me with the lyrics."

Harley seems pleased with my answer. "You two make a great team. I'd want to keep that if I signed you."

"Keep that how?"

"Get Ryder to produce your music."

That right there is almost enough for me to yell "Sold" and shake his hand.

Cameron doesn't let me get that far. "I can have the hottest producers in town gagging over working with you."

Harley cringes. "Old man, don't say *gagging* like you're a contestant on *RuPaul's Drag Race*."

Cameron ignores him, but his lips twitch. "I have all the contacts in the world."

"I have what you want," Harley counters.

Brix clears his throat. "Babe, could you not make it sound so sexual when you say that? Thanks."

"Aww, jealous, Rambo?"

Cameron seems to know about Harley's relationship, which is surprising, but it shouldn't be. He would've had to have known about Harley's sexuality back in the Eleven days. Is he one of the ones who made Harley and Ryder stay closeted throughout their boy band days?

I turn to him. "How do you plan to pitch an out and proud gay artist? I won't step into a closet like—"

"Like Ryder and I did?" Harley asks.

I don't answer.

"Those boys came out to me after the fact," Cameron says. "After the contracts were signed and the label had put their rules in place. Being up-front is a lot easier. Some labels will turn you down because of it, I'm not going to lie, but being out from the beginning is key in this industry."

Harley sighs. "I really want to debate why I would be a better choice in this area, but I think we both know that's not the case. Actually, in a lot of areas, Cameron is by far the better choice."

"That really fills me with confidence," I say.

Harley shakes his head. "I'm never going to lie to you either. That I can promise. I will work you hard. You and I will fight over songs, over lyrics, and everything in between. But I will always listen to you. I will always work with you."

I glance at Cameron. "And you won't?"

"It's my job to be the go-between for you and the label. I will go to bat for you—"

"But he'll also bat for the label," Harley adds.

Cameron can't deny that.

"Sign with me and I'll cut out the middleman," Harley says. "My label is going to be small starting out. Just Eleven and one artist I want to promote the shit out of. Then I'll think about adding more artists."

"What about the fact that my sound is so much different than Eleven's?"

"Not an issue. Eleven will bring in the money. I want different acts. I'm getting bored recreating the same crap over and over again. I need new blood." Harley's passionate. There's no doubt about that. But he's also a little too excited about the *new-blood* thing.

I tilt my head in Brix's direction. "He is still talking about music, isn't he?"

"I have no idea," he answers.

"In all honesty," Harley says, "it's a risk working with me."

"I'll get you signed within a month," Cameron promises.

My head hurts, and I rub my temples.

"Think about it," Harley says. "This industry moves fast, so Cameron can't wait for an answer as long as I can. My label will take months to get off the ground."

"I'm a little overwhelmed," I admit. And then something occurs to me. "How did you two know where to find me?"

"Total fluke?" Harley squeaks.

I narrow my eyes.

"Shit, is that the time?" Harley checks an imaginary watch. "It's way past my bedtime."

He goes to leave.

"What happened to not lying?"

"Okay, fine. Ryder told me where you *might* be, but trust me, it was only because I'd been calling him nonstop about you. I even tried to trick him into giving me your demo, which is how Cameron got involved in the first place, but he saw right through it. Now Cameron's interested in you too, and if I was going to lose you to anyone, I'd be comfortable with it being him. Even if, right now, I really want to tell a guy who is like my dad to fuck off."

Cameron smiles. "With Harley going to extremes to get your demo, it piqued my interest. It's business."

Right. It's business.

"I … I have a lot to think about," I say. "And I'm not considering anything unless you send me contracts with all your terms." Thank fuck my brother is an entertainment lawyer.

"Give us your contact details, and we'll send them," Cameron says. "Unless you're going to make us go through Ryder again?"

"I'll give you my information."

They each give me their phone, and I put my email address and phone number into their contacts.

Harley steps closer to me. "Please don't be mad at Ryder for telling me where I could find exactly what I was looking for. I wouldn't be fighting for you if I hadn't seen something out there." He points toward the stage. "Neither would Cameron. I admire you for wanting to get this the right way, but I also have to say that you need work. You need to grow as an artist. We both see that thing inside you that you need to be great. Eventually. No free rides. Got it?"

I nod.

The way this is happening is not how I ever wanted to get a deal, but I believe him when he says he wouldn't be here if he didn't believe in me. Neither of them would be willing to sink time and energy into me.

The weight of my decision claws at my throat.

My head says Cameron. He's one of the biggest managers in the industry and could make me a huge star.

Harley … he's offering me more, but it's a risk. His new label, no matter how big his name is as an artist, is a risk. He might suck at running the business side of it.

I really have no idea what to do, and the only thing I want to do right now is go home to Ryder.

CHAPTER 27
RYDER

I'M PACING my bedroom and starting at the text I sent to Lyric a few hours ago. As soon as I hung up with Harley, I knew I'd done the wrong thing and needed to confess.

It took a few hours to work up the courage to type a half confession.

So, I did something. Please don't hate me.

I figured he was onstage, maybe, or hadn't seen it.

By now, Lyric would know for sure if Harley had turned up, which I assume he had. He wouldn't have been hounding me for details on Lyric only to drop it the minute he was given them.

So I guess the only question now is how much trouble I'm in.

The front door clicks open, echoing up the stairs in the silence of the late hour.

I pray to the God my parents forced down my throat, even though I don't believe in Him, and hope it's Lyric and not some stalker situation like what Harley dealt with this past year.

I open the door to my bedroom and come face-to-face with the most gorgeous man I've ever seen in my life.

From his loose, long, wavy blond hair, expressive hazel eyes, and strong jaw down to his usual attire of tight jeans, plain T-shirt, and a suit vest, I love everything about this man.

Even the scowl he's … wait … not wearing?

He smiles at me, and now I'm wondering if maybe this is a dream.

I should be getting yelled at. I should be—

Not getting cut off by his mouth on mine. Yet, here we are.

I stumble back, but he comes with me. His tongue probes my mouth, making my lips part for him as he dives in and kisses me with everything that he is. Passionate. Caring. *Mine.*

I kiss him back just as hard, hoping he can taste how sorry I am for doing something he didn't want me to. I'm hoping he feels how much he affects me, not just physically but mentally as well.

My cock tents my sweatpants, and I pull our lower halves together so Lyric can feel every inch of me against him.

"I want inside you," Lyric murmurs against my lips.

I don't hesitate to step back and shuck off my shirt and pants, leaving me naked for him in record time.

Lyric slips his vest off, then his shirt. "Get on the bed for me."

I walk backward toward the bed, not taking my eyes off him for even a second. Sitting on the mattress, I wiggle my way to the middle and then lie back.

I'm exposed and hard. I go to reach for my cock to stroke it and try to give it some form of relief, but Lyric doesn't let me.

He grunts. "Hands and knees will be better for this. I really wanted to make love to you, but I know this is going to be hard and fast."

Part of me wonders if this is my punishment—an angry fuck—but I have to say, it's not much of a punishment.

I do as he says and roll onto my hands and knees.

"You look so good like that."

I stare at him over my shoulder while he drops his pants and gets supplies from my bedside drawer.

He doesn't lie. The minute he has the condom on, he's fucking me with lubed fingers, trying to get me open for him as fast as possible.

I moan as my ass clenches around his fingers. I'm craving more, craving the burn. I don't care if I'm not ready, I want all of him. Now.

"Tell me if you need a minute."

I shake my head, my throat too dry to make sounds come out of my mouth.

His hand goes to the back of my neck as he lines up his cock and sinks inside me.

We let out a collective groan, but mine cuts off when he rotates his hips and pushes in deeper.

No other sounds pass my lips. All I can do is feel.

The hand on my neck creeps up into my hair and holds tight so my head is pulled back.

Lyric moves in and out of me, the burn still there but diminishing slowly with every thrust. It's hard and rough but not in the hate-filled or angry way I was expecting. It's just rough enough to sting in between bouts of pleasure, and his hand on my hip is soft and gentle. He's supporting me while still fucking me.

Tingles shoot down my spine. My toes curl and go kind of numb. Precum leaks onto the bed beneath me, my cock hard and untouched, and I struggle to catch my breath.

Lyric trembles, and I feel it in his thighs when they meet mine over and over again.

"This is …" He lets out a loud breath, and the hand on my hip tightens.

I want to say it's *amazing*, but my voice is still gone.

Probably a good thing because all I keep thinking is how gone I am for him.

I'm in love with him. There's no doubt about that.

"Fuck, Ryder." He shudders inside me and holds his breath while he slows his thrusts.

Just when I think he's going to pull out of me, his arms come around me, embracing my chest as he pulls me up onto my knees with my back against his front.

His cock is still inside me, still slowly jerking as he continues to come. I suddenly wish there was no condom between us and make a mental note to have that conversation with him sometime soon.

Lyric nuzzles my neck, and I lean back against his chest and rest my head on his shoulder.

His hand snakes around me and goes to my cock. The head is slick, and he strokes me languidly.

From the rough way he took me to the care he's giving me now, my head swims.

Lyric's lips trace my shoulder, and his hand grips me tighter. He jerks me off until my hips take over, and I fuck into his hand as he holds me close.

He peppers soft kisses over my skin.

And when I come all over his hand, he uses his free one to turn my head and kiss me deep.

By the time we've both recovered, our muscles are liquid.

Lyric releases me, and I don't even care that I turn and collapse onto my back in a pool of my own cum.

He stares down at me warmly and leaves briefly to clean himself up, but then he's right there next to me again, holding me.

"Hi," I say.

Lyric laughs at me. "Hey. Probably should've started with that."

"I thought you were gonna start with yelling."

He kisses my nose. "No yelling."

"Didn't Harley—"

"Oh, he did. And he brought Cameron Verikas with him."

"Cameron. And you're not yelling at me why? I didn't mean to tell Harley where you were. I mean, well I did, but I knew it was wrong the second I did it, and I'm sorry, and I'm not butting in, I swear. I—"

"They, uh"—a shy smile crosses his face—"both offered me a contract."

I grin. "Fuck, baby. That's amazing. You should've led with *that*."

"I … I don't know what I'm going to do."

"What are the terms?"

"They have to send me their contracts and exactly what they're offering, but basically, Cameron is promising to make me huge, and Harley is offering me creative freedom."

I wince. "That's a hard choice."

"It is."

"Though, creative freedom is what you wanted, isn't it?"

"Cameron says he'll go to bat for me as an out artist."

"Depending on what label he'll want you to sign with, you'll have to deal with them having input on your sound."

"Harley said even he and I will get into arguments over that."

"Though with Harley, you get me as a producer."

He doesn't smile at that like I thought he would. In fact, there's a hesitance behind his eyes I've seen before. That unsure emotion he gets around performing is now directed at me.

But then he finally breaks. "I don't know how much work we'd get done."

"Hey, we got your demo done … eventually."

"I don't think Harley would be happy if we do half the shit we did while on his dime."

"Whatever gets the songs cranked out."

"Now I feel like a whore. Or, wait, are you the whore in this situation?"

"Why do either of us have to be whores?"

Lyric shrugs. "Either way, sounds like a fun role-playing thing we could do."

I laugh.

"I'm going to have Chord look over the contracts and get his opinion. Then I'll make my decision."

"Smart." But I already know what Chord is going to say. From a business standpoint, he'll choose Cameron. "Are you leaning more toward one or the other?"

"You know I was never in this for the money, and I only want fame if it's as myself, so Harley's offer makes sense. But on the other hand, I don't want to be the moron who turned down Cameron Verikas."

"It's true. No one turns down Cameron Verikas, and he is a great manager."

"Less risky. Harley's new label might fail."

"That's true too." Damn it.

I don't want to throw my opinion out there because I know it'll be biased. He has to do what's best for him, and signing with Harley is too much of a risk. If Cameron wasn't interested, it'd be a no-brainer, but getting Cameron Verikas's attention is like finding a unicorn in this industry.

"The only thing I will say about Cameron is he's loyal and he does fight for his artists, but generally speaking, labels are like casinos."

"It's a gamble?"

I snort. "No. The house always wins. Look at Harley and me."

"Couldn't the same be said for Harley's label?"

"I don't know. The thing is, Harley's intentions are pure, I can promise you that, but you know what they say about good intentions."

"You're being very philosophical tonight."

"It's late and I'm tired." *And I'm using all my energy not to tell you to pick me.*

Which is stupid because his decision isn't between me and something else. It's between two men who can do amazing things for his career, but when it comes down to it, the choice he makes will affect how our relationship works.

I knew this was going to happen sooner or later. I was hoping for a lot later. Lyric has too much talent to not be discovered, and the only thing holding him back was himself.

"I'm not going to make a decision anytime soon." Lyric kisses the top of my head. "Let's get some sleep."

I curl into his side and try to forget about our uncertain future. Maybe if he signs with Cameron, I can renege on the Eleven deal. I haven't signed anything yet, and I don't expect contracts to be drawn up until Harley gets all five of us on board. That'll take time.

If Lyric signs with Cameron, he will be thrust into a world he probably can't even fathom. It was an eye-opener for me at eighteen.

Holding him back from that isn't fair.

"Stop thinking," Lyric mumbles.

"I'm not."

"You are. You're all tense. It makes me think I didn't fuck you hard enough to turn your brain off."

"You might have to do it again."

He rolls on top of me. "I'm suddenly not so tired anymore."

Neither am I. Though I'm going to be wrecked in the morning.

CHAPTER 28
LYRIC

RYDER'S BEEN ACTING weird ever since I told him about the offers from Harley and Cameron. It's been days of forced smiles and soft kisses. Whenever I've asked him what's wrong, his voice has gone high-pitched and squeaky as he lets out a weak "Nothing! I'm fine."

Mmhmm, fine. Everyone knows when someone says they're fine, they're not fine.

It's why I didn't tell him the contracts came through yesterday, and I promptly sent them to my brother.

I expect him to call me any moment to tell me what he thinks, even though I already know.

What Cameron is offering is a once-in-a-lifetime opportunity. One my father never got to see.

Harley's contract is a risk. A big one. But it sounds so damn perfect.

My gut clenches.

I think that point is in both the pros and cons column. I loved working on my demo with Ryder. He makes me a better artist while not stepping on my creative side. But Harley's offer is still tainted by Ryder's connection to it, and signing with him and what I'm sure will be seen as a boy band label feels like selling out even more than signing with the biggest manager and possibly the biggest label in the industry.

My prejudices are pushing me toward Cameron.

Choosing Ryder and Harley's venture would feel like choosing my boyfriend over my future, and when did I become *that* person?

"I think it's buttered," Kaylee says.

I look down at my hands to find them making a sandwich. Huh.

Can anyone say distracted?

"What was I making again?"

She folds her little arms. "Peanut butter."

"Oh. Of course."

"You're dis-tacted."

"Distracted? Me? Never."

"Now, you lie!"

I ruffle her dark hair. "Nothing for you to worry about."

Kaylee is another factor in all this. We've bonded. This time last week, I was spending quality time with Ryder and Kaylee, and it felt like we were a family. I don't want to leave her.

I love being her nanny.

If I choose Harley, I could keep that even if it's only until she starts school. It's more time.

I finish making her lunch and slide her plate over to her. "There you go."

She takes it and moves toward the dining table.

"You're welcome," I say sarcastically.

She giggles. "Thank you, Lyric."

"That's better."

My phone rings in my pocket, and my heart leaps into my throat when I see Chord's name. I sink to the tiled floor and lean against the kitchen cabinet.

I'm scared of what he's going to say because I really, really, really want him to pick Harley so I have a business reason to go with the riskier choice.

"Hey," I answer.

"Did you win the music lottery?"

"Huh?"

"Cameron Verikas."

"Oh. Right. That."

"*And* Harley Valentine? When you said you'd been offered

contracts, I was prepared to tell you how slimy and crappy they were."

"So, they're both good?"

"For a first-time artist? Yeah, they're really damn good."

"Which … who do you think I should sign with?"

Please say Harley. Please say Harley. Please say Harley.

"Cameron. Duh. No-brainer."

Damn. "That's what I thought."

"You don't sound happy about that."

"Of course I'm happy."

Chord hesitates. "This is because of Ryder, isn't it?"

"With Harley's contract, I'd be working with Ryder and staying here for a while. With Cameron, I could be anywhere next week."

"I didn't realize it was so serious with Ryder."

"It's not. I mean, I don't think it is. I have all these stupid fantasies of being a family, and how dumb is that? We haven't even used the L-word and I'm thinking about rearranging my life for him. I'm thinking of turning Cameron down for him. Could you imagine if Dad were alive right now? He'd kick my ass for not going with Cameron."

"Dad would be proud of you for landing any contract." Chord's voice is soft and sincere.

"I'd be an idiot to pass on Cameron's offer."

"Nah, not an idiot. I think you're looking at this all wrong."

"Wrong how?"

"If Cameron's offer was the only one, yeah, I'd think you were an idiot for turning it down. Harley's contract is riskier, no doubt, but it's also an actual record deal. Cameron could sign you and dump you in a few months if you don't get anywhere with labels."

"He's Cameron Verikas," I point out.

"Okay, yeah, that argument would probably fly with any other manager. My main point is that while Harley's advance on your album is nowhere near what you'd get from a big label with Cameron's help, the royalty rate he's offering makes it more than a fair deal. What you've got to ask yourself is what's more important to you, family or your career? Maybe you could choose the option Dad never had—a world where he could have both."

I think back to all the times Dad was away on tour while we sat at home eating ramen because even though Mom worked, three kids on a waitress's salary barely kept the roof over our heads.

Dad would send money when he could, but he was paid peanuts and spent most of it on his rock star lifestyle.

I have the choice here—fulfill my selfish father's dream of being a solo artist with a major label or redo history and become the family man he never was.

"Oh, hey," my brother says, "here's an idea. You could talk to Ryder about it. Crazy, I know."

"We fight a lot when it comes to this topic."

"You know the best thing about fighting? The makeup sex."

I wince. "I don't want to know what you and Brenna get up to. Thanks."

"Think about what's more important to you and tell Ryder. Maybe he's willing to do long-distance."

He might be willing to do that, but I'm not.

And I think I have my answer.

CHAPTER 29
RYDER

I DIDN'T HAVE any artists in the studio today, but I still found myself unable to work on the stuff I need to get done.

When Lyric finds me, the computer screen in front of me is off, it's dark outside, and I realize I've spaced out again.

"Looks like you've got some real productivity going on in here."

"Hey." I force a smile. "Is Kaylee already asleep?"

"Yep."

"It's so gonna suck when you leave." Which is what I've been dwelling on all day. Because I know it's going to happen.

"When I leave?"

"Yeah. When you sign with Cameron."

Lyric looks at me as if my words hold some significant meaning. "You want me to sign with Cameron?"

"I can't make that call, but I do know it's the smart decision."

He pulls the spare chair next to me and takes a seat. "This studio has so many memories already attached to it. Our first kiss. Our first … more than a kiss. My first demo. Recording my first original single."

"What's your point?" Is this goodbye? This sounds like the beginning of a goodbye speech.

"What if I told you I was seriously thinking about taking Harley's offer?"

My heart stutters. I can't have heard that right, but I try to keep things light. "I'd say you're an idiot, and your brother must be a shit contract lawyer if he didn't tell you Cameron is the right choice."

"Oh, he told me to go with Cameron."

"Then why would you—" *For me.* Oh, shit. "Don't sign with Harley for me. I mean, it's a nice gesture, and I want that more than ever, but like you've been saying this whole time, you have to do your career your way. I shouldn't be a factor when it comes to making this decision."

Lyric looks like I just punched him in the heart.

I turn to him and grab his hands. "I don't want to be the reason you pass up an opportunity with Cameron. I know what he can do for your career. And if you make the wrong choice here, I can't be the one you grow to resent because of it."

"What if you were a factor but not the deciding one?" Lyric can't look me in the eye.

"What was the deciding one?"

"When Chord called me, I was holding my breath and hoping he'd tell me to sign with Harley. My gut is leaning in that direction. Creative control. I get to work with you. I get to spend the next year creating an album and a brand with you and Harley while still being here with Kaylee."

"You … want that?"

Lyric lets out a loud breath. "I don't want to scare you off, but yeah. I fucking want that. My father would absolutely think I'm making the wrong decision, but the thing is, I promised myself, and my mother, that I would do things differently. I want to be smart about this, and Cameron's offer is shiny and pretty and one of those insane *change your life* type deals. My dad wouldn't have even hesitated to leave his family for an offer like that. But you have to remember the last thing I wanted was to become like him."

His words begin to sink in, and hope starts to grow. I didn't think he'd make this choice. I haven't allowed myself to believe he would.

"What happens if Harley's idea fails?" I ask. "What if he can't get the other three Eleven guys on board and doesn't have the funding to even cut your album?"

I'm not trying to push him away, but I need him to be sure.

He leans forward. "Then I'm hoping my *family* will be there to cheer me on while I put myself out there time and time again to find another contract like it."

"Your family …" The pounding against my rib cage grows.

Lyric shrugs. "Yeah. You know, Chord. Brenna. Chase."

"Oh." My heart sinks, and I turn away.

"There's the reaction I want. I'm gonna say something that you're probably not going to like, and then I'm going to hold my breath and pray you don't run away. Or kick me out …"

"What?"

"I want you and Kaylee, and hell, even Maggie to be part of my family too. I want you to ask me to move in with you for real, and I want *everything* with you."

"Yes," I blurt. "Sign the contract with Harley. Move in. Be with me."

The idea of it is perfect, but there's one problem we haven't discussed.

Lyric moves to kiss me, but I stop him. His face falls.

"I know you want to come out to the media, but—"

Lyric cups my face. "Being an out artist is important to me. You know that. But I will do anything to protect our little girl. The media doesn't need to know who I sleep with, just that I'm gay."

"*Our* little girl." I love the sound of that.

"If she'll have me. She's known to be picky, you know."

I huff. "She loves you, but if you're living here, it might tip the paparazzi off."

"We'll work something out—a cover story. They already know I'm Kaylee's nanny. Maybe we formed a bromance during that time. Maybe my awesome producer is letting me crash with him while we work on my album which might take a really, really, really long time to get out."

"Because of all the sex we'll have in the studio?"

Lyric laughs. "Yeah, we just won't tell them *that* part. I promise you we can both be in music and still protect Kaylee. And with Maggie on board …"

I suck in a sharp breath. "We're really doing this?"

"All you have to say is yes."

"*Fuck yes.*"

Lyric grins. "Even better."

A hot, wet mouth makes its way down my chest, and in my half-asleep state, all I can do is moan and hope it's real.

My hand seeks Lyric's hair and tangles in the loose locks as my hips thrust upward.

I have no idea what time it is, but that nagging father instinct is on alert. "Where's Kaylee? Do we have time before she wakes up?"

Lyric chuckles against my skin.

I crack open my eyes and stare down at him.

"It's past ten, sleepyhead. Kaylee's been awake for hours."

I blink and then glance around the room. "And you got up with her?"

"It is my job. Technically."

I beckon for him to come up higher. "I know it's still your job, but I hope you don't feel that's all you are to her."

He climbs my body so we're face-to-face, and I feel his hard cock against mine. "I don't." He bites his lip. "How do you think she'll take the news today?"

"That you're moving in? She won't even blink. You practically live here now anyway except for the days you have Chase. And speaking of Chase, how do you think your brother and Brenna will handle it?"

He lowers his head and buries it in my neck. "I don't know, but it's not like I won't still be able to take Chase. We'll just have to work out a different schedule."

"You won't be able to once your work with Harley starts."

"I know. And Chord already knows that too."

I smile up at him. "Today's going to be a good day. It's all happening for you."

Lyric cups my cheek. "For us."

I nod. "For us."

It's a monumental day. Lyric signs with Harley today, and we decided to throw a little signing party. While we're all here, with Lyric's family and mine, we'll tell them our big news.

"We should get up and start setting up for the day. And no doubt Kaylee will be running up here any minute." I grind my hips beneath him. "As much as I'd love to stay right here. I'd only need a couple of minutes."

Lyric meets my thrusts. "Lucky for us, Maggie took Kaylee to go buy a cake for today. It was my job to come wake you."

"Then why the fuck have we been chatting?" I run my hand down his bare back to find his naked ass in my palm. "And you're naked? Since when?"

"Since I tried to wake you with a blowjob and you wouldn't let me. You're the reason we're chatting."

I reach between us and grip his cock. His eyes flutter closed, and his hips thrust forward. The friction on my dick makes my eyes roll back in my head.

Lyric's hot breath lands on my skin, and my brain short-circuits to the point my hand stops moving.

"I've got you," Lyric says and takes over.

I'm right. It only takes a few minutes of stroking and grinding for me to come without even having taken off my underwear, and it doesn't take Lyric much longer.

"That's a nice way to wake up," I murmur, sleep claiming my voice.

"Sounds like I almost put you back to sleep."

"Mm, I want to sleep more."

"One full-night's sleep in five years and you want even more? So greedy. But I think Maggie and Kaylee will be back soon, and we should probably clean up the mess in your underwear."

I laugh. "Yeah, that's probably a good idea. Shower?"

"I will never say no to showering with you."

"I'll never say no to you for anything." I don't realize how much I mean that until the words are out there.

I'd do anything for the man on top of me.

I've never had this kind of fullness in my heart with anyone but Kaylee.

Lyric has wormed his way inside, but instead of it feeling like an intrusion, it's comforting.

It's a complete feeling—an infinite promise.

I just have to build up the courage to tell him so.

Lyric tries to climb off me, but I stop him and suck in a sharp breath. I prepare to say the words dancing on the tip of my tongue. "Lyric, I …" *I'm falling for you. I've fallen for you.*

I don't know how to not fuck this up.

"You're still so out of it," Lyric says lightly. "I think you function better on less sleep." He moves off me. "You're never allowed to sleep in again."

Moment lost.

After another mind-blowing handjob in the shower—where I have to bite my lip to stop from blurting out my thoughts about Lyric and me together forever at the wrong time—Lyric leaves me to recover and actually wash myself without getting distracted.

When I finally amble downstairs, I find Lyric fussing over a fruit platter.

He's staring at it like the kiwi fruit's arrangement on the plate is offensive.

I wrap my arms around him from behind. "Nervous?"

"Were you when you signed your first contract?"

"Fuck yes, but my excitement outweighed my nerves."

"How were you recruited into Eleven? Had you signed with a label first or—"

"I wanted to move to LA. Joystar was holding auditions—first video auditions and then face-to-face. I sent my video in, got a callback, and the rest was history. Unlike you, I didn't mind selling out if it gave me a ticket out of Texas."

Lyric turns and leans against the counter. "What if …"

"What if you made the wrong choice?"

"I'm wondering if I'll forever be known as the dumb idiot who turned down Cameron Verikas."

I press myself against him. "Not if you become the first platinum-selling artist on Harley Valentine's label."

Lyric touches his forehead to mine and whispers, "Damn, that sounds amazing."

"It's normal to be anxious over your first ever record deal. It's scary and exciting, but you deserve all of it. You deserve everything, Lyric."

"I want it all with you."

The words bubble to the surface again, threatening to spill out. I want to tell him. I want to say those three little words that scare the crap out of me.

Before I can, Lyric's lips touch mine, and like every time he kisses me, my brain goes fuzzy, my heart feels full, and words like love float around in my head.

I get lost in him, so much so I'm taken off guard when Maggie's voice interrupts us.

"I thought I gave you two plenty of time to get all the kissing out of your systems for the day."

We pull apart with wide smiles, but mine falls when I see Kaylee's little face screwed up.

"Kissing is yucky, Daddy."

"Oh, so sorry." I run after her while crouching. "I guess you'd hate it when I do this, then." I grab her and pick her up, planting kisses all over her face.

She squeals while trying to fight me off. "Stop, Daddy. Stop!"

I let out an exaggerated sigh. "Fine."

As soon as I put her down, she runs behind Lyric for protection.

"Ooh, don't think he'll save you," I tease.

"Kaylee, run!" Lyric yells.

This time she runs around the counter while I try to chase her, but Lyric's in my way. He wraps his arms around my waist.

Kaylee runs behind Maggie this time.

"Oh no. She's found my weakness." I pretend to be in pain and sink to my knees.

"Women?" Maggie jokes.

Lyric snorts.

I glare. "Not cool, baby momma."

She cocks her eyebrow at me.

I hang my head. "I won't call you baby momma ever again."

She smiles as I get to my feet.

Lyric leans in. "She really is your weakness." He lifts his chin in Maggie's direction. "You're gonna have to teach me how to do that."

"Sorry. It's a gift. It can't be taught."

They share a look, and shit, it's moments like this when I really think we can make this all work.

Of course, we're going to have to get Maggie on board with my plan, but I don't know if she will be.

"Hey, Kaylee, how about you help Lyric set up the backyard for the party while I talk to Mommy?"

Lyric holds out his hand. "Come on, little one."

Once they're gone, Maggie gives me an inquisitive stare.

"I have some news," I say.

She beams. "You're pregnant!"

I flip her off. "Funny. But, uh, can we sit?" I gesture to the small dining table.

"Uh-oh. Sounds serious."

"It is, but it's good news. I promise. I just don't know how you're going to take it."

"You want me to move out?"

"Oh my God, woman. Just sit."

She does, but her green eyes that are so much like Kaylee's stare at me with worry.

"Lyric's moving in."

She doesn't appear surprised. "That's amazing. He's really good for you. I've never seen you happier, and that includes when you were this big pop star with the world at your feet."

"To be fair, I don't think I was overly happy back then."

She reaches for my hand. "Was that all you had to tell me?"

"No. There's more." I swallow hard because this is the part she won't like. "With Harley and me starting this label and Lyric being signed, we're both going to be busy in the upcoming months."

"Which reminds me. You know that Brix guy? He's ex-army as

well, and while Harley was here and he was playing with the kids, we got to talking. He offered me a job on Harley's security team."

"A job …" I'm not sure if I can work all of this out without Maggie's help, and if she's on tour with Harley, and us, that means Kaylee would have to go back to the life I took her away from on purpose.

Maggie leans back in her seat. "I told him I'd have to think about it. And now with Lyric signing to Harley's label, it will probably mean you'd need a new nanny, and—"

"Okay, well, that's the thing. I was hoping … I mean, you said you wanted more time with Kaylee, and I've always had full custody, but maybe it's time to change that. I figure if we work out a custody agreement where you become the primary carer and Lyric or I are on tour or whatever, you could bring Kaylee to see us on weekends when she's not at school. Unless it's too much for you, and—"

"Oh my God, I'll do it." Her brow furrows. "But what does that mean for me getting a job and working?"

Yep. There it is. "If you can get a job that works with our hours, then that'd be perfect, but …" Fuck, I'm sweating. I bumble the words in a hurry. "Do you know how much child support I would have to pay if we changed custody agreements? You wouldn't have to work. And I know you *want* to work, and you're independent and don't want my money, and I can already hear you yelling, and—"

"You know me too well, but—" She bites her bottom lip. "— getting to know my daughter is more important right now. Eventually, I will want to work, but if this is a way I can get close to Kaylee and make up for lost time, I'll take it. I just thought you would never let this happen. I mean, in the past, you've been worried about me trying to change our custody agreement."

"I'm not going to lie, and you know I love you, but you coming to take Kaylee away from me has always been in the back of my mind because you left her with me so she could have a 'good life.' But the media hasn't left us alone for five years. My fear comes from feeling like an inadequate parent, not thinking you're an evil person who wants to steal her, and if I can overcome that, I'm certain we can do anything."

Maggie's eyes soften. "I understand, and I'm just thankful you're giving me enough trust with this."

"It's hard thinking of leaving Kaylee. We might have to have some practice weekends for a while first, but Lyric has made me rethink how I see the world. That maybe there's more to life than sacrificing everything for a tiny human I created."

"A *cute* tiny human," Maggie says.

"The adorablest."

"I don't think that's a word."

"Don't care. Anyway, I realize Lyric's right. I can't always protect Kaylee from all the bullshit, and I can't put my life on hold trying to do it either. It's possible to have a career and protect her, but I know she'll still be exposed. There's not much we can do about that except teach her how to handle it. It will be manageable if we have the right people on board, and there's only one person I'd trust to make sure that happens."

Maggie smiles at me. "You must really love Lyric. For you to even contemplate all this for him when you've been the most uptight parent I've ever known."

My mouth drops open, but nothing comes out. Apparently, I can't even say the words to other people even if they're right there waiting to explode from my mouth. "I should probably tell him first before saying anything."

Her eyebrows arch. "He's moving in, but you haven't told him you love him yet?"

"It's been *implied*."

"How special for him," she says. "Just tell him. Go out there, march up to him, and say, 'I love you, you big, gorgeous idiot' and kiss him. There. Done."

I cock my head. "You think my boyfriend is gorgeous?"

"So much so I have no idea what he sees in you."

I burst out laughing. "Thanks for always being you."

She stands and pulls me into a hug. "I can't thank you enough for giving me the chance to make it up to her."

"Aww, Mags." I hold her close.

Lyric's voice comes from behind us. "Should I be worried?"

Maggie moves out of my arms. "Yeah, right. The only time you'd have to be worried is if Ryder and I were both in emotionally horrible places at the same time."

"Recipe for disaster," I joke.

"Hey, not that much of a disaster." She nods in Kaylee's direction as our daughter comes running in from outside.

I pick her up as she runs into my arms, and I find crumbs around her mouth. "You got into the cookies already?"

She licks her lips. "Uh-huh."

Definitely not a disaster.

Totally worth it.

CHAPTER 30
LYRIC

THE PEN in my hand hovers over the spot where I need to sign. I'm excited and ready to change my life, but I also want to make sure I don't rush it and forget what this feels like.

I'm surrounded by my family old and new, Harley and his partner, Harley's assistant, and even Cameron.

"He's hesitating," Cameron whispers. "My offer's still on the table," he calls out.

"Not hesitating. Just taking it all in."

"Suck it, old man," Harley mutters.

Cameron smiles.

Maybe Harley's venture will fail. Maybe it will take off. Right now, it doesn't matter. What matters is taking this new opportunity and running with it. With Ryder by my side.

I slide the pen across the page, signing my future away.

I'm the happiest I've ever been in my life.

When I straighten up, Ryder's right there, kissing me and making my dreams complete. After Ryder releases me, everyone else shakes my hand and offers me their own congratulations.

"We need a photo," Harley says and turns to his assistant. "Jamie, get a snap of this so we can use it as promo when we announce the label."

We take a photo of Harley and me shaking hands and smiling. I probably look like an absolute goofball. My first official public photo is going to haunt me for years.

Cameron approaches us. "I'm heading out, boys. Best of luck to you both. And remember, either of you can call me for advice whenever you need it. I have high hopes for this." He shakes our hands.

"If you weren't so obsessed with money, you could get in on this," Harley says.

Cameron scoffs. "It's not me who's obsessed with money. That would be wife number four."

"Divorce her!" Harley says. "Get into business with us."

Cameron laughs. "You'd think I'd learn after the first three. I'd be more broke divorced."

"Prenups, man." Harley claps Cameron on the back. "We told you that with the second one."

"I know, I know." Cameron sighs. "But if your man over there asked you to marry him, would you ask for a prenup?"

Harley stares at his bodyguard boyfriend, who's talking with Maggie right now, and then hangs his head. "No."

"Exactly. I'm a romantic at heart."

"I'd sign a prenup," I say. "But, you know, that's me wanting to protect Ryder."

Ryder's voice comes from behind me. "Wait, we're getting married?" He wraps his arm around me and pulls me close. "Were you planning on telling me? I thought that was a long, long, long, long, long way off."

I nudge him. "Hypothetically."

"Oh, well, in a hypothetical situation, I wouldn't make you sign one." He kisses my cheek.

"Thank you! My point exactly," Cameron says. "I knew my boys would see it my way."

"Speaking of your boys," Harley prompts. "You wouldn't happen to know where Mason is, do you?"

Cameron looks at his phone which is most definitely not ringing. "Oh, shit, I have to take this." He walks toward the house with his phone pressed to his ear.

"I'll get it out of him," Harley says with determination.

I love the dynamic between Cameron and Harley. I like that

Cameron isn't bitter I didn't choose him. That says a lot, and it makes me realize no matter what I would've chosen, I would have been okay, but going with Harley, I know I'm getting the type of family environment I could've only wished for.

Ryder's arm around me squeezes tighter. "You all right? No regrets?"

I smile at him. "None at all."

Kaylee bounds up to us and tugs on my hand. "We're ready."

Chase is behind her.

My nerves kick up a notch.

"Ready for what?" Ryder asks.

"My gift to you."

"You got me a gift? This party is for you."

I put on a confident face even though I'm shitting bricks. "Let's go, guys." I usher Kaylee and Chase toward the middle of the backyard, grabbing my guitar from where I stashed it under the cake table earlier.

As we take our positions to perform the song we've been practicing together, I take a deep breath.

I look out at the small group, and doubt begins to cloud my mind.

This is a mistake.

This is the worst.

I can't believe I'm doing this.

Ryder's smiling.

Harley looks confused.

My brother is just plain trying not to laugh at me.

He won't be able to contain it soon.

"Okay," I croak and then clear my throat. "Some of you probably don't know how Ryder and I met."

"Oh, I told everyone I know," Ryder cuts in.

"Thanks. No, really, thank you. Anyway, I might have said something about boy bands being lazy, cliché, and, well, sucky."

Brix puts his fingers in his mouth and lets out a loud whistle. Harley elbows him.

"While I still think their songs are a bit cliché, I'm not ashamed to admit I was wrong about the other two. Ryder's one of the most hard-working people I know, and I can't wait to begin this journey with him. Both professionally and personally." I glance at my brother and Brenna. "Oh, by the way, I'm moving out." I don't give them a chance to react before I strum the opening chords to a song that should burn in hell. "Ryder, this one's for you."

The kids start with the *Ooh, ooh, oohs.*

I join in with the first verse, and everyone in the backyard erupts into laughter.

Yes, I'm singing an Eleven song.

And I'm not spontaneously combusting. Who knew?

Because I like you. Ooh, ooh, ooh. I like you.

My soul is dying.

But as I lock eyes with Ryder, I realize I'd sell my soul ten times over for that man.

I think I might've been a little bit in love with him since the moment he didn't get offended at the rude, jealous comments I made the day we met.

I fell a little more when I saw him with his daughter.

Was completely enamored by the time he helped me with my demo.

Now?

We may not have said the actual words to each other yet, but I'm so in love with him it's been hard to keep it in until I thought he might be ready.

And maybe he's still not ready.

But it's too late now.

The kids sing the last chorus—the one we changed.

Ooh, ooh, ooh. I love you.
I love you.
I love you ...

The song finishes, and while everyone claps and cheers, Ryder's eyes remain locked on mine.

I try to approach him, but my feet refuse to move.

He didn't even blink at the notion of me moving in, but this? This is huge.

This is massive.

I want to put the words back in my mouth—take them back and continue to wait for him to catch up—but they're out there now.

The world blurs around the edges as if tunnel vision is kicking in and only letting me focus on Ryder.

He's the one to approach me.

My guitar drops to my side as I rest it against my leg.

Ryder stops so we're toe-to-toe, his face a mix of fear and awe.

"I might've changed the words," I rasp.

He huffs. "I like your version better. Especially if it was directed at me."

Damn it, I wish I could read him better. I don't know if he's shit-scared right now or begging for me to answer truthfully.

"It might have been."

He takes my hands. "Just in case it was, I love you too."

A relieved whoosh leaves me. "Thank fuck for that."

Ryder leans in to kiss me.

"Swear jar!" Kaylee's little voice interrupts us. Of course it does.

I slump.

"That's what life is going to be like living in this family," Ryder says. "You up for it?"

"I'm up for anything when it comes to you."

"I love you, Lyric."

"I love you too. So. Fucking. Much." This time I make sure to keep my voice low so little ears can't hear my curse words.

"We're about to start something massive together," Ryder whispers. "Are you ready?"

"Forever ready."

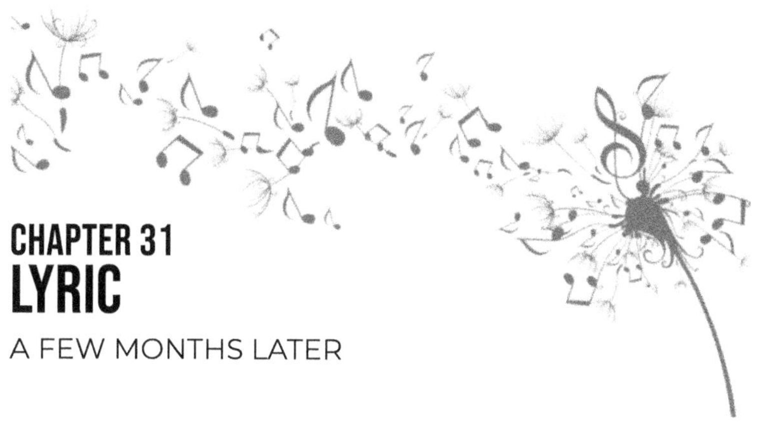

CHAPTER 31
LYRIC

A FEW MONTHS LATER

MY PALMS SWEAT. The stage lights are blinding, hiding the audience. That's probably a good thing.

Singing, I'm good at. Talking … shit, I don't even think I know how to do that anymore.

It's my first appearance on a talk show, and I'm nervous as fuck.

Shit. Don't say fuck on TV.

I swallow hard and think about Ryder and Kaylee at home in LA. Ryder said he'd let Kaylee stay up to watch it tonight even though by the time this airs, I'll be in my hotel room watching it too.

Sean Rushton, the newest, fresh-faced host of the latest late-night show, smiles at me. The reason I got booked on this show is because of how new we both are.

Turns out, Harley Valentine knows this business better than I ever could've imagined. Three months after signing with him, I had a single on the charts and my face in the tabloids.

It's been a crazy whirlwind I wouldn't change for anything. Except maybe having Ryder and Kaylee here with me.

"So tell me," Sean says. "I hear the way you were discovered is unique."

I recite the rehearsed speech Harley gave me and that Ryder approved. "I was actually working as a nanny."

"A nanny?"

"You might have heard of my boss, Ryder Kennedy."

The crowd goes wild like only boy band fans do.

I laugh. "Harley was over at the house—"

"He says, like it's completely normal to have Harley Valentine as a house guest," Sean says.

"Exactly! I got used to seeing him and the guys from Eleven dropping by. They're all still great friends." *Lies.* I only recently met them all, and not all their receptions were warm, but that's not what I'm supposed to be selling.

"So, Harley was over, and ..." Sean prompts.

"He overheard me singing with Ryder's daughter. Then he chased me down where I was gigging on weekends and convinced me to sign with his new label, Valentine Records."

There you go, Harley. I got in that plug you wanted.

"I think a heap of struggling artists just signed up to nanny agencies across the country."

I would tell them how I met Ryder for real, but we want people to like me.

"Is it true you almost appeared on *Fandom*, the reality show in which Denver from Eleven is a judge?"

"I did audition for that show." And it's laughable that I walked away from it because the producers wanted me to sing a Harley Valentine song, and now Harley's not only the head of my label but my manager.

It's only temporary until he finds me someone we both want to work with.

Sean holds out his arms. "Turns out, you didn't need it."

I smile. "Turns out."

"Okay, so you're new to this scene. How much has your life changed in the last few months?"

"Well, I'm not so invisible anymore. When I used to go out with Ryder and his daughter, the paparazzi always ignored me. It worked in protecting little Kaylee from the media. Oh, actually, I promised her I'd say hi to her if I ever made it here." I turn to the camera and wave. "Hi, Kaylee." Then I point. "You should be in bed."

The audience snickers.

"Are you still in contact with Ryder, then?"

Still in contact? We share a bed every night and make each other come as many times as possible while the kidlet is asleep.

"Ryder produced my single, and we're working on my album together. I'm actually crashing at his house while we're recording. It's a real family vibe at Valentine Records."

Boom, another plug. If I wasn't the only act on Harley's label, I'd say I was the favorite.

"You know, when Harley announced the label, fans around the world started screaming for an Eleven reunion. You wouldn't happen to know anything about that, would you?"

Yeah, I know both Mason and Blake are holding out harder than Harley thought they would, but I'm not allowed to say that.

"They don't tell me anything. Apparently, I tell stories I'm not supposed to."

The crowd laughs again.

"That's right. I read an article where you told the interviewer about throwing up on Cash Kingsley."

The audience gasps.

"Great memories," I say.

"Wait, so it's true?"

"Oh, have I got a story for you."

As I get into it, I think back to a promise Ryder made me in his small studio in his large house. That one day I'd be on a talk show just like this one and I'd tell this story.

I don't think either of us assumed it would happen so soon, but it makes me wish, not for the first time since arriving out here, that he was with me.

I know without a doubt that signing with Harley was the right thing to do now.

I get the best of both worlds, and I get to go home to a man who loves me, our child, and the work-slash-family balance my father was never able to achieve.

I have everything I've ever wanted.

All because of Ryder Kennedy.

We finish up the interview, and I take my time getting back to the hotel. I've never seen New York City, so I wander around Rockefeller Center until I'm recognized by someone on the street.

No fucking shit.

Someone stopped me for a selfie and an autograph. *Me.* I love it, but I don't think I'll ever get used to it.

At home, it happens, but more often than not it's when I'm with Harley or Ryder. Very rarely on my own. I'm not that recognizable yet.

I can't wait to get back to the hotel so I can call Ryder and tell him about it.

I'm itching to get to my room, pulling up Ryder's number as soon as I get into the elevator.

I hit Call when I get into the hallway, and it starts ringing when I get to my door.

Fiddling with my key and juggling the phone at the same time, I don't even register the ringtone echoing around the place.

When I open the door and see my man and Kaylee on my hotel bed, my heart melts.

"What are you guys doing here?"

Ryder holds his finger to his lips, pointing at where Kaylee is napping.

He slowly climbs off the bed and approaches me. "We missed you."

"It's a school night," I whisper.

"She was going to stay with Maggie, but when she found out I was coming to see you, she put her foot down."

I can't help smiling. "Our five-year-old put her foot down, so you both flew five hours to come see me?"

"Yup. Because we love you." He glances back at Kaylee. "Both of us. I know we won't be able to do this for every show or every appearance, but this is your first time. We belong here with you." He seals it with a kiss that makes my knees weak and my heart full.

I could live without fame.

I could live without creating and making music professionally.

I can't live without Ryder and Kaylee.

They're like the melodies I can't get out of my head and the lyrics that itch to be written. They're part of me. They consume me.

"Ryder?"

"Mm?"

"If I haven't said it enough, you guys are my everything."

He smiles. "Careful, Lyric. You're sounding a hell of a lot like a boy band cliché."

I gasp. "Never. You take that back."

"Never," he mimics. "Because I know, deep down, you love my boy band-ness."

"I love everything about you," I whisper. "Even your demons."

Ryder bursts out laughing. "We should wake Kaylee up and go have dinner so we can watch your big interview together."

Epiphanies and big moments are supposed to happen at monumental times in someone's life.

Standing in the entryway of a cheap hotel room is not where I'm supposed to have a giant romantic revelation.

"I want to marry you," I blurt.

His eyes widen.

"I mean one day. When Kaylee's old enough to kick paparazzi in the nuts."

"Wow. What a … romantic proposal?"

"Not a proposal. A revelation."

"That … you want to marry me. And what exactly brought on this revelation?"

"The perfect picture of what I want my future to look like. You—" I lean in and kiss his cheek. "—me—" I kiss his other cheek. "—and Kaylee eating dinner together."

"That sounds positively boring and unexciting."

"But it's my boring and unexciting. With the kind of crazy our lives are, I can't think of anything more permanent and normal than sitting down with the two people I love most and shutting out the rest of the world so it's just us in our bubble."

Ryder's face softens as his bright blue, hypnotic eyes fill with warmth and love. "Now that you put it that way, it does sound perfect."

THANK YOU

Thank you for reading *Spotlight*!

Where is Mason?
Why is Denver so against getting back together?

Find out in *Fandom*! Available now: https://geni.us/jDflqR

Want more Cash Kingsley? Go on tour with Cash Me Outside in *Rockstar Hearts*: mybook.to/rockstarhearts

I need to give special thanks to my readers for their suggestions. Thank you to Jeannie Cooper for suggesting the name Eleven for my boy band. When I hear that name now, I can't help thinking of my boys.
And to Samantha Blundell for giving Harley, Ryder, Denver, Blake, and Mason their names.

Want to stay up to date on everything Eden Finley?
Join my reader group here: https://www.facebook.com/groups/absolutelyeden/

ALSO BY EDEN FINLEY

https://amzn.to/2zUlM16

https://www.edenfinley.com

FAKE BOYFRIEND SERIES

FAMOUS SERIES

MIKE BRAVO OPS

CU HOCKEY co-written with Saxon James

PUCKBOYS co-written with Saxon James

STEELE BROTHERS

Headstrong

Football Royalty

Can't Say Goodbye

Unprincely (MMF)

ACKNOWLEDGMENTS

I want to thank my long list of betas, especially Leslie Copeland from Les Court Services, Blue Beta Reading, Susie Selva for development and line edits, and Sandra from One Love editing for copy-edits. Thanks to Lori Parks for one last read through for those ninja typos that have the ability to sneak through four rounds of editing. Lastly, a big thanks to Linda from Foreword PR & Marketing for helping get this book out.

9 781922 743534